TULIP
TAYLOR

ANNA MAINWARING

Firefly

First published in 2019
by Firefly Press
25 Gabalfa Road, Llandaff North, Cardiff, CF14 2JJ
www.fireflypress.co.uk

A CIP catalogue record of this book is available from the British Library.

ISBN 978-1-910080-97-9

This book has been published with the support
of the Welsh Books Council.

Typeset by Elaine Sharples

Printed and bound by: Pulsio Sarl

TULIP TAYLOR

To Anne Mainwaring and Sarah Mainwaring-Parr
Thank you for your love and support over the years…
…and for helping me survive that camping holiday.

CHAPTER ONE

Word: Blunder (noun or verb)

I'm sitting at my desk, staring into the webcam with my heart racing. 'So, there you go. As you can see, it takes a bit of time and effort, and a helping hand...' here I nod to Anjali who waves manically for the camera '...but I hope you think the end look is worth it. Bye, guys, and see you soon for some more amazing looks.' I lean forward and stop recording. Then, and only then, do I relax my smile. 'Cut. And chill.' I stand up, stretch and throw myself back on my bed, narrowly avoiding Kate and my menagerie of soft toys. 'That was intense.'

Kate finally looks up from her book. 'Oi, you've made me lose my page. Intense? That's a bit over...'

Anjali tuts as she wipes down the make-up brushes. 'Don't listen to her, Tulip. She just doesn't get it.'

I sit up, my heart still getting back to normal after the last twenty minutes of adrenaline. 'Not many other vloggers do that, you know. They spend ages editing videos to get them perfect. I just...'

'*We* just,' Anjali interrupts, letting down her hair so that when she goes home her parents don't see either her undercut or the fact that she's dyed a huge section of her hair purple.

'*We* just created magic in twenty minutes. Live. Mistakes and all.'

I can see that Kate's still not impressed. 'But it's just…'

Leaning over, I put a finger to her lips. 'Don't say those words. Kate, you are better than this. Thousands of people just watched me commune with my art. So don't you go and ruin the moment by saying "but it's just make-up".'

'Well, I think you look awesome,' Anjali says, and looking in a mirror I agree. My boring, bland face has been transformed into a mask of glitter, flowers and gems. A perfect festival look. If only I had any hope of going to a festival or anything else so exciting. My next social engagement is double maths.

'How many views so far?' I ask Anjali.

'Hundreds. Look at all your likes.'

I watch the number under my post move up and up and up. Every one of them means that someone has taken the time to like my work. To like me. It feels like a little hug, giving me a warm glow.

'Great. At least that will keep Mum happy. She starts hassling me if my reach doesn't increase. She's obsessed with my metadata.' Mum is a bit – zealous – that's a good word and I do love my words. She keeps a spreadsheet to track how popular I am on all my social-media sites.

Kate peers at me over her book. 'Don't take this the wrong way but your mum is a bit weird.'

'I totally agree. Any ideas on how to change her will be gratefully received. But she never listens to me and, to be honest, I like doing the videos, so I don't mind. It's cool.'

Kate thinks about what I'm saying. 'I know but…'

Anjali, whose phone has just vibrated, interrupts us with a gasp and then a very loud squeal. 'Lads. Lads. Lads.'

Kate and I share a glance. What news has our gossip queen heard?

'What is it this time?' I start playing with the make-up removal bottle though I can't bear to take it off just yet. 'Has Simon Brodie realised that he's been dumped? Surely he'll realise that Lorna hasn't spoken to him for a month soon.'

'No, oh no, this is so much better than that.' Anjali leans back, squinting at her phone.

By now, Anjali has got what she wants. Both Kate and me are gazing at her, desperate to find out the latest news.

'Well?' I say. 'Come on. Spit it out, or do I need to use force to get you to talk?' I grab the nearest thing to hand, my huge dictionary that always takes pride of place next to my bed.

Kate bats it away. 'Put it down, you'll knock someone out with that thing. I mean I love a good read, but you are way too obsessed with that book. Can't you read something with – you know – a story?'

I put down the dictionary gently and dust down its cover. 'Don't listen to her,' I whisper to it. 'I wouldn't really throw you at Anjali. You might get hurt.'

Anjali and Kate are now staring at me. 'Am I doing it again?' I ask.

'If by "it" you mean talking to inanimate objects, then yes,' Kate says. 'But…'

I grab Mr Snowy and throw him at her instead. She squeals

which is a bit of an overreaction to being hit with a fifteen-year-old soft toy.

'Will you both stop!' Anjali is now on her feet and squawking. She shoves her phone under my face. 'This is more important. *This* is starting at our school tomorrow.'

Kate and I scrabble to get the phone. I, of course, win.

'Show me! What is it? I want to see.' Kate sounds just like one of the twins now. I forgive them normally, given that they are five.

I keep staring at the screen as Kate finally gets a look. 'Oh, now he is pretty. He is really pretty. He is so boy band. Who is he?'

Loving the fact that she has now got our full attention, Anjali starts to explain. 'Okay so you know Precious – her mum works in the school office?'

'Yes, of course we do. We've been friends with her since Year Three.'

'Okay, Precious' mum told her that there's this new boy starting tomorrow. At our school. And this is him.'

I look at him again. He looks older than us, shinier. Deep brown eyes, so dark they could be black. Brown hair with a hint of gold that falls in just the right way. Cheekbones you could cut yourself on. Lips that curve in a way that makes me jealous. How can any human be so naturally gorgeous? I mean it would take me ages and lots of very careful contouring to create that cheek effect. I can't stop looking at him; my fingers wander towards the screen to brush his virtual cheek.

'Tulip. Tulip. Back off.'

'What?'

4

'You were drooling. Not cool.'

Anjali takes the phone back and actually checks for saliva.

'Sorry. But he is lovely.'

Anjali looks at me with scorn. 'He's more than lovely. He's tabasco sauce hot and then some jalapeno on top of that.'

Kate peeks too. 'I agree. I think he's lush. What do you think, Tulip? You must have a better word than lovely.'

I stare again and think hard. 'I'd say he was pulchritudinous.'

They both roll their eyes at that.

'I'm not even going to ask,' Anjali says. 'Kate, you shouldn't encourage her. She's not normal. Anyway, there's more,' she continues. 'His name is Harvey McManus.'

Kate grimaces. 'Harvey's a cute name but McManus is a bit of a mouthful.' She lies down on the bed and goes back to her book.

'Hang on,' I say. 'Isn't that the name of that guy who's opened an outdoor centre up in the hills?'

'Yes,' says Anjali, 'you are correct. You get all the bonus points in this round. His father is Hugh McManus.'

'Yuk.' Kate sits up. 'Isn't he the guy from TV that makes people drink their own wee? I'd rather die.'

'I'm with you, sister,' I agree. 'Yes, he does a kind of show, doesn't he, where he dumps people in the wild and they have to fend for themselves.'

'That's the man,' Anjali says. 'TV star. Wilderness expert. And his son is coming to our school.'

There's silence. I'm pretty sure that all three of us have the same image in our minds – our shabby, grey school, always

5

shrouded in cloud, and at least a hundred miles from anything interesting.

We all turn to each other and say at the same time. 'But why?'

Just as we are about to dissect the most interesting thing that has happened since Amy Dutton bit Tyler Leach to prove that she was really, truly a vampire, Kate suddenly says, 'Is the record button supposed to still be on red?'

I flap a hand at her. 'I turned it off. It's not red.'

'Tulip…'

'What?'

'It's definitely red. I know what the colour red looks like and this is red. I think you're still recording.'

Finally, I turn away from the image of Harvey on Anjali's phone. 'Look, I know what I'm doing. I've done this hundreds of times. I turned it…'

The screen of the computer shows us talking. The webcamera's light is on. It's red. I'd go so far to say that it's vermillion. So, we're still live.

As I squeal, launching myself across the room to turn the camera off, a word comes to mind. A pretty rude one. So much for me knowing what I'm doing… Stupid, stupid Tulip.

Hector: Yo bruv. Nervous for your first day with the savages? Bro. Bro. Don't go cold on me. I know I'm the favourite son, but you don't need to be so salty about it.

Harvey: Stop talking like you're a road man. You sound ridiculous.

Hector: Whatevs. You need to know the right slang, man. That's how they'll all be talking. Or grunting. Everyone back at school is dying to hear about it. Especially the girls. I want the lowdown on the chavviest girl you can find. You know the type. Thick. Eyebrows like slugs. All that ridiculous make-up.

Harvey: I'm not going there to socialise. I'll just do the hours and then get out as quickly as possible.

Hector: That's your plan? No human interaction? You do know that you're weird and you let the family name down? McManuses need to be Alphas, not zeroes. Anyway, it would be a waste of an opportunity to study the lower orders in their natural habitat. You'll never rub shoulders with the like of this lot again. Unless you disappoint Dad for a second time.

Harvey: You do know that it was my choice to go there. Not that I'm intending to hang out with them much, but they might be alright.

Hector: HAHAHAHAHAHAHAHAHAHAHAHAHAHA-HAHAHAHAHAHAHAHAHAHAHAHAHA

YOU ARE IN HICKSVILLE. CHAVLAND. They will tear you to pieces unless you show then that you are a superior being (though obviously not as superior as me as I am the chosen son). The girls will fall at your feet. Just project confidence and bring them to order. Then collect the spoils of war.

7

Harvey: It's just a school. With kids my age in it. Stop making such a big deal.

Hector: Harvey. Listen to your big bro. Do I ever get bullied? Do I get hot girls? Do I ever show weakness? Do I get what I want? Does Dad love me more than you? If you want to survive in Chavland, then you need to do one thing.

Harvey: What's that?

Hector: Kill shy, nice Harvey with the puppy dog eyes who gets nervous around people. Be More Hector and you will carry all in your path. Think about it. Maybe things didn't work out for you at our school because you were always in my shadow. I mean no one can compete with Hector McManus. I was named for a Greek god after all, whereas you were named after Grandmama's favourite brand of sherry. So, repeat after me: Be. More. Hector. You know it's true. Laugh at them and then they'll know that you are superior.

Harvey?

…

Harvey?

…

Loser. You won't last one day unless you do what I'm telling you. Be. More. Hector.

CHAPTER TWO

Word: Auspicious (adjective)

'Tulip, come on. If we're late again, she'll turn us into toadstools or something.' Kate's voice gets particularly high-pitched when she's scared. And she's scared of Ms Regan. Which is fair enough but I'm more scared of being seen without my face looking perfect. Kate bangs on the scruffy toilet door but I'm safely on the other side, scrunched up on the toilet seat with my bag of magical tricks and potions safely on my lap. I sigh, as I try desperately to repair the damage that forty minutes of hockey in a freezing Pennine March wind has done to my appearance. I mean I quite like running around with a wooden implement in my hands – it brings out the inner warrior. But now the inner warrior needs to be transformed into a bronzed goddess with precision-engineered eyebrows.

'I'll be a minute. I mean, you can't be the teen queen of make-up vlogs and be seen in real life with a shiny face. It would be bad for my brand as Mum would say.'

Outside I can hear Kate and Anjali muttering. 'I can hear you, you know,' I remind them. 'I know you think I'm being ridiculous. You might not mind going au naturale to lessons but it's not for me.' The thought of being seen without my mask of primer, foundation, concealer, bronzer, highlighter, mascara,

9

eye shadow, lipstick (matte of course), eye liner and finishing powder AND fixing spray makes me shudder.

'And that Harvey is going to be in our English lesson. He can't see me like this first time.' I wave my hand at the bulging bag that's threatening to fall over in my lap. Then it strikes me that they can't see this gesture so it's a bit pointless. 'It takes time to achieve natural beauty.'

'Um, I think natural beauty is a bit of a paradox in the current…' Kate starts.

'Stop whining,' I interrupt, '…and I'll be done. You know I can do this quickly.' She mutters something under her breath and thumps the door with what sounds like a particularly thick book, but she stays like I knew she would. I try to distract Anjali by moving on to her favourite topic. 'So, Tiffany told me that the new boy…'

'Stop right there. Tiffany knows nothing. I have all the info.'

'Well then…'

'Rumour has it he had to leave his last school because he threw a javelin at a teacher.'

'I heard that he looked a bit nervous in form this morning,' Kate suggests.

Anjali clearly takes offence. 'That's not likely. Why would someone who's clearly an athletic psychopath be nervous about coming here?'

'The bit I still don't understand is why the son of a TV star is coming to this dump?' I've laid down the base now and I'm on to the eyes, but I still need time, so my question is completely there to hook Anjali in.

Anjali is now fully warmed up to her topic. 'That remains a mystery. But I will find out. Do you think he knows we were talking about him?'

I shudder at the thought. I mean I'm sure he's not a great watcher of make-up tutorials, but it would be pretty embarrassing if he found out. I deleted the bit at the end when we were talking but even so, maybe thousands of people were still watching. Suddenly I don't need any blusher. It's not that we said anything awful after all, just that he was hot. And he is. Or at least he seems to be in that photo. It's more that I hate the idea of a private conversation being heard by loads of other people – strangers at that. That bit was not for public viewing at all.

'Let's not talk about that. What else do you know?'

She shuffles. 'Not much more really. He went to a boarding school, though.'

Kate says, 'Like Hogwarts? I bet it had an awesome library.'

I can only imagine Anjali's withering stare. 'No. No magic, all boys. Pretty strange if you ask me. He'll probably be one of those arrogant posh boys who thinks he's better than us.'

'He might be nice,' I suggest. 'Especially if he was nervous. That doesn't show arrogance.'

Anjali tuts. 'Keep dreaming, make-up girl. You just think he's the only boy round here who might actually be good enough for you. You are the closest thing to a celebrity that we have.'

Kate pipes up. 'Oh, I hadn't thought of that. You and him could become the new power couple on Instagram.'

'The thought has never crossed my mind,' I lie as I aim to line out the perfect brow. That the gorgeous son of a TV star might be a suitable boyfriend had struck me yesterday. There was something in his eyes that I liked. A rather sweet expression.

Anjali starts hammering on the door. 'Tulip, come on. No boy, son of a TV star or not, is worth missing a party for.'

'A party? What party? Where does a party come into this? All I'm asking for is sixty seconds,' I yell back. 'Nothing bad is going to happen if you wait sixty seconds.'

Anjali hisses through the door. 'Tulip. If you put as much energy into your make-up as you do into talking we'd be done by now. At parents' evening last week, I had to sit there while Ms Regan told my parents that you were a bad influence on me and that I was constantly late to lessons because of you. If I'm late again, then Mum will ground me. And you and I both know she means it. There's Ravi's party next week. I have been promised boys. Fit boys. Not from this school. I. WILL. NOT. RISK. GROUNDING. Come on, Kate. Let's go.'

I can hear moving. 'You're not going? It's like a war movie. You don't leave one of the team behind,' I plead.

Kate opens the door, knocking my legs so that my precious bundle of beauty products starts to wobble. 'Anjali's right. We can't afford to be late again.'

'But…' I start to protest. 'You're making me walk to a lesson ON MY OWN. People will think I've got no friends. *He'll* think I've got no friends.'

Anjali adds, 'Which will be true if you keep being late all the time.' And with that someone (probably Anjali) slams the door.

'Haven't you heard the term "fashionably late"?' I shout. 'Well, at least give her a good reason why I'm late.'

No response.

'But I've got no one to talk to!' I cry. I hate being on my own, so I talk to myself instead. 'I would never leave them behind.'

At this moment, the Instant Beauty Flash starts to roll off my lap at the same time my beloved Kissable Lip Kit (that no one else in school has – in fact hardly anyone in the country has because someone sent it to my mum from America) starts to go in the opposite direction.

No. No. No. Two of my beautiful products are about to fall on the petri dish that passes for the floor. I try to grab both at once. But in the process, I lean too far forward and the whole bag on my knee starts to tip.

I get the lip kit and beauty flash. Hurrah!

But can I get the bag too?

No.

Bottles roll, containers burst, brushes hit the grimy floor. All my lovely, lovely stuff shoots off in different directions like beautifully packaged fireworks.

Squealing like a Year Six who's seen her favourite YouTuber in real life, I stand up and grab as much as I can. The three-second rule applies to make-up surely? I'm not going to have to throw it all away, please Goddess of Cosmetics… I'm juggling expensive products. I can't keep hold of them all. Some of them start to fall out of my arms.

Not the Kissable Lip Kit. It's heading for the toilet bowl.

No, no, no, no, no, no.

There's a splash. I whimper.

You guessed it – it's gone. Lost in the scummy, suspiciously dark recesses of a school toilet.

Today is not going the way I've planned. Today is not – what's the word – auspicious at all.

CHAPTER THREE

Word: Altruistic (adjective)

For a moment, I look at my hand. Could I really put it down there and fish it out? I mean, how much do I love that lip kit? Enough to put my hand – where – where – oh for goodness sake, I can't even bear to think about it.

The answer is no. I could not. I might love my make-up, but it is, of course, make-up. Something new will always come out to replace it. My cosmetics, scuffed in the dirt of the girls' toilet, have suddenly lost their glow.

With a sigh, I round up what's left rolling round the floor. I dust it all as best as I can and then start to wipe it down with tangerine-scented hand sanitiser. But my heart's not in it. I might as well chuck the whole lot away. What I've always loved about make-up is that it's like magic. You get all the right ingredients – they smell HEAVENLY. Then you mix them all up in the right way with a bit of skill and *voilà* – you can transform yourself into whatever look you want. I can make every day beautiful. When you live in a place like this, making life shiny is what keeps you going. It's been my obsession for the last two years and keeps me connected with the big, wide, exciting world beyond the hills.

Just as I begin to consider how Ms Regan will begin to kill me – I jump as a door bangs, then rattles as if it's been hit. Is someone after me?

'Isabel Smellabel? Are you in there?' It's the soft tones (not) of Jade Montgomery. A door lifts on its hinges as she smacks the wall of the cubicle next to me. I curl up in a ball though it's not even me that she's after. Jade makes Year Sevens leap out of her way just with a glance and I swear I've even seen teachers hide in cupboards so they don't have to deal with her. An old feeling I've not had for a while returns in a very unwelcome way. I touch my face, hardly even realising what I'm up to. Four years ago, in Year Six, Jade and her crowd called me ugly every day for over a year. You don't need to be a psychoanalyst to work about where my love of cosmetics came from.

'Isabel Smellabel. I know you're in there with your disgusting skin. You make sure you stay in there. I don't want to catch the plague or whatever makes you look so hideous.' The door rattles again and then she's gone. Phew. That one really needs anger management.

I hear crying. I need to go but I also don't like the idea of leaving one of Jade's victims behind. I tap softly on the ancient wooden partition.

All I get in return is a sniff.

'Isabella?' I say. It's a risk beginning a conversation with a crying girl you don't know that well. I mean, you never know what you're getting into. But I decide the risk is worth taking. And after all, I do like to chat.

I try one last time. 'Whatever it is, I bet you're not having a worse day than me.'

'You wanna bet?' I hear the door slowly open. 'They say you're the queen of the makeover. Make over this.'

Intrigued, I leave the safety of my cubicle and see what horror awaits me.

'Oh,' I say. 'Well,' I say. Before me is Isabella McCormack, blessed or cursed depending on your outlook with Celtic genes that gives her skin that would make Snow White look like she'd fallen asleep on her step-mum's sunbed and hair so bright I need sunglasses. And there's nothing wrong with that. Nothing. Nothing at all.

It's just that the huge red spots, the size and ferocity of super-volcanoes, really stand out.

'They're not that bad,' I lie.

Isabella scowls at me. 'They are. I hate them. I tried to stay off school today, but my dad made me come in.'

Even I think missing school because of spots is a bit of an overreaction but figure out that saying that wouldn't be helpful under the circumstances. I begin to feel virtuous. My friends may have left me behind but I, Tulip Taylor, am better than that.

'I can help if you like,' I hear myself offering, even though I am going to be even later to my lesson.

'Oh yes, please.' Isabella looks like she'll burst with joy. 'Will you really?' She turns away from me and says quietly, 'They're always on at me. You heard Jade. She's spreading rumours I've got some contagious disease and now no one will come near me.'

'Don't listen to them. Okay, I'll help but it'll have to be quick.' It's funny really. Seconds ago, I was repulsed by the toilet. But here I am, applying my make-up to a stranger's spots. For a trained expert like myself, it doesn't take too long.

17

'Here,' I say, pushing a mirror in her direction. 'What do you think?'

'They've gone,' she says in a voice that's dropped in actual awe. 'You're a witch. You made them go away.'

'Just cosmetics and a bit of knowhow,' I say, though secretly I am quite proud of what I've done. One minute there's a girl hiding in the toilet scared of a bully and then I, Super Makeover Girl, with my amazing powers of blending, concealing and contouring, come along and send her out into the world, all sparkly and confident. I really could change the world, you know, with my skills if only I got the opportunity.

'Thank you,' Isabella says, 'but…'

'Time to go,' I smile. 'Look I'd love to chat. Talking is one of my favourite occupations. Maybe message me later and I'll run you through what I just did but I've got to go. I'm in so much trouble.'

'I know.' She's trying to stop me going now. What is wrong with this girl? 'But before you go, I've really got to tell you…'

'Look.' I put my hand on her hand and peel it off my arm. 'No need to thank me. I'm just glad to spread a little happiness in the world. I'll send you a link to my vlog.' With that I'm off and out the door but Isabella is still shouting after me.

But I haven't got time to listen. I have a new boy to impress with my aforementioned natural beauty. My heart is starting to pound with excitement at the thought of meeting him. Someone new, someone who might share my dream of getting out of here, one way or another. Until I'm old enough, the internet is the only way to escape.

As I walk as fast as I can without breaking into a run, I wonder what excuse Kate and Anjali have made for me.

I hope it's a good one.

Otherwise I'm dead.

CHAPTER FOUR

Word: Mortification (noun)

As I open the door, the lesson is in full swing and Ms Regan is attacking Destiny Richard.

'It may surprise you, but I do know a little about the Illuminati. I also think you'll find that people who consider the Illuminati to be a demonic force set on world domination are generally stupid. Are you stupid, Destiny?'

Ouch. Ms Regan takes no prisoners. I attempt to breeze in – big grin, confident stance, looking like I don't have a care in a world. At the same time, I'm quickly scoping the class for this Harvey. Freya described him at form time as having 'a face chiselled by angels'. I think this was a compliment, but I didn't know that angels were supposed to be handy with DT tools.

Then I see him, already sitting with the loud, cool boys, making them look ordinary, and I understand.

Well, hello.

It's like a ray of sun has pierced the clouds and picked out the chosen one. He's just like his photo – perhaps even better in real life. He's so tall and I see how broad his shoulders are. He is perfection. I try to see if his eyes have that thoughtful expression that was in his photo.

I flash my best, most rehearsed smile his way and await his

flattered acknowledgement back. Most guys consider me pretty, so I'm confident that he'll like me.

But he's not smiling. He's staring. And not in a good way. His eyes are not soft and thoughtful. In fact, he's looking at me as if I'm the world's biggest loser. My stomach lurches, my palms go sweaty. What is his problem? Why doesn't he like me? He must be an arrogant posh boy after all, who looks down on us mere mortals.

Patrick Adeyemi takes one look at me and shouts out, 'What's the smell?' and falls under the table as if killed by gas. Then next to him, Callum Stewart leans over and opens the windows. 'Miss, you've got to save us. We'll all die from the stench.'

I stare at Kate for an explanation and mouth, 'What have you said?' But she doesn't stare back. Instead, she's hiding behind her book. This is not good. What did she say about me? Whatever it was, New Boy is finding it all funny. He's finding me funny and that was not part of my glorious plan.

I head to my table while Ms Regan yells at Patrick and Callum.

'What did you say?' I hiss at Kate.

The book wobbles a bit but doesn't reply.

'I know you're there, Kate Morgan. Just because you can't see me doesn't mean that I can't see you.' I push down the top of the book, but she's pulled her fringe across her face, so we can't make eye contact.

'Don't get mad at me, Tulip,' she whimpers. 'Regan put me on the spot and I found words coming out of my mouth.'

'What words?' I don't want to know but I also need to know at the same time.

'You were still in the toilet and that sort of got stuck in my mind. Regan stared at me the way that she does, and I think she hypnotised me. Anyway, I said…'

'She told the class you had diarrhoea,' Anjali says.

Inside, I'm screaming, just like Callum who now appears to be in his final death throes, pretending to choke on his own vomit.

'I asked you not to tell her,' Kate cries.

'She had to know. Honesty is the best policy.' Anjali is enjoying this too much.

Eventually all I can manage is, 'But she wasn't honest. It was a lie.'

'What was I supposed to say?' Kate is now wailing. 'That you were doing your make-up. And Tulip, while we're on the subject, I hope you don't mind me pointing out…'

'Don't you change the subject,' I say. 'We're not finished with this. I am never going to live this down.'

'I know,' says Anjali, with a touch too much enjoyment.

By now Callum is a twitching corpse on the floor. But Patrick has seen the glint in Ms Regan's eyes and has decided that sitting down and looking vaguely interested in the lesson might be a good idea if he is ever to achieve his life-long dream of becoming a dentist.

'Tulip Taylor, you've finally come to join us.' There is something vaguely hypnotic about Ms Regan. Now those icy eyes are fixed on me. I think about trying to come up with a better, different excuse, but my mind goes blank. 'I am not interested in why you are late. The fact that you are indeed late is all that is of any importance. You have detention after school every night this week.'

I think that my interrogation is over but it's at that moment a strange expression comes over Ms Regan's face. She's staring at me as if she can't quite put into words whatever's troubling her. I've never been scrutinised by a teacher quite like this. I'm like a small (I'd like to think rather cute) hamster transfixed before a boa constrictor.

'Tulip.'

'Er – yes, Miss?'

'I don't wish to make personal comments but as you have missed half of my lesson I am going to skip over the usual rules of engagement.'

'Er – what was that, Miss?'

'I don't know quite how to put this but there's something wrong with your face.' The class explodes. Even Callum, who has been lying on the floor dead, starts to sit up and howl with laughter. New Boy looks amused and shakes his head. This is not how it was supposed to be.

My fingers instinctively move to my face. What can she mean?

Anjali 'I'm very honest' pipes up next to me. 'Tulip, you only did one half of your make-up. You've got one eyebrow on fleek and the other's non-existent and then…'

'I get the picture,' I say, though I really don't want to. It all falls into place. I was halfway through my routine when the

23

great cosmetic disaster happened. Then I decided to be nice to Isabella. This led to me being late so I, Tulip Taylor, queen of make-up tutorials and the empress of the selfie, have walked into class with make-up which is not only less than perfect but makes me look ridiculous. I'd rather them all think I was stuck in the toilet with – well, with what Kate said. And to think, I wanted to impress the new boy. Yup, I might as well walk right out of here and flush myself down the toilet.

'Why didn't you tell me?' I hiss.

'I tried,' Kate returns, 'but you wouldn't listen.'

I feel my face go red and I reach into my bag for my make-up wipes.

'No, no, no,' Ms Regan says, 'whatever you're looking for, Tulip, you don't need. We'll continue with our debate and you can just listen. Unless of course, you want to contribute, as it's a topic I believe is close to your heart.'

I stare at her in disbelief. Is the woman some kind of sadist? She's going to make me sit here for the rest of the lesson looking like this? Her eyes seem to gleam all of a sudden and it's not because she's used eye-brightening gel. No, it's because she's taking pleasure from my humiliation.

Not cool, Ms Regan, I think. Not cool at all.

I ease my phone out to try and take a picture of myself, so I can see exactly how bad it is. It's bad.

Callum starts to get up. 'No,' Ms Regan says, 'you made the foolish decision of lying on the floor. You can stay there for the rest of the lesson.'

'But the floor's hard.'

24

'You should have thought about that before you began to impersonate a corpse. You're dead. Now lie there.'

Callum whimpers and goes back down on the floor.

'Tulip, I hope you're not getting your phone out because I would confiscate it. Put it away. Now is not the time for selfies.' My cheeks burn again and the phone edges away. New Boy is looking at me again and I'm pretty sure he's smirking at me now. I feel that I've been judged and categorised.

'Now,' Ms Regan continues, 'this afternoon's topic for debate is … Callum, do a drum roll, it's all the dead are good for … the internet. Is it a power for good or evil?'

CHAPTER FIVE

Word: Plagiarism (noun)

There are moans but I let out a small squeal of joy. I hate talking without having rehearsed it but at least I have all the opinions on this subject.

I put my hand up. Might as well try to get back into Ms Regan's good books. 'Can I start then?'

She nods. 'As our resident blogger, it is only what I would expect.'

I hear Patrick say to New Boy, 'Yeah, she has a channel on make-up' and then I hear New Boy snort. This is still not going well so I leap in before I get too nervous. 'Okay, well my starting point is that the internet is not only a force for good but the greatest techno – techno – technoligical? No – technological development ever.' So that could be more polished, but I've not had time to prepare. How could I not get technological out?

Just as I'm about to continue, New Boy says, 'Greater than penicillin? Greater than the printing press? Can you really defend that comment? How is the internet technoligical? That's a new word on me.'

I burn with embarrassment. He's teasing me for stumbling over words. Does he think I actually don't know how to say it? Before I can say anything more in my defence, there's general

laughter at me again. First the eyebrows, now 'technoligical' –
I'm never going to live this down.

Ms Regan waves a regal hand at New Boy. 'Pray, continue.'

He leans back in his chair, shifting a bit. 'Er, surely it's
someone else's turn to say something.'

All of a sudden, everyone's staring out of the window or
fiddling with their hair.

'Surely, you have an opinion,' Ms Regan says. 'What, for
example, are your thoughts on the selfie?'

Harvey twiddles his fingers, breathes deeply and seems to
mutter three words under his breath. Be. More. And I can't
catch the last one. For a moment, I think he's going to wimp
out but then he begins. 'I think that selfies are what's wrong
with today's society. With today's young people. I mean it's just
pure narcissism.'

'What?' I spit out.

'Narcissism. It means being in love with yourself. It's from…'

'The Greek myth of Narcissus who fell in love with his own
reflection. I am familiar with the story,' Ms Regan repeats and
I want to shout, 'Yes, I knew that', but then I'd look weird.

His accent is starting to annoy me. He speaks like Prince
Harry. And it's not just that that's annoying. He's suggesting
that a) I'm narcissistic and b) I'm too stupid to know what I
am. This is not cool at all. I lean back, fix him with a glare of
my own (admittedly some of the impact is lost in the one eye
brow situation).

Bring it on, Posh Boy, bring it on. What have you got to say
for yourself?

27

'We live in a huge, fascinating, varied world full of adventure. But what do teenagers look at? A few square centimetres of glass, metal and plastic made from the world's precious resources. The world is stripped of these to make these little boxes. Which might be okay if we then used them for the greater good of mankind.'

I am listening. You can't help but listen because his voice is so loud. I can multi-task though so I'm also removing my solitary eyebrow while taking a selfie to check it's all gone.

'But what we do is use these items for a pointless activity.' I look up again and see he's looking at me. I see where this is going. 'We use them for selfies.'

The class look at me and react. 'Caught in the act, Tulip, caught in the act,' Callum comments.

'Get down, corpse,' Ms Regan says. 'Continue, Harvey.'

'The internet seems to rule our lives. We post food on Instagram instead of enjoying it. We message each other instead of talking. We spend hours putting filters on photos instead of looking out of the window. And please don't think I'm being sexist but we all have to admit that girls are the worst at this. I mean, come on lads, don't you agree?'

Patrick whistles. 'You have to admit it's true, Tulip. You're never off your phone.' Harvey nods in agreement as if he knows.

This is an act of war.

A thought strikes me. Whilst I disagree with all he's saying, he is putting his points pretty well. Suspiciously well. After the girls left, I spent quite a while googling his dad. Okay, I should have been doing homework, but I do like a bit of procrastination.

28

I ended up watching some TED talk that his dad delivered. And now I'm experiencing déjà vu.

'What is better – a life spent looking at a small screen, sending out fake images, wasting time on fake friendships. A life lived in pixels and megabytes. Or a life spent out there – for real. In the wild, real world.' He nods.

Two girls on the front row applaud him.

Even Callum dares to sit up and contributes, 'That's deep, man, that's deep.'

Ms Regan shouts at him, 'Dead, Callum, you're dead. The dead don't speak.'

Kate whispers, 'He seems nervous.'

'Don't be ridiculous, he's the most arrogant person I've ever met,' I say, not looking up.

'If you looked up from your phone, you might actually see what I mean. He's shaking. You've just judged him already.'

'That's harsh. I think you'll find that he's judged me. Ha.' Something interesting pops up on the screen. I put my hand up.

'An excellent and refreshing contribution there, Harvey.' Ms Regan sees my hand up. 'What is it, Tulip?'

'Can I respond? The debate's not over yet, is it?'

A flicker of confusion spreads across her face. 'If you insist. I thought you might have had enough attention for today.'

Nick slaps Harvey on the back, 'You're cool, man. You need to lose that accent but you're cool. You can hang round with us if you like.' Then Nick goes for that annoying man hug.

This time I need to say what I want to say without any

mistakes, so I do what I always do when I'm nervous – internally, I recite a list of my favourite words. *Shrike, sunfish, viniferous, pernickety.* Deep breath. And then I begin.

CHAPTER SIX

Word: Confrontation (noun)

It's my turn in the spotlight, Posh Boy.

'I would like to contradict some of these comments. For lots of reasons. I mean, not having a phone is social suicide for any modern teenager. But we've heard how girls spend all their time taking selfies as if that's the worst thing in the world.'

I pause for effect. 'Really? Really? Taking a photo that you're proud of is the worst thing in the world that you can imagine? Believe me, I can imagine a whole lot worse. I'm sure most girls can. As girls, our appearance is judged every second of the day. We're surrounded by perfect, airbrushed photos in adverts of what we're supposed to look like. We walk down the street and boys and men...' I stare at Harvey, who's suddenly looking less confident than before '...they think that it's okay to comment on what we look like. As if our whole purpose is to get their approval. So, when I take selfies I do it for this reason. To take back control. It's me saying, "This is what I look like. And I'm proud of it." It's a way of boosting self-esteem.'

Anjali shouts, 'Go, sister. You tell them.' A glare from Ms Regan soon silences her and Kate's applause suddenly stops mid-clap. I risk a quick glance at Harvey. He's looking at me in an odd way. He's not smiling anymore. He looks like a dog has just got up and started playing the piano. I try to hide a smirk. Smirking makes you look smug.

'Another thing I love about the internet is that you can connect with people whenever you want to on your terms. Some people have anxiety. Some people find it hard to make conversation with people. Social media means you can reach out to people and find support whenever and wherever.'

Okay, I know that's not completely true but I'm trying to make a general point there. 'A few years ago, I would have been too nervous to speak out like this but vlogging has helped me develop my confidence. Connecting with people online has made it easier for me to connect with people in real life.' I breathe. This is a bit personal but it's all true. I suddenly feel vulnerable saying something like this but then I do truly believe it.

'So, this little grey, black, rose gold or white box is not a fashion accessory. It's so much more. It means you can have a world of knowledge at your fingertips. You want to find out something – a few seconds later, you get the answer.' I flourish my phone like a prop, hoping Ms Regan doesn't swoop in and take it off me.

'For example, a few minutes ago, I had an idea. I heard a talk and thought I'd seen something similar before.' Now I really eyeball Harvey whose smile is not looking as secure as it was a few seconds ago. In fact, he looks as nervous as Kate said he was. 'And what I found was really interesting. It turns out that Harvey's rousing speech is not as original as you might think. It turns out that he's copied what his dad said word for word.' He's not looking quite so shiny now. In fact, he's sinking down in his chair.

'In case you don't believe me, let's hear Daddy in action.' I press play on the video clip I've found, and Harvey's dad's voice can be heard on my tinny speakers saying pretty much exactly what Harvey has said.

'What is better – a life spent looking at a small screen, sending out fake images, wasting time on fake friendships. A life lived in pixels and megabytes. Or a life spent out there – for real. In the wild, real world.'

'Perhaps someone should look up the word "plagiarism".'

Shots fired. Burned. Mic drop. I am done. I don't look to see what effect this is having. I don't need to.

As I sit down I'm a bit wobbly. I know I can project confidence but that's all it is – a projection. I practise and practise things a bit like taking a selfie until it's right. That's how I deal with stuff. Anyway, Anjali and Kate are applauding loudly. Even Ms Regan's frosty face has melted to something that's coming a bit closer to approval. I can't resist sneaking a look at Harvey who now looks like a different person. It's like he's shrunk.

'Well, that was a good response there, Tulip. Perhaps Harvey needs to look "plagiarism" up and enlighten us on its meaning next lesson.'

The bell goes at this moment. We all start to move. 'Not so fast, Harvey, not so fast,' Ms Regan says, 'you and I need to have a little chat.' He gives me a look as I go past. Funnily enough it's not a dirty one. But I don't care what he thinks about me anymore. No, I'm done with any little daydreams I might have had about getting to know him better. I'm out of here. I don't want Ms Regan to remind me about my detention, so I keep my head down and walk past her as quickly as I can.

'That was cool,' Kate says, jumping up and down a little bit with excitement.

'You still told the whole class that I had diarrhoea,' I remind her. 'I haven't forgotten that yet.'

Her head drops. 'I know. I'm sorry. I panicked. I'm not cool under pressure like you.'

I'm about to say, 'Well, you're not cool at all,' but stop myself.

Only, that's what she says. 'I know I'm not cool. I don't know why we're even friends.'

'You are cool,' I say and hug her. 'In a nerdy, not-cool sort of way you are very cool. Not cool is the new cool. That's what everyone says.'

We shoulder bump.

'Right, enough of this emosh stuff. My face needs sorting. Call me superficial if you like but I need my eyebrows back.'

Kate is reading something on her phone that's making her eyebrows disappear under her hairline. 'Tulip…'

'What – don't distract me. I need to do my contouring.'

'Tulip, really, I think you should see this. Your mum's tagging you on Instagram again.'

I grab the phone, the old horror rising up inside me.

'We have a deal,' I shout. 'She has Facebook and Twitter and I get Instagram and Snapchat. What's she done now?' I stare at the scratched surface of Kate's phone and then gasp.

She just has no idea how awful it is for me. It's okay for Willow and Rowan, they're only small, so they don't care about

34

their digital footprint and how their peers will judge them. They're not fifteen.

Thanks to Levityuk for these revolutionary pads. Sure @Tulip will feel #fresh and #protected when using these

She's tagged a photo of me in with pads. Oh, Mum, you've really done it this time. Because it's not any old photo. Oh no, this is one from the most hideous party ever held. My Moon Party. Where Mum invited everyone she knew round to 'celebrate' my first period. That's the kind of mum she is.

I text her furiously. 'Delete that post NOW. We need to talk.'

Hector: So, bro, how did it go? Do you like my rhymes? Think I've got a chance to be a rapper. Were you more like me?

Harvey: It went. I'm still standing. But I don't think pretending to be like you is going to work for me.

Hector: Course it will. You just need to give it time. It'll take a while to work up to my level. So, give me the chav report? Did they treat you like a superior being or chase you down the corridors and flush your head down a toilet?

Harvey: Neither.

Hector: Well, what then?

Harvey: Not much.

Hector: You're being very unsatisfactory. I'm bored and I need entertainment. Tell me what they're like. Are they really, really awful? Are they morons? Were the girls entranced by your manly good looks?

Harvey: Hector. Chill. I had five lessons. I was stared at. I took part in a debate and got some applause.

Hector: That's my boy!

Harvey: Yeah, but I was nervous so I borrowed some of Dad's TED talk. But then this girl realised I'd copied Dad and called me out for it.

Hector: YOU GOT OUTWITTED BY A CHAV GIRL. SHAME ON YOU, MAN, SHAME. YOU ARE AN EMBARRASSMENT TO THE CLAN OF MCMANUS.

Harvey: It was weird. She was one of those try-hards who wears far too much make-up but then she spoke and she seemed alright.

Hector: GOD, I FORGOT TO TELL YOU.

Harvey: What and will you take the caps lock off?

Hector: You know Charlie in 6E?

Harvey: Yes.

Hector: Well, his girl (bit of a tart but she's hot) watches some make-up video and the girl on it was discussing you. Apparently this girl (not Charlie's girl) said you were hot. And what was it? Used some ridiculous word to describe you.

Harvey: What word?

Hector: Can't remember. Never heard of it. But yeah, three girls at your new school were all drooling over you. One of them literally apparently. How stupid is that? And gross.

Harvey: Really? What were their names?

Hector: I can't be bothered with stupid details like girls' names. Apparently one of them is the vlogger/blogger/whatever. Though I do remember she had a ridiculous name like Hyacinth or Blossom.

Harvey: Tulip?

Hector: Who would call their child that? That's child abuse. You might as well call her Chardonnay and get it over with.

Harvey: That's the girl I was talking about. She seemed okay.

Hector: Well she's got the hots for you so you go for her if you like her. Then again, the thought of you with a make-up vlogger is too disgusting. Dad will send you to outer space if he hears that.

Harvey: I'm pretty sure she hasn't. I don't think she likes me. And how many times do I have to tell you? I CHOSE TO COME HERE. Dad didn't send me anywhere. Look, you've got me shouting now.

Hector: You can tell yourself that as much as you like. But the truth is you just couldn't handle our school. Dad's old school. Where I'm Head Boy. But you just couldn't take it. You just hated coming second to me all the time.

Harvey: Just give it a rest, will you.

Hector: So, this girl, she's a make-up vlogger? STOP THE PRESS I HAVE HAD THE MOST AWESOME IDEA OF ALL TIME. Send her the link to Dad's TV show. That would be so funny. Imagine someone like her trying to survive in the wild. What was her name?

Harvey: I don't know her. I've not talked to her. I'm not sending her any link.

Hector: Wimp. Go on, do it. DO IT. DO FOR THE BROTHERS. DO IT FOR THE BANTZ. DO IT TO PROVE YOU ARE A MAN AND WORTHY OF THE MCMANUS NAME.

Harvey?

…

Harvey?

…

Loser.

CHAPTER SEVEN

Word: Capitulation (noun)

By the time I get home, even though I've had a detention to think about it, I am not any calmer. She's not answered any of my increasingly angry texts. I've even resorted to sending threatening gifs but it's having no effect. The post is still there. Even when I finally get home, she seems to have left a number of cunningly placed obstacles in my way.

First of all – Rowan who, as normal, is dressed in full Disney princess regalia. Cheap-looking polyester replica dress? Check. Hideous blonde wig with plait? Check. Impossible to wear plastic mules with fake diamonds? Check.

'Tulip…'

The whining has begun.

'I need to talk to Mum, Row, I'll talk to you later.'

'But Mummy said you'd help make me beautiful.'

'You're already beautiful, Row, you don't need any help from me.'

'I know, but I tried and it all went wrong. I tried to do it the way you did it but I couldn't get the eyes right.'

Row's little face looks downcast and for a second I feel a pang of sympathy but then a horrible thought strikes me.

'Rowan, when you say you tried to do it the way I do it, whose make-up were you using?'

When Rowan tries to hide in my skirt, I have my answer. I try to control the irritation welling up. 'How many times have I told you not to mess with my stuff?'

Whimpers emerge from behind the wig. 'I want to be pretty like you.'

You would have to have a heart of stone not to fall for that one.

I clearly have a heart of stone.

'Rowan, all of that stuff is expensive. And lovely. And mine. You get your own. I don't want to have your five-year-old snotty germs over everything. Never touch my things again. In fact, don't even go in my room again. You are banned!'

This leads to full-on tears, but I've had enough. I need to talk to Mum and I can do without make-up crises with a five year old.

A final howl emerges behind me as I march to the back of the house to track Mum down to her lair. 'You hate me because I'm a boy and boys shouldn't wear make-up.'

My heart of stone softens so I turn and go back to Rowan. I sit next to him on the floor and wipe a few tears away. 'You're crying on your dress, Row. Don't mess it up.'

He continues, 'If I was a girl, you'd do my make-up. You do Willow's and Mummy's.'

I sigh. Sometimes I wonder if there's another house like ours in the world. Is any other girl having to comfort her brother because he's crying over make-up while about to have an argument with her mother over linking her on the internet with sanitary products?

Welcome to my life.

Hugging Rowan, I try to avoid his face as it is pretty much shiny with snot now. 'Row, I will do your make-up later. Full-on princess makeover. But haven't you got rugby practice soon? You better get changed for that and then if there's time I'll do it before bed.'

I get a full-on bear hug for that. 'I love you, Tulip. You are the best of bestest sisters.'

'I know, and don't you forget it.'

I'm free – but Mum has left another trap for me in the kitchen. Willow is dancing around wearing only a unicorn headdress. And I mean, ONLY a unicorn headdress. She attempts to engage me in conversation but all she gets is the hand.

'No, Willow, I do not know where your unicorn onesie is. I expect it's lost in Unicorn Land (her bedroom). You need to go on a mission to Unicorn Land to find your lost fur. The Queen of Unicorn Land told me herself that only you can do it. I will only get in the way. Go forth, child, and fulfil your destiny…' I point majestically towards her bedroom and she trots off, doing a pretend gallop, whilst still butt naked chanting, 'I am the Chosen Unicorn, I am the Chosen Unicorn.'

Another small child dilemma sorted, now it's time for Mum. I think I need a few calming words before I find her. *Cleave, egress, glibbery, ligate.*

It's not that hard as she's in her pod. No, she is not a pea. Peas would be easier to deal with. Her pod is a wicker construction that she's had built in the piece of land next to our

41

house which we call the orchard. It does have trees, so that's partially true but it's not exactly what you'd call beautiful. Mum calls it 'unspoiled' but really, it's just neglected. She bought this house for the orchard as she likes to pretend that we live in the country. This is sort of true. It does smell of cow poo a lot and there are a quite a few older people.

Anyway, Mum loves 'the orchard' as it's full of good energies there. It's certainly full of something. Mum spends most of her time in her wicker pod all at one with nature, while at the same time connected to Wi-Fi (and heated against the spring cold with a heater on a long extension which just about reaches from the house). She doesn't seem to see any contradiction in this. As I push the door open, Mum, all wild hair and big smiles, raises up her hand while she talks on the phone. 'Of course, that would be lovely, the children would love that. Send those samples through and I'll do some lovely pictures. Normal fee? Normal fee. That's lovely. Always lovely doing business with you.' As you can see Mum loves the word 'lovely'.

She used to be a copywriter (someone who writes the words on adverts). She worked when it was just me but then she started blogging about the joys of having children when the twins came along. Some other mums liked what she was writing (mostly because she seemed to think that drinking gin at all times was some kind of cure for feeling down about being a mum) and before you know, she's actually making a living out of her blog. This is mostly because advertisers pay her to feature products and then her million followers might be fool enough to go out and buy them. The only good thing about this is that I get free stuff. All the cosmetic companies now send us the latest shades and products so that I can use them and feature them in my videos. I suppose you could say that selling ourselves on the internet is our family business. Which is sort of fine if a bit weird. But sometimes, like today, she's gone too far.

Finally, she leans back in her sheepskin-covered chair where she conducts all her 'business'. 'Now, pumpkin, what seems to be the matter? Why are you being so sensitive?'

'Firstly, don't call me pumpkin. Secondly, I'm not being sensitive. Thirdly, we had a deal. You use Facebook and Twitter. I have Instagram and Snapchat. And you linked me into one of your stupid posts on Twitter. For pads. Using a photo. We agreed no photos. Do you have any idea how uncool that is?'

'But darling, it was one little post. One little post that made us some money. I thought your generation were cool about periods. I mean why be shy about it? Maybe you should make it a new campaign to be more open about periods. I think it's a thing on Twitter – livetweetyourperiod.'

Where do I even begin on this? 'It doesn't make us money; it makes you money. And yes, girls have periods and if I wanted to post about it, I would. But you didn't give me that choice did you. You thought, "Oh look, I can make some money here and who cares if it embarrasses Tulip?" You keep telling me that I need to grow my online presence, that I need to think about my brand, that I need to have a strategy. And I do. And you've ignored what I want and what I'm trying to do and pleased yourself like you always do.'

43

She sits up at that moment and I think I might have gone too far there. It's all gone a bit Antarctic in here all of a sudden.

'Tulip. Stop thinking about yourself for one moment.'

Well, that's hardly fair. I start to answer but she puts up one hand and suddenly I'm silent. Why do I always do this? I can fight my own corner with everyone else but with Mum, I just can't.

'All this…' she indicates the phone, the laptop, the contracts all around her, '…is what puts food on your plate. It pays our bills. This is how we live. This is what puts a roof over our head. Don't think I love it all. I don't. But until someone comes up with a better way of making a living this is what we do. This is our family business.' All of a sudden, she looks very tired. 'I'm at this eighteen hours a day. You get time off when you go to school. But I have think of new posts. I have to find new and better photos. And now it's all about videos. Because without it we go under. You might not like it. And to be honest with you, some days I don't like it either. But currently I don't have another plan. Do you? If so I'm all ears.'

I stand silently. Maybe I've been a bit harsh on her.

'I'm a single parent. God knows when and if your dad will pay any maintenance. He's months behind. Years even.' She's right. Dad is useless. Word of caution. Don't get involved with a guy called Storm. Not unless you're prepared for him to live up to his name and blow in and out whenever he feels like it.

'Well, Tulip, I will unlink you from that post. Perhaps after all it doesn't fit with your online profile as you suggest. Is that a deal?'

'Deal,' I find myself saying.

'We're a partnership, you and me. I can't do it without you. A lot of people have let me down over the years, sweetie, please don't be the next one.'

I put my hand on hers. 'I won't let you down, Mum.'

'Fabulous.' A huge smile spreads across her face. 'That's such a relief. Because I am going to have to ask you to do a teensy-weeny bit more work than normal.'

'But…'

'So, here's the latest contract. I signed it for you today.' She produces a list and hands it to me. 'Now they have asked for one change. Instead of doing a vlog on them all, they want you to do one for each product.'

I look at the list. It's huge. To make a video for each would take hours … days…

'You mean I can't do what I normally do, make a video using all the different products at once.'

'No can do, kiddo. New rules. Separate vlogs for each company. Yes, it's more work but it's also more money.'

That word again. Money.

'Don't look like that, sweet pea. Think of all the lovely things you get. And I thought you liked vlogging. You're extremely good at it. This could be the start of something great. You could really go somewhere with this, Tulip, you really could.'

'But…' I try to say, looking at the list, some of this stuff isn't any good. But then I see Mum's hopeful face.

Looking at this list of vlogs to be made, it doesn't feel like fun. It feels like work. Possibly dishonest work at that – saying stuff is good when it's not. And let's not mention the fact that this stuff is probably tested on animals, wrapped in plastic and has goodness knows what chemicals in it. Mum and I just ignore that even though it doesn't quite fit in with the pod in the orchard. We appear to have made a pact with the Devil. I might not have sold my soul – yet – but I clearly seem to have sold my life away for the time being to help put food on the table.

And I've said I won't let my mum down. I don't even know what I can do to get myself out of this.

I've been deceived, beguiled and hoodwinked.

CHAPTER EIGHT

Word: Entrammelled (adjective)

Even back in the sanctuary of my room, I don't feel much better. My webcam seems to be staring at me in an ominous way. I have a hug with Mr Snowy, my ancient, huge polar bear and then re-arrange my other fifty plus soft toys. Some may say they are tacky; I say they are cute and offer a great contrast to Mum because: a) they give me unqualified support and cuddles and b) they don't talk.

After Mr Snowy has silently reassured me that everything will work out, I flick through my dictionary to see what word best expresses how I feel. Entrammelled. Well and truly trapped.

But I'm not one to sulk for too long, so I spend the next hour looking at the list of things I have to do. This doesn't make it any shorter. No point in going on Google for any advice. It's going to take days. I'll probably be thirty-five by the time I finish all of this and who wants a middle-aged woman preaching on about the best liquid eyeliner? I'm doomed. Mum will lock me in here until I'm finished. I'll be found years later, gibbering things like 'perfect matte finish' or 'if you're going for a dewy look' whilst staring desperately at an out-of-date webcam. I'll be like Rapunzel but without the amazingly well-nourished hair.

I think I might be rambling now. Pull yourself together, Tulip.

My phone suddenly starts to buzz like a bee that's drunk too many caffeine drinks. Obviously, I grab it to have a look.

I've been tagged in a post. Not that unusual. What is more unusual is that the person who's done it is Harvey. Yes, Mr 'Who Needs the Internet' clearly has a social media account and knows how to use it. Hypocrite. But what does he want with me? We've not even spoken, and our eyes met only to prove that we dislike each other intensely.

He's posted 'Make Up Girl – Think you're up to the challenge?'

And then he posted a link. I click on it, despite myself.

It's an online application form for his dad's show.

I watch the publicity clip. It consists of a man shouting, with lots of shots of scary activities and close ups of terrified faces.

'Ten teens. Eight days. One elimination every day. Are you tough enough? Could you live wild with only your wits and survival skills to save you? Can you prove that you are the best?'

I've seen clips of the adult version before, but this is for teens. Hell, no. It sounds like my personalised version of hell. Scotland, even in June? Wild camping? Outdoors? No luxuries? What kind of madness is this? We live in the twenty-first century. We moved out of caves for a reason. It's generally considered a sign of civilisation that we build things called houses and move into them to keep the dark, cold and any random murderers at bay. And now this guy wants us to give all that up and embrace nature? Maybe he and Mum should get together. They sound like they'd have so much in common.

Then he tags me again. This time it's a gif of a chicken, running around in the most ridiculous way. My heart starts to pound, and I feel a bit sick. This is just how Jade and co made me feel all those years ago. I'm being called a coward for the whole world to see – I'm the butt of some stupid internet joke. Only a few hours ago, he was basically saying the internet was for losers and now he's using it to bully me. He's turning into the most inconsistent and annoying person I've ever met, and he only came into my life today. And I called him 'pulchritudinous' when, really, he's abhorrent.

My phone starts to explode with notifications. Basically, most of school are finding this funny. 'Tulip – in the wild? No way she can do it.' Comment after comment, some from boys, some from girls, all thinking that me going into nature is the funniest thing since Mr Reynold's trousers split in assembly.

Another ping. 'Can Tulip take the heat or is she just a Wilting Tulip?' And there's another gif of flowers flopping down pathetically.

I look at my phone and feel something new towards it. It feels like it's harassing me. First, Mum and her endless blogs. Now Harvey and the whole of school, all thinking that I'm too pathetic to go without my make-up. All these notifications are not like little hugs anymore.

I think the unthinkable. For once, I feel like switching off the Wi-Fi; then they'll leave me alone.

But that only solves one problem. I can't switch off Mum.

I'm called down to dinner. Lentils. Yum.

One hangover from her time living at one with nature is

that she cooks mostly vegan food. On Instagram, vegan food is generally green and lovely – all smashed avocadoes and shiny tomatoes. Not for us. We eat very unlovely, stodgy gloop that looks more like something the world's worst dinner lady has made for her entry into Most Unappealing Food Ever competition.

I pick at it without any enthusiasm. Rowan, all sweaty after rugby, is making his into lentil mountains while Willow is writing her initials in the slop in front of her.

Mum meanwhile is chomping hers down. She doesn't even seem to notice that it smells like bark and tastes like soil. Note to self – search up some yummy vegan food. It's out there, I know, I just need to find it.

Willow is now eating hers with her mouth open which means Rowan decides this is an out-grossing competition. He picks up a handful and smears it over his face. I suppose I could tell them to stop but a) I'm not an adult and b) it's pretty funny. Rowan flashes a look at Mum who is still oblivious. So he grabs the bowl and pours it over his head.

Now Willow is screaming and I'm laughing so much I can't breathe.

'Damn, did something good happen?' Mum was too distracted by her phone and she's missed it. 'Do it again, Rowan, whatever it was.'

Rowan is looking confused. 'You want me to put more food on my head?' he says, as lentil Bolognese runs down his face.

'You're right. You need to go and get cleaned up and then do it again.' Mum's in full bossy mood now. 'Off you pop then.'

Rowan looks at me and then at Willow. Even he, at five years old, realises that this is a bit mad.

Mum's back on her phone again, completely oblivious to the fact that she's currently lost touch with her more sensible side.

'Mum…' I start.

'Yes, twiglet?'

When have I ever been remotely like a twig, sapling or branch? But I refuse to be distracted.

'Mum, don't you think it's a bit weird to get Rowan to do that again? I mean, it was funny the first time, but it'll look rehearsed if he repeats it. He's not an actor, you know.'

Mum sighs deeply. 'Oh, I do know. It would make life easier if we could do a few takes.'

'So, we're a reality TV show now, are we?'

Mum stares at me as if I'm suddenly made of gold. 'Tulip. You are an inspiration. I knew I could rely on you to help. Have I ever told you that you are my favourite child?' She's lit up in a way that I've not seen since she got a free case of organic gin. 'You are a genius.'

'Er, exactly what have I said?'

'You know what you said. And yes, we should, my brilliant girl.' I get my cheeks pinched for this.

With that she's off, roaming through the house with me trailing after her. 'We could put cameras in every room, activated by movement. Or you could wear a GoPro when you're in the house. Then we'll never miss anything. You can edit the best bits into a daily highlights show. This could be huge. This could save us.'

The trouble is I still don't know if she's being serious or not. 'Mum, you're not actually suggesting we film our lives twenty-four hours a day?'

'Why not? This family is what the world needs. Us sharing our wonderful lives here is an act of love to the world.' She leans back and sighs with bliss.

'I thought this was all about making money.' I can't help but point this out especially if I'm the one who's going to be doing all the work.

'Well, of course it's about the money. This could set us up for life but we're not selling out. We're sharing our lovely family life, so everyone can enjoy it.' She's drifting off humming, but I have to try to make her listen.

'How am I going to have time to do all the make-up vlogs and then edit daily highlights? There aren't enough hours in the day.'

Mum stops, and I begin to have hope. It looks like she's finally seeing my point of view. 'You know, that is a very good point, my little chicky.'

Yay – finally.

She takes a deep breath. 'You know I've wanted to do it for a while. But now is definitely the right time. I'll ring your school tomorrow and tell them.'

'Tell them what?'

'Your decision of course.'

She's looking at me like I'm an idiot. What have I decided?

'To be home-schooled.'

I open my mouth, but no words come out.

Mum continues. 'You don't need formal education. You could stay at home with me all day, wouldn't that be lovely?'

Delete my previous comment about camping being the Worst Thing Ever. Spending twenty-four hours a day with my mother while she works me to the bone with editing endless videos – that is now my new definition of Worst Thing Ever. Deep breath time. Someone has got to make her see sense. 'But Mum, we can't have cameras in every room. I don't want my life broadcast to the world. And I really, really do not want to be home-schooled.'

'What's got you all hot and bothered, blossom petal? Do you want Mummy to make you some lovely, relaxing jasmine tea?'

'No. I don't. I want you to think…' But she's standing up and is now walking to the door. 'Rowan, are you ready? We need to do it now and I want you to do it exactly as you did before. Have I told you that you're my favourite child?'

She's not listening.

She never listens. And even if she did listen, she'll say we need to do it for the money. I don't have any answer for that one.

I'm going to come home tomorrow and find that every room is kitted out like a spy film with lenses whirring in on every move.

How can I stop this?

Harvey: What are you playing at? TAKE THAT POST DOWN

…

Harvey: Answer me.

…

Harvey: Hector, I know you're there. STOP PRETENDING TO BE ME ONLINE. You've made an account that looks like it's me. That wasn't cool. I don't know the girl.
Hector?

…

Hector?

…

Hector: It's all about the bantz. Look at the reaction. She's just some chav anyway. What do you care about her? Or do you LEURVE her? Are you going to bring her home to meet Mum? Do you think Dad would be impressed with your choice? Okay I'll take it down if you say that I am the superior son.

Harvey: …

Hector: I'm waiting. I am the superior son. Go on, say it and I'll leave your precious chav alone.

Harvey: Hector.

Hector: What?

Harvey: You're a loser.

Hector: TRIGGERED. Hahahahahahahahahahahahahaha-hahahahahahahahahahahahahahahahaha.
So the post stays… Or… Okay, Harvey, I've got a proposal for you.

Harvey: Leave me alone, Hector. Haven't you got friends you can torment?

54

Hector: But you're the most fun. Look, I've had a brilliant idea.

Harvey: I bet you haven't.

Hector: This chav girl…

Harvey: She's not a chav and she has a name. She's called Tulip.

Hector: Whatevs. Anyway, get her to sign up for the show.

Harvey: Why would I do that?

Hector: Because it would be funny.

Harvey: No.

Hector: I will admit that you are the superior son if she goes on the show.

Harvey: …

Hector: I will publicly admit to everyone that we know that you are superior in every way if she signs up for the show.

Harvey: …

Hector: Well? Will you accept the challenge or continue in being an embarrassment to the McManus name?

Harvey: I'll think about it

Hector: Use the chicken routine on her. It always works for me.

Harvey: The chicken routine that you use on me all the time?

Hector: Yup. Use it on her. It always works. Be. More. Hector.

Harvey: You'll stop all of this and delete the account?

Hector: Of course. I promise. Scout's honour.

CHAPTER NINE

Word: Sublime (adjective)

The next day at school, as Anjali picks over yesterday's events in minute detail, I am in a quandary about pretty much everything but all anyone wants to talk about is Harvey's post. Do I ignore the challenge which everyone else is finding so hilarious or confront him? Everywhere I go, some guy seems to be shouting at me. 'Going on that show, Tulip?' 'Bet you're not so hot without all that make-up, are you?' I have never been spoken to like this in all my years at high school. All of a sudden, this Harvey turns up and everything has started to go wrong. He must be a bad omen. Or my nemesis.

Deep in concentration on my notifications, I march across the yard, Anjali trailing behind me. Next thing I know I've walked into some guy's barrel of a chest and dropped my phone. Then a camera hits me and falls to the ground. I pick it up and look at what's in the screen on the back. It's really rather nice – a shot of cobwebs all shot with water, so it looks like it has jewels on it. I flick back. The next shot is beautiful too – a panorama of the hills, all grey and mysterious with the late spring sunlight hitting the very tops of them turning them to gold. There's someone artistic at this school? Well, I never.

'These are awesome,' I murmur. 'You've really got a good eye.' I look up to see whose camera it is. I didn't know anyone at my school even had such a hipster thing as a camera.

'Oh,' I say, 'it's you.' Inside, I'm thinking, really, it's you? Anjali gives me a look and a smile that I don't quite like.

'Very observant,' Harvey says, shoving his camera away in his bag. 'I think this is yours.' He gives me my phone without looking at me. It's like he can't look me in the eye.

'Well, as I've proved to you already, phones are really very useful. And not for taking selfies.'

'You got me,' he says, 'but the points I made…'

'The points your dad made…' Anjali flings back at him.

'Were still right. People our age look at phones all the time. You two were even doing it just now.'

Guilty as charged.

'You say that like it's a bad thing.'

Harvey starts to get agitated. 'It is a bad thing. There's much more to life than a few notifications.'

'So you say. But what about tagging me in that post? That was not cool.'

He shifts from side to side, staring over my shoulder at some distant horizon. He'll look at anything apart from me then. 'Yeah about that…'

I interrupt. 'Yes about that. That was uncalled for. We don't even know each other, Mr "I don't use social media". And then you go tagging me.'

'There's something I need to tell you about that…'

I put my hand up. 'You know, I'm not interested.'

'But…'

'No. I'm not going to even dignify what you did with any more attention. Just stop talking now. I need to communicate with my followers.'

He finally looks at me, with an odd expression that I can't work out. 'Don't you feel that you're a bit dependent on that thing?' he motions to my beloved phone. 'I mean, you're clearly not stupid. Can't you see you're addicted?'

I bridle. 'I don't need you to tell me whether I am stupid or not. Yes, I like my phone, but I could do without it if I wanted.'

Anjali draws breath. 'Tulip, stop talking now and walk away.'

'You've met me for one day and you think you know me. I could go five days without my phone if I wanted. I could go for five weeks.' This clearly is a lie. But for some reason I don't quite understand I feel a very strong need to prove Harvey wrong. I got him yesterday and I'm not letting him get the better of me now. 'You turn up here, thinking you're something special. You know nothing about me.'

He shuffles around. 'I do know one thing though. I know what "pulchritudinous" means.' His voice has gone quite soft for a moment and he won't look me in the eye again. Then he does. He steps closer for a moment and I can see myself reflected in his pupils.

I don't think I can bear it. How did he find out? Right, I have to show him that I don't care about him one little bit.

'It's funny how someone can have a nice exterior, but you can really go off them when they start talking.' I step back, throwing as much shade at him as I can.

I can feel Anjali fidgeting next to me, putting an arm on my shoulder, whispering, 'Tulip, stop now.'

I'd be okay if only I could have rehearsed this. Improvised arguments are not my strong point. He can't have the last word.

'Look,' he says, 'the whole tagging thing was not cool. But you might like being on Dad's show. It's going to be in a beautiful part of the world. You could show that there's more to you than being a vlogger. That's if you really could live without your phone for ten days.'

Anjali looks at me. I look at my phone.

'I'll think about it,' I say, and start to head away, heading for safety. This whole conversation has me so confused. Then he mutters something under his breath. It sounds like 'Be more…' and his whole face goes from sincere to weird.

'Here goes nothing,' he says and then he starts clucking and waggling his arms, like he's a demented chicken nugget.

'What in the name of mascara are you doing?'

'Are you a chicken, Tulip? Too scared to go without your phone?'

He's clearly mad. He's waddling round the playground, squawking repeating, 'Tulip's a chicken.'

I stare at Anjali. 'How do I make him stop? He's possessed.'

Anjali can't stop looking at him, appalled but entranced. 'This is the best story ever! I can't wait to tell everyone.'

I decide that the best idea is just to run away but he follows me. Inside, I slam the door to the girls' toilet in his face.

'What an idiot,' I mutter.

How can someone take such beautiful photos and then be such a freak? What was the whole chicken thing about? It was like he was possessed by another person.

I just can't work him out.

CHAPTER TEN

Word: Progenitor (noun)

Back at home I try to forget all about Harvey, his beautiful photos, his annoying behaviour and his gorgeous eyes. Mum does her best to distract me by telling me she's phoned school to start the move to home-schooling. ARGH. What does a girl do when she's desperate and has no way out?

That's right. She rings her dad. When all else fails, you turn to your parents for support, especially when one of your problems is the other parent. But I do need to remember that my dad at some point looked into a mirror and said, 'I know what. I don't think I'll be Nigel anymore. I'll call myself Storm.' That is all you really need to know about how my dad's mind works.

Back in my bedroom (or the shrine to soft toys as Kate calls it but she's just jealous), I sit in front of my ancient laptop and check out Dad's latest posts. He's somewhere in south-east Asia. That's as specific as it gets and it all looks the same in his photos. Him, bit wrinkly, with dreadlocks that you might call blond if you're feeling generous (or white if you want to be honest) and skin the colour of shiny mud. Then there's always bright blue sky or sea in the background. Add in a beach bar and assorted bikini-clad women and that is all that Dad ever posts. He clearly thinks he's won at life and, as I look out the window at grey skies and distant hills, it certainly looks more attractive than round here. I've sent him a message that I'll be ringing tonight but beer and women might be more interesting than me.

Rowan trundles in and nestles on to my knee. 'What are you doing?'

'I'm going to ring Dad.'

His face glows. 'I want to talk to him.'

'It depends. We might not get a connection and I need to talk to him about something.'

'Please, Tulip.'

And there's no saying no, so he snuggles in and tries to get a good look at the screen as I set up the video call.

It rings.

Nothing.

Rowan sighs and starts to fiddle with the fabric of his princess dress.

But then Dad answers. His face seems huge in the screen and I'm not sure if it's because he doesn't moisturise, but he looks a bit older than last time. Obviously, I don't mention this.

'Hey Dad.'

'Hey, girl. Rowan, how are you, little man?'

Rowan can hardly sit still with excitement. 'Daddy, Daddy, have you seen my dress?' He gets up to show the full synthetic glory of his sparkling layered outfit and plays with his tiara so that it sits straight.

Even five thousand miles away, I can see Dad struggling to find the words. 'Right, son, yes, that's great. Very – very – well, dress like.' Rowan basks in the praise while Dad slides his eyes over to me. 'Did you choose that for him?'

'No, he does it all himself,' I say.

'Right and what does Raven think?'

'She thinks it's cute and posts videos of him dancing on YouTube a lot. Don't you follow Mum on anything?'

He makes a face. 'Tulip. Your mother makes her presence felt even when I'm half a world away. Don't blame me if I don't track every single one of her movements. It's not that I'm not interested in you lot. It's – well – life is simpler if we don't communicate directly.' Then he smiles. 'But you're doing great, aren't you? I met this girl and while we were hanging out, she was watching a video of how to do party make-up. And there you were.'

I do feel a touch of pride. Like Rowan, I want Dad to show a bit of interest. Then I think of Dad hanging out with a girl who likes make-up. Yuk.

'So, you're all AOK then? Raven's not posting too many videos of Rowan I hope. I mean, you're cool, son, but I'm not sure the whole world is ready for how cool you are.'

This goes right over Rowan's head. 'I need to show you my other dresses,' and off he goes to get changed.

'Exactly what kind of videos does she post?' A shadow of something like concern crosses his face.

I sigh. 'You need to check her blog out, Dad. She's going too far. She shares everything, and I mean everything.'

His face shows the struggle. He cares; I know he does. But there's always the pull of the fun lifestyle. And we're hard work in comparison. But that's not good enough now. We need him, and he has to know and this time he mustn't let us down.

'What's the matter? Are you in trouble?'

'No. Yes.' I should have rehearsed this. 'Mum says she's only doing this to make money. Apparently, the more posts and vlogs she does, the more sponsors she gets and that means more money for us.'

He shakes his head. 'She never used to be this materialistic.'

'That's the thing,' I say, 'I don't think she really is. It's more about the bills being paid, I think.' Dad's face now looks old. I'm burdening him with our problems, but I don't feel sorry. He has this amazing life and hardly ever thinks of us. Or so it feels.

'So, what you're saying is that your old dad needs to pay his way. I've fallen behind on the money I'm supposed to pay Raven to help look after you guys. I'm not a regular payment sort of dad, I suppose.'

'Well, you need to be.' He flinches at my honesty and I try not to react. He has to understand. 'Dad, apparently we're in a bad way. Mum seems to think this is the only way we will make any money. And now she's now got this idea of putting cameras in every room and filming us all the time to create our own reality TV show. She thinks it will be our big break and we'll be the next big thing.'

'That is…' I better edit what he says.

'Yes. It is. Can you talk to her?'

'I don't know if you've ever noticed this about your mother, but she doesn't listen. To anyone. She never has.'

At least it's not just me.

I try again. 'But what do I do? I don't want her to do it, but she keeps going on about it.' I don't tell him about the home-schooling because it's only me that thinks that is a terrible idea.

There's a pause. 'If I pay the money that I owe, do you think that will change things?'

Relief floods though me. 'Yes. I do. I think that will make all the difference in the world. Can you pay it now?'

'Not right now. But I've got a big deal coming through in the next few weeks. Once that money's in, I'll send her what I owe her.'

'Will you really though? I'm not being funny, but you have said this before. You really will pay up?' I try to give him a hard stare via the webcam but I'm not sure that it's working.

My dad holds the laptop at his end and stares down the lens thousands of miles away. 'I promise to you, Tulip, that I won't let you down. Anyway, how's school? Any boyfriends I need to be worried about?'

No. Last date I went on involved going to Subway, eating a salad bowl, not talking at all. Hardly romantic.

'No, boys seem to want to annoy me rather than impress me.'

'That's a sign that they like you, love. Take it from an old sea dog.'

'Dad, we're in the twenty-first century now. No one falls for the old "treat them mean, keep them keen" thing any more. It's verging on abusive.'

Dad doesn't look convinced. 'You might be right, but I think boys might be a bit slow on the uptake with that one. Boys can find girls very intimidating you know.'

At that moment, Rowan swans in dressed as – yes, you've guessed it – the Swan Princess herself and there's no chance to discuss things further.

But for the first time I feel something like hope. If I can just stall her somehow then Mum will agree to postpone the 'Plan'. Then when Dad's money comes through, we'll be saved. Hurray for dads. But my mind is already working overtime: what can I do to gain us time for Dad's money to arrive?

CHAPTER ELEVEN

Word: Bibliotheca (noun)

A few days later, I'm in the local library.

It's not very high tech or the most glamorous place to hang out but I've been coming for years and I like it. The building is old but beautiful. I suppose these places were the internet of their day. I'm not expecting it to solve the 'how do I stop my mother ruining my life' problem. I've looked for a section called 'Crazy hippy mothers and how to tame them' but funnily enough it's not there. I suppose when I've finished working through the endless list of vlogs that I have to create to keep Mum's sponsors happy, I might write the book myself. Except of course for the one big problem. I haven't worked out how to tame her. Currently it's like trying to talk to an out-of-control steam train. She just keeps moving forward at speed while never stopping to listen.

Anyway, as I say, that's not why I'm here. I'm checking out the old books in the art section, looking for inspiration for colours or patterns to use in my vlogs. Yes, I could use the internet but so does everyone else. No one else is looking at these books and I might just find some things to inspire me.

I sit there for a while, sneezing as I turn the pages of these lovely books, which clearly haven't been opened for a while, scribbling down notes in my notebook as I go and occasionally snapping a shot when I find something interesting. Runny eyes and snot are not a good look – thank goodness no one I know will be seen dead in a place like this, so it doesn't matter.

As I scrabble for a tissue, I see a tall figure sitting on the other side of the library. It's Harvey. I shrink down. I do not want the repeat of the whole, strange chicken incident. Then I sit up. I will not hide from him. But he's not noticed me. I peer through my streaming eyes and see he's sitting next to some Year Seven boy. They're reading something together. Harvey is pointing things out and they both laugh. My eyes must be defective, but it looks like he's helping him with his homework or something. Which would be a very kind thing to do but also incompatible with my idea of who or what Harvey is.

I sneeze again. This time he sees me and starts to come my way. I hold up my hand. 'This is a library, a temple to learning. There must be no repeat of the whole chicken incident, for my sanity and for your reputation.' Really, I should just blank him but there's just something about him that intrigues me. Things always seem to happen when he's around. Not always good things but at least it makes this place a bit more interesting.

'Yeah, sorry about that. I don't know what came over me.' I check his expression. It seems genuine. He's smiling. His eyes are a soft brown with gold and green flecks.

'Of all the places in the world, this is the last place I would have expected to see you.' Harvey says, as he towers over me. My eyes still stream with tears making my mission to find a tissue difficult. I scrabble in my bag to no effect.

'Here,' he says and offers me one from his pocket.

'It is clean?' I ask. 'You're not trying to take me out with chemical warfare by offering a used tissue?'

He laughs. 'I don't know much about girls, but I do know that.' It's the first time I've heard him laugh when it doesn't seem to be at me but rather with me. I mean, I think I'm funny but not everyone agrees.

I stare up at him. 'Harvey, I'm getting neck ache looking at you. Can you move away and let me get on?' I gesture at my pile of books and notes.

But he doesn't. He sits down and starts to turn pages. I hit at his hands. 'Don't mess this up. I've got the pages I want; don't make me lose them. Anyway, what are you doing here?' I grab my emergency make-up bag and wipe away the mascara that's running down my cheeks.

He looks away from the books to me with a puzzled expression. 'What makes you think I don't like libraries.'

'They let anyone in here, you know. It's not members' only.'

'So?'

'So, I didn't think it would be your sort of place. I mean, you speak like a minor royal. You clearly think that we are all stupid. You went to an expensive school where you have to be on a waiting list since birth, and you've treated me like I'm a prize idiot since you've arrived. Not to mention all the bullying about getting me on your dad's show…'

Harvey looks startled. 'Bullying … it was just a bit of banter. And anyway, it wasn't…'

I sigh. 'When a boy calls something banter and a girl calls it bullying, then it's clear there's a problem.' Scanning my face, I see that it will do.

He's looking confused and as if he's about to say something.

'Go on, spit it out,' I say, 'as we're having this rare chat, we might as well get everything in the open.' I'm kind of enjoying myself, I have to say. It must be because I'm proving him wrong. There's nothing else to enjoy about his company.

Harvey points to the make-up bag. 'Don't you ever get tired of applying that stuff? Isn't it all just a bit…'

'A bit what?'

'Superficial.'

I take a deep breath to quell the anger that's bubbling up inside. 'Superficial?'

'Yes. It's all about how you look. Isn't there more to life than that?'

'You think this is all about vanity?' Our eyes hold each other's gaze steadily. 'You think I'm vain.'

'A bit, yes.'

I lean back and break our stare as I gesture at the books. 'Does this look vain?'

He shakes his head. 'No, that's why I don't get you.'

'You don't get me because you've too blinded by your own stereotypes. You just see make-up and see stupid, vain and self-obsessed. What you don't see…' I jab my fingers at the books, '…is creativity and hard work and self-expression. You take photos. I create looks with make-up. It's the same thing.'

'Make-up? Creative?' He couldn't be more incredulous than if I told him the moon was a highlighter. 'Photography is an art form,' he says.

I sigh. 'Because mostly men do it it's Art. Obviously make-up will only become serious when men start doing it. Run along then, Nature Boy. As you say, apparently you don't know much about girls. Well, you're not going to learn much more unless you listen to one.' He looks at me uncertainly and then gets up. I see the book he's got. *The First Ascent of the Eiger.* So, he's into mountain climbing. 'You struggle with insomnia then?'

Harvey continues to look confused.

'The book – it's hardly light reading.'

'Oh, it's just preparation for my next expedition.'

The arrogance of the boy! 'Your next expedition?'

'Dad wants some ideas for the new show.'

'The show that you want me to go on, so everyone can laugh at me?'

'Tulip, you've made your point. Maybe I was wrong.'

'Ha!' That feels good.

'But maybe you are the perfect candidate. Anyway, wouldn't it be good for your brand? Ten days of exposure on TV?'

As he finally leaves, I try to throw a few last shots. 'Hey, I don't think about my brand, it's my mum…' But then I stop myself as I realise how lame that sounds.

Then, entirely appropriately as I'm in a library – a church to learning, after all – I have an amazing breakthrough. I need time for Dad's money to come through. I need something that will persuade Mum to get off my case and keep Rowan and Willow offline for a bit. And Harvey has unintentionally shown me the way.

I smile to myself. Tulip Taylor, you really are amazing. You've cracked it.

CHAPTER TWELVE

Word: Bucolic (adjective)

Kate whimpers as Anjali falls forward and grabs on to her for support. 'Remind me exactly why we're climbing a mountain,' Kate says as she rights herself, 'in the middle of winter.'

I regard her with a touch of scorn. 'I'd hardly call this a mountain. And it's hardly winter – it's Easter next week.' I gesture around us to take in the slight incline that leads up the hill in the local park. From the top, you get a view of some proper hills that are still considerably short of being mountains, but Anjali seems to be getting out of breath looking at them.

Anjali stops for a moment. 'Mountain. Hill. Lump of dirt. Call it what you like but, as Kate says, what are we doing here?'

'I need to take a shot of me looking at one with nature to put on my application,' I say. 'Isn't it obvious?' I get out my phone to check what the view, with me in it, looks like. The wind keeps whipping my hair across my face in a most unflattering way. 'I've got to look like I could survive in the wild. So I want to look like an explorer but not a withered and sunburned one. More sunkissed. What about this?' I angle my head and turn into the wind so my hair flares about behind me. But I don't get the best view of the trees.

I feel a hand on each shoulder and then I'm being pushed

to the ground. 'Have you two gone mad?' I shriek. 'These are good jeans. I'm not sitting on the dirt.'

But I have no choice and, before I know it, my behind has made impact with the earth.

'Right,' Anjali says, 'stop squeaking and stop looking at your camera.'

'I'm not squeaking,' I protest. 'I've not been this close to dirt since we went on a bug hunt in primary school.

'You put mud packs on your face,' Anjali says. 'Isn't that the same thing?'

She's clearly gone mad. 'That's not any mud, it's been purified or something. What kind of person would put dirt on their face of their own free will?' Don't get me wrong – I do like nature but I just like it better online with a filter on.

Then Anjali puts her finger in the earth and wipes it across my cheek. Okay, now I'm squealing. I pull out some wet wipes and start to scrub at my face. 'What exactly do you think that you are doing?'

'That's a good question and one that we'd like you to answer.'

I turn my head from side to side like a hyperactive meerkat, looking from Kate on one side to Anjali on the other. 'I told you. I'm going to apply to the TV show and I have to send a photo. Obviously, I have lots of great images, but I thought I should send one that makes me look like a real explorer.'

Kate starts a bit hesitantly. 'But we're sitting in a park. It's hardly scary.'

I give her a look. 'It's four o'clock. Give it a few hours and it will be the most terrifying experience of your life. Anyway, with a bit of editing, I can make it look like I've climbed Everest.'

'The thing is...' Kate keeps going, '...Anjali and me were wondering if you've really thought this through.'

'I told you,' I say impatiently, 'weren't you listening before? Mum is threatening to home-school me and turn our house into a reality TV set. This is my way out of it.'

'Yes,' Kate says, twiddling her hair, 'but I'm not quite getting how you going on a TV show where your every move is televised is an improvement on what your mum is suggesting.'

I breathe deeply. 'I didn't say it was a perfect plan. But it's something. I've been in touch with Dad and he says he's got a deal coming through. Then he can send home all the maintenance money that he owes Mum and then I can talk her out of the reality TV show idea.'

'Okay, but I still don't see...'

'I told Mum I was applying to go on this TV show and how it would increase my "brand awareness". She got very excited. Then I told her that she couldn't post anything about me until after the show was broadcast. And the show's not until June so that's loads of time.'

'So why can't she post anything in the meantime?'

'I have to look grown up and independent and that is kind of ruined if your mum keeps tagging you with tacky products and tells stories about you from when you were three.'

'And she bought it?'

'Amazingly, she did. So, I've bought time. Six weeks at least. If she stops posting stuff about me and the twins for a while,

Dad's money will come through and then she'll forget about the whole thing.'

But Kate won't give up. 'But even if all this works, which seems a bit of a long shot, you hate being outside. You hate the dirt, you hate being away from electricity.' She grabs my arm. 'There will be no Wi-Fi. Did you watch the last series? One woman had to be airlifted with hypothermia and a man lost the end of his finger in a bizarre woodcutting accident. Have you really thought this through?'

I am really getting hacked off with people thinking I'm useless, though I make a mental note to watch some old episodes. It probably would be a good idea to do some research. 'I have thought this through. I know you think I wouldn't survive and I'm not saying I'm looking forward to it, but seriously how bad can it be?'

No one says anything. The wind blows round us. No tumbleweed comes moseying on through but that's probably because it's not native to these parts. A few crisp packets and an empty soft drink can scuttle along but that isn't quite the same thing.

'Look,' I say, 'I know it sounds a bit crazy and it's not an obvious choice for me. But I need to get away from home for a bit and actually I could do with a break from the whole being on the internet.'

Anjali's eyes lock on me. 'I think we should take you to the doctor. Or get you exorcised.' She shakes me. 'Are you in there, Tulip? Can you hear me? Some nature demon has taken over you. Don't worry, we'll get it out of you as soon as we can.'

'Stop it,' I giggle. 'Is it really that ridiculous that I'd want to do this?'

'You hate being outside. You check your phone about every second. If you don't post a vlog every forty-eight hours, people start messaging you to make sure you're not dead because you're so punctual. You are a make-up vlogger. A very successful one. And now you want to live in the wild. Without make-up?' Anjali raises one perfectly formed eyebrow. 'You've got to admit it's a bit unlikely.'

It's hard to explain. 'I know. It's Mum. She's making it all hard work and she keeps posting things that are embarrassing. I had to stop her posting naked pictures of Willow the other day.'

'Yuk.'

'I know. She keeps saying how cute she looks and how I'm being silly when I stop her.'

'Doesn't she realise that not everyone online is lovely?'

'That's her problem. She thinks everyone out there loves us and everything we do. But Willow will grow up one day and it's going to be a bit embarrassing when she goes for a job interview and there's photos of her wearing nothing but daisy chains still going around.'

'But how does you going on this TV show stop any of this? That's the bit I don't get.'

I sigh. 'It doesn't stop that bit, I know. But I've told her that she can't post anything about me. That if I'm going to make it as the next big vlogger, she can't be involved at all. That I'll look sad if my mum's involved. I've made it sound like this is all part of a great strategy to launch me on the world and she's agreed to stop mentioning me at all in any way. At least until the show's over.'

'Okay,' Kate agrees. 'That does make sense. But I've got two more questions.'

'Fire away.'

'One, what happens once the show's over? Won't your mum be back to her old tricks again?'

'I'll think about that when it happens.'

'And secondly, and this is the big one.'

'Right…'

Kate looks serious. 'You might not even get accepted on this show. Have you even considered that?'

And she's right. And I have. My whole deal with my mother could go horribly wrong. What can I do to make sure that I get accepted? Perhaps a photoshopped picture of me up a small hillock in a park isn't going to do it. But what will?

CHAPTER THIRTEEN

Word: Pusillanimous (adjective)

In the dining room at school the next day I'm still thinking about how to do the best application I can while Anjali recounts what just went down in French. I've got to fill in a form, add a profile picture and upload a video. For the queen of vlogs, this might sound easy but I'm not so sure that my normal, 'Hey, guys, want to see my latest eyeliner flick trick?' is going to be the right thing. What would an intrepid explorer do? Drink my own wee? Well, that's not going to happen for a whole load of reasons.

Just as I'm thinking all this through, I hear my name and out of the corner of my eye I see Harvey and his new crowd of hangers-on sitting on the next table. I don't look. I have yet to acknowledge his challenge to apply – I'm trying to think about the best way to do it. One of the girls with him is nudging him and pointing in my direction. Rude. He tries to put her hand down and looks embarrassed.

I sigh and smile the smile of someone who knows their inner worth, the smile of someone with 300,000 followers and 100,000 likes on her latest video. I find myself saying very loudly, 'People really do underestimate how make-up is a truly creative process.'

Anjali looks at me as if I've gone mad. 'What's that to do

with Amber and Ava having a fight over who burned who on Snapchat?'

'Nothing,' I say, 'I was trying to make a point.'

She looks around and sees Harvey nearby. 'I wonder who for.' She pauses for a moment. 'Tulip, for someone you don't like, you seem to spend a lot of time thinking about what he thinks of you.'

I spear a chip with particular ferocity. 'And exactly what do you mean by that?'

Anjali puts her hands up in surrender. 'I made a statement. No food stuffs need to suffer as a result.'

'He just annoys me. One minute he's bullying me, next he's saying he's wrong about me. Then he takes nice photos and is randomly helpful to small children. I mean, is he okay or is he an idiot? I just can't work him out,' I sigh. 'And he's so tall. It's a small school. He's just there all the time. It's annoying.' I find myself repeating things. This is not a good sign.

Anjali sniffs. 'You're not going to like this. But for what it's worth, this is what I think. Because you're pretty, you're used to boys wanting to impress you. You can't cope with one who doesn't seem to fancy you.'

'No.' I need to get her to see. 'I'm not pretty at all.' I still re-live that year of being told I was ugly by Jade. How I used to cry myself to sleep every night. How I used to spend hours looking at my reflection, picking out every flaw in what I could see. But I did something about it. 'Without make-up, I'm nothing special. I have learned a few tricks to make the best of what I've got. That's not to get boys to like me, it's…' Then my words run dry. Why exactly do I do this? 'It's more about looking the mirror and feeling okay. I'd like to be able to do it without make-up but I can't.'

'But isn't okay meaning you want to look hot?' Anjali suggests, less than helpfully. 'I mean let's face it, that is generally a good thing in society, isn't it?'

I glare at her. 'It's not about that. It's about being in control of how I look. But if you like make-up, people assume you're stupid. And I'm not. I might not be in the top set for everything but I'm not daft.'

But our conversation is drowned out by the loud voices nearby.

'So, what's the most outrageous thing you and your dad have done?' one of the hangers-on asks.

I listen even though I don't want to.

'The most extreme? I'm not sure I'd call any of them extreme really…' he begins. I notice how he's shifting in his seat a bit and glancing around. If I didn't know better, I'd say he was looking awkward. Then he sees me looking. I glance away. But I still hear him talking. 'There was the time I free climbed a sheer rock face. But that was when I was a kid.'

There's one thing I really, really hate. Heights. I get scared when I put a pair of high heels on and I once cried in the Trafford Centre when Anjali made me go down the big escalator in Selfridges. It was only thinking about a particularly gorgeous purple sparkly lip-gloss that kept me from screaming.

'Then there was the time with the polar bear. It was in the Arctic, of course. Melting snow for water. Carrying your own food. But one day a hungry polar bear got wind of us and nearly had us for lunch.'

All eyes are on him, apart from me. I catch Anjali staring, her mouth wide open. 'Stop it,' I hiss at her. The only polar bears I have experience of are the fluffy ones on my bed.

'You stop it,' she hisses back. 'You're listening too, you hypocrite.' Which I am.

'What happened?' breathes one of the girls. She looks like she's about to collapse at his manly feet at these tales of his manly feats. And they think I'm stupid!

'Well, what I've learned about dealing with hungry polar bears that weigh several tonnes is this…' He waits until he knows everyone's looking. Okay, I'm looking. He seems to know that I'm looking which makes him happy and me very cross with myself. 'You find a flare, fire it in its face and then you won't see it again for weeks.'

Everyone laughs. Except me. I look at him with new respect. If that's true, then he is ten trillion times braver than I ever could be.

Polar bears? I like my stuffed polar bear but if I'm being honest I'm not sure how I'd get on with the real thing. What would I do in that situation? Poke it in the eye with an eyeliner and run away? I'd be a human chicken nugget before you could say, 'It looked cute from a distance.' At least they're not thinking of anything like that for this show. I think. I suddenly realise I need to read the small print before I even think of sending in my application.

'This new show won't be like that. But Dad's really pushing

the boundaries of what kids our age are allowed to do on TV. There will be dangerous climbs, they'll have to hunt and kill their own food. No baths or toilets – living under the stars. It'll be wonderful.' I find his eyes on me. Is that an invitation or a challenge?

I slump in my chair.

Weeing in the bushes?

Hunting?

I think of all my stuffed toys. Kill Bambi? Rip Mr Bunny's heart out?

Who am I trying to kid? It's not Harvey and the rest of the world who don't think I can do it.

The word I need here is pusillanimous. I am wilting Tulip. The girl who can't stand upright in a stiff breeze. The real problem is not the rest of the world. It's me. I don't think I can do it either.

CHAPTER FOURTEEN

Word: Epiphany (noun)

I trudge home, feeling a rare sense of defeat. Mum has texted me ten gazillion times today, chasing up the beauty vlogs I'm behind on, which doesn't add much to my mood. I suppose I should do a few tonight but then the application needs to be done too. My heart's not in it right now. Something that was fun, creative and – well – mine, has now started to feel like work. Aren't there laws that are supposed to protect me from child labour?

But the thought of a big hot chocolate and some comfy clothes keeps me going. I'll chill for a bit and then start on my List of Doom. Cue dramatic music. Inside the door, I slip off my shoes and dump my bag before starting my search for yummy food in the kitchen. I realise then I've made a rookie error. I should have bought popcorn or chocolate on the way home but if I'm lucky I might find a few raw cacao bars or a handful of unsalted nuts. That's as close as Mum gets to comfort food.

At this point, I bump into a man dressed in black with a huge screwdriver.

I squeal.

He jumps.

It's all a bit awks. Is he one of Mum's 'friends' who she meets online? If so, her taste has changed quite a lot. No manbun, tattoos or interesting hair arrangements? This guy is surprisingly ordinary looking, apart from carrying the aforementioned very large screwdriver.

'Um…' I begin, completely unsure of what to say.

'Tulip, my little moonbeam, this is Dave.' Mum wafts in and waves a hand towards Dave who is now beginning to rummage through a large bag of cables with grim determination.

'Right,' I say, but I'm not any clearer to what's going on apart from now knowing the man in black has a name and he owns about three miles of cable.

'And it's all down to you that he's here.' No, the situation is not getting any clearer.

At this point, Rowan swans in dressed as Ariel. 'We're going to be famous, Tulip.'

My mental fog begins to clear. Dave the cable man.

Oh no.

'Mum, can I have a word with you?' I hiss.

'Of course, I'm going to make a turmeric latte. Do you want one?'

Turmeric latte or hot chocolate? Think I know which one I prefer. I stalk into her pod and she drifts in a few minutes later, holding on to her yellow 'latte'. 'You really should try this you know, it's very soothing. You need to think about eating more healthily with you being on TV.'

Where do I even start? 'I'm not on TV yet and, even if I am, I'm not sure drinking horrible spiced milk is going to help me light a fire or fight a polar bear.'

She looks at me oddly which is fair enough. No one has really mentioned a polar bear before this.

'Okay, forget about the polar bear. Who is Dave and what is he doing in our kitchen?'

Mum's eyes twinkle with excitement. 'Well, after your brilliant idea, I've been thinking about it and I think we should launch ourselves on the next exciting part of our journey.'

'Dave's a boat builder?' I suggest, a bit confused by Mum's metaphors here.

'Don't be ridiculous,' she snaps. 'He's installing the camera system you suggested.'

I knew it. 'Mum, I did not suggest it and I don't want to live in a house where my every move will be filmed. I don't want to be in a bad version of a reality TV show.'

'But you suggested it.'

'I really didn't,' I say.

'Ah,' Mum looks happy with herself. 'You see, if we had had the cameras then we'd have been able to prove who said what.' She nods at me as if she's said something very clever. 'Anyway, you teenagers post every detail of everything you do every day. What's the difference between that and this?' She picks up her phone and clicks on an icon. 'Look. There's your account. What you had for lunch. What you were thinking about in Science when you should have been working. You post updates all the time. What's the difference between that and this?' She goes in for the hug and smoosh of my hair. 'I love how thoughtful you are, Tulip. You are creative and caring. You have nothing to hide. You're a role model to other young women. So, don't put yourself down. You should have the confidence to share yourself with the world.'

'But you promised you wouldn't do this until after the show?'

'I know, and I am a woman of my word. You might not even get on. And if you do, well then it's all ready for when you get back.'

Before I have a chance to say a word, she's gone. 'Dave, now let's discuss what we're going to do about the bathroom…'

I feel sick. I must get out of here. In my currently camera-free room, I barricade myself by pushing a set of drawers in front of the door. I need to be on my own. I really didn't think that she'd go through with this. Who do I ask for help?

I've only got me, and I've got to sort this out. I re-read the printout of the application. I need this. But what kind of video do I do? I look at the make-up I put out this morning to help me. I was going to do full camouflage like some action hero or soldier. 'Hi, I'm Tulip. And I eat raw polar bear liver for breakfast.'

No. That's what everyone else will do. Try to show that they are the hardest, toughest, outdoor freak adrenaline junkie ever. Just like Harvey seems to be.

If you want to stand out, you have to be different.

If you want to stand out, you have to be yourself.

That is your Unique Selling Point.

I turn on the camera on my laptop and begin.

'Hi, I'm Tulip and I'm a make-up vlogger. My superpower is making the world a more beautiful place.'

Harvey: Rollo, I need some help.

Rollo: Course you do. Why aren't you asking Hector though? I thought Big Bro was your go-to-guy for advice.

Harvey: I'm not sure he's got all the answers somehow. I've tried being more like him but it's not working that well.

Rollo: So, fire away.

Harvey: There's a party. There's a girl I like.

Rollo: Go, man. Get your lady. What's she like? Hot?

Harvey: Sure. And smart and funny.

Rollo: Sounds great. What's the problem?

Harvey: I'm not sure she likes me. Sometimes she seems to and then I'm not so sure.

Rollo: You're you. Rich, good-looking, son of someone famous. What's not to like?

Harvey: That doesn't seem enough for this girl.

Rollo: She's picky then. She's probably just playing hard to get. Just be confident.

Harvey: You know, she seems the confident one. Maybe I need to be a bit more like her.

Rollo: What does Hector say?

Harvey: To stop being such a big girl's blouse and just go for it. And on the basis he's dad's favourite son, maybe I should follow his example.

Rollo: But you're not sure?

Harvey: No.

Rollo: Be bold, man, be bold.

Harvey: Bold. Yes. Go for it.

Rollo: This is so weird.

Harvey: Why?

Rollo: You're are frightened of a girl!

Harvey: I wouldn't put it like that. I just get nervous around her.

Rollo: Just kiss her.

Harvey: Just like that?

Rollo: Just like that. I mean it's a compliment, isn't it? She'll be pleased. You have to make the first move anyway.

Harvey: Yeah. Right. I hate that rule.

Rollo: It's the law of nature. Men ask, women swoon at their feet.

Harvey: Swoon?

Rollo: Swoon. I promise you. Be bold and she will swoon.

Harvey: Hmmm. Okay. Can I just be myself?

Rollo: Do you want her to like you or not? No. Do not be yourself. That's the worst idea ever. No. Give being more like Hector one last shot. You won't be disappointed.

Harvey: There's one more problem.

Rollo: Hit me with it.

Harvey: There are two things I really need to tell her. But I never know what to say. And she never listens.

CHAPTER FIFTEEN

Word: Magnetism (noun)

'You've sent it then?' Anjali asks, eyes shut as she reclines on my bed.

'I have.'

'And did you go for the "Hey, I'm Tulip and I'll try not to cry if I get dirt on my hand" thing?'

'Not really. But it's gone now. I just have to wait.' But what I don't say, because I don't want to sound pathetic, is that I'll be devastated if I don't get on but also that I'll be terrified if I do. I am in deepest do-do either way and there doesn't seem to be anything I can do about it.

Good job I've got a party to go to and people to make fabulous!

I sigh with a touch of intense joy at the sight of my room. It's full of clothes, make-up, my best friends and lots and lots of positivity. I suddenly realise why I've not been able to make any product vlogs for a while. If it's me and a camera, it's not that much fun. But here with Anjali and Kate, suddenly it's like someone's turned the colour and volume up to 11 and a half, and all the fun has flooded back. Kate, having actually put down her new book, is oohing and ahhing at the latest products and Anjali is taking the wild colours that I wouldn't normally know what to do with and owning them.

'Blue lipstick is so me,' she pouts in front of the mirror. And she's right. With just a bit of lipstick, she's transformed into a goddess. I sigh with satisfaction. This is what I'm all about, this is what I love; this is what makes me feel safe. We squeal, laugh and muck about for a while and at the end of it we're feeling on top of the world, drunk on friendship and fun.

A bit later, Kate's mum picks us up and drops us off at the party. We walk through the door and I sigh as if I'm about to expire.

'What's up with you?' Anjali says. And I know what she means. It's a normal party. Boys and girls, music and food. But the food!

'Are those Pringles? Do my eyes deceive me or are those chocolate biscuits? Hold me back or I'll eat them all.'

Anjali is looking at me like I'm an idiot. 'You forget,' I explain. 'I've been on a mostly macrobiotic diet for the last six months. We even had beansprouts for Christmas dinner. I'd have sold my soul for one solitary real sprout. One tiny, mini fake cabbage and I'd have been happy. And now I'm in a room with free access to chocolate-related comestibles and you want me to act all cool.'

Kate shakes her head slightly. 'Just take her to the chocolate and keep her under control.' She looks round the room. 'Would it be weird to go and sit in the conservatory and read?'

We look at her. 'You do whatever floats your boat. But I am eating forbidden food.' With that I'm off to find sustenance.

In short, I eat chocolate. This might explain why I then start to dance very energetically and talk manically. Who needs alcopops when you can have sugar? I have a great time! It is, in fact, a really good party. Not one of those awkward non-parties where everyone stands at the edge of the room and sips on diet cokes, being too cool to dance or talk or look like they are capable of fun. Even Kate edges in, puts *Anna Karenina* down and has a little dance when they put Beyoncé on.

I have so much fun that I think I'd better go and check my face. I'm sure some damage will have occurred in the last few hours which means a trip to the bathroom to check a mirror.

After performing all the necessary adjustments, I find my way back down stairs. There's a shape looming at the bottom of them. A large, now familiar shape. My stomach churns with something – nerves? Anticipation? Who cares – I take a deep breath and fix my best 'celebrity on a red carpet' smile on my face.

It is, of course, Harvey. What is he doing smiling at me? Is it going to be bully Harvey or 'I got you all wrong Harvey'? I just never know.

'Tulip, taking a breath from entertaining us with your dancing?'

That's a bit snide. Is he telling me I'm an awful dancer or what?

'I like to spread joy and happiness wherever I go if I can,' I reply. I'm going to have to squash past him if he doesn't move. Currently there's no sign of him moving.

'Great mission statement,' he says, still smiling.

Is he for real? What teenager talks like that. Then I remember Mum and her 'brand awareness' chats. Touché.

'If you say so.' I take a step down the stairs but still he won't budge. He is really like an iceberg. Won't move, too big and generally lowers the temperature. 'Now if you'll excuse me, I have to go and entertain people with my dancing. My fans will be lost without me.'

As I edge past him, he grabs my arm.

'Er, unhand me. Or as they say round here – get your mitts off me before I mash you.' I glare at him with disbelief.

Hands up, he backs off. 'Sorry. I just need to talk to you.'

'I really don't see what the two of us have got to talk about. It's not like we have anything in common,' I spit out.

He steps closer. 'Rumour has it you've applied for my dad's show.'

'And?' I say, stepping closer still to show I'm not afraid of him. 'Maybe I'm out to prove you wrong.' As soon as I say it, I regret it. It looks like I care about what he thinks. It looks like he matters to me. Which, of course, he doesn't. We are now centimetres away from each other.

But he doesn't react the way I thought he was going to. He's not triumphant at all. 'There's something I need to tell you though. If you have applied.' I'm finding it hard to concentrate and not swipe that one lock of hair that always falls the wrong way.

'If you think I need any advice or inside information, then you're wrong. IF I do this, I'll do it my own way.'

Harvey looks exasperated. 'You're getting this all wrong. You need to listen to me.'

Okay, now he's got me mad. It's my turn to edge nearer. 'I don't have to do anything you tell me. You told me you didn't know anything about girls. That's the only thing we agree on. Stop telling me what to do. Stop thinking I need your help. I don't. I'm a perfectly competent human being all on my own.'

As I stare into his eyes, I notice how they are flecked with gold within the brown, rather like topaz.

'Get a room, you two,' Isabella says as she shoves past. 'I didn't even know you two had a thing going.'

We fly away from each other as if we've had cold water thrown over us.

'Me and Harvey? Don't be ridiculous.' I mutter as I march past.

For a moment, he looks hurt. 'Like I'd go out with a plastic girl like you,' he sends back.

Me? Plastic?

This party is suddenly not quite so much fun as it was.

Rollo: How did it go?

Harvey: Disaster. I was bold. She was bolder. From now on, I officially give up on being like Hector. I'm going to be more like me.

Rollo: Bold move indeed, my friend, I wish you well. Are you going to tell her the big secret?

Harvey: I want to. I know it would be the right thing. But if I do, then she might withdraw her application. And I really would like her to go on it.

Rollo: To laugh at her?

Harvey: No, not at all. No, the reason is this…

CHAPTER SIXTEEN

Word: Sorority (noun)

Time passes as the Easter holidays come and go. Back at school, Harvey and I keep an uneasy distance from each other, never talking, sometimes glaring. Because he's so tall, he just seems to get everywhere, always as if he's about to say something but then never does.

'What is he even doing here?' I hiss, while trying to work out some map coordinates one geography lesson. 'Is this a church or a hotel?'

Kate sighs, puts her book down, grabs the map and turns it around. 'You put the North to the top remember?' She taps the map to make her point. 'Now can you get on? I'm just getting to a good bit.'

'But why?'

Exasperated, Kate waves the map in front of me. 'Because that is WHAT. YOU. DO with maps.'

I waft it away. 'Not the map. Harvey. Why is he even at this school?'

It's head in hands time now for Kate. 'We've been through this before. Harvey's dad has set up an activity centre in the Peak district. It's only about ten miles away.'

'Yes,' I say, 'that doesn't explain why he's at our school. Who joins halfway through Year Ten? Listen to him. Listen to his dad.

Why is Harvey at some shabby comprehensive, where the closest to civilisation you get is when you see the lights of Manchester through the rain?' Kate starts to reply but I continue. 'And he called me plastic.' I look at her for some kind of outrage. 'Me. Plastic.' She doesn't say much but her face is contorted.

'I know you're not plastic. You know you're not plastic. So, does it matter?'

'Yes,' I bridle, 'because he's wrong about me.'

'This is just a friendly question, but did you say anything mean about him before he called you plastic?' Kate is filling in the coordinates with keen interest all of a sudden so as not to make eye contact with me.

'I may have said something. But he deserved it.'

Kate sighs. 'I know he did. But it sounds like it was a heated conversation. Things can be said in heated conversations that aren't always meant.'

'I know but why did he...'

'You know what, Tulip?' Kate suddenly sits up. 'I've got a great idea. Why don't you ask him if you're so interested? And then I might just finish this map.'

Defensively, I say, 'Who said I was interested in him? I know what it looked like at the party, but he just invaded my personal space.'

Kate is now staring at me as if I'm wearing the wrong-coloured foundation. 'What exactly happened at the party? I didn't hear anything. Does Anjali know? If anything happened and you didn't tell her, you know that she will hunt you down and kill you.'

'Oh well, nothing then.'

She stabs my hand with a pen.

'Ow, what was that for?'

'Do you fancy him or what?'

'NO!' I yell. A bit too loudly because now the teacher is paying too much interest in me. I scribble down any old coordinates just to keep him happy. 'No,' I whisper. 'I just think it's weird he's here. And remember I never had a problem with him. He attacked me first.'

Kate sighs. 'He just thinks you spend too much time on your phone and you are interested in things that he's not interested in.'

'Exactly.' I'm about to respond in more detail when my phone buzzes to tell me I've got an email. I fumble inside my blazer pocket to get it. It's from the TV company so I try to open it.

'Tulip. What are the coordinates for the slate mine?'

I hesitate and send Kate a desperate glance. She slides her work at me, so I can read them out.

'Okay but concentrate and remember if I see a phone in class I will confiscate it.' He's not kidding. Last time a phone went off, he confiscated it for a week, which is theft if you ask me but apparently is in the Home/School Agreement, so we can't challenge it.

I look desperately at the clock. Forty-two minutes to wait. If he's distracted, I'll go for my phone. I try to get Kate involved in a complex plan to create a diversion, but she just gives me a look. 'You can wait a few minutes, Tulip. You won't die.'

Which is not very supportive, so I huff and puff to myself and count down the very long seconds to the end of the lesson.

Eventually, after several millennia have passed, after ice ages have come and gone, the bell rings. I run outside to the corridor, leaving Kate to pick up all my stuff. I can't bear to read the email. What if it's a no? But then do they even send emails if it's a no?

My thumb hovers over the icon. Someone jogs me from behind and I end up pressing the email icon anyway.

'Dear Tulip…'

I burst into tears. Kate puts an arm around me and gives me a hug. 'I'm sorry, Tulip. I know you had your heart set on it. Maybe it's for the best.'

As I wipe my eyes, I say, 'No, that's not it. I'm not crying because I didn't get in. I'm crying because I did.' I wave the screen in her face. Squealing, she grabs it off me and reads it. 'You've been selected. You're really going.' She looks at me, 'You've only flipping gone and done it.' Then she grabs me, and we dance around the corridor. 'You've got to tell Anjali. You've got to tell your mum.' Kate pauses. 'Are you going to tell Harvey?'

Suddenly my shoulders slump. 'Either way, he's won. He'd have won if I hadn't been selected and now he's won because I have. The only really good thing is that I'll be away from here and everyone, including him, for a bit.'

She slides down to my level. 'Okay, you're going to have to run that past me again, but I don't get it.'

'Kate, we both know the truth. I'm just not up to this.'

She grabs my face as I stare vacantly at the wall ahead and

turns it so I'm looking at her. 'Okay, Tulip. You can be vain, you can be annoying, you are never on time. BUT, I don't know anyone like you. You research, you plan, you practise. You solve problems. You project confidence even if you don't feel it. You make things happen. So, *you* might not believe that you can do it. But *I* can, and I do.'

'Really?' I say, in a particularly pathetic way.

'Really. How many teenagers have the energy, imagination or creativity to make your videos? You're one of a kind. You just need to see that. I wish I could be more like you. I just escape from the world into books. You actually go out and try and do things.'

I would like to sit here longer and listen to how Kate thinks I can do this. But then some Year Elevens trip over our legs and it all gets a bit nasty for a while. Even as we make our hasty escape, I try to remember Kate's words.

I'm going. I just have to believe that I can do it.

CHAPTER SEVENTEEN

Word: Diligent (adjective)

Three weeks later, I have spent the time doing what I do best. Research. Thinking of every possibility and planning for every eventuality. It's been hard, but I hope it'll be worth it. In my room, I survey the fruits of my preparation and I have to say, I'm quite pleased. I've not had as much time as I'd like but I've done what I can.

A knock on the door. I scowl in response. My brother has been driving me crazy this last week, endlessly asking me for fashion and make-up tips. Normally this would be fine but just at the moment all I've got time for is me. 'Rowan, I'm too busy to play make-up with you. You'll have to do colour blending on your own. Here's an idea – why don't you watch one of my videos? That'll show you how to do it and then you can LEAVE ME ALONE.'

But rather than follow my very clearly enunciated words, the person on the other side of the door slowly pushes it open.

'I said I'm too busy!' I repeat but then I stare with confusion as the unseen intruder waves a piece of tissue from behind the door. 'I hope that's not used tissue or World War Three is just about to start in this house.'

Kate and then Anjali edge into the room, their eyes scanning around as they enter.

'Wow,' Anjali says, 'you've really gone for a new look in here. What is it you're aiming for – nature in chaos?'

Anjali is standing next to my research wall, with an odd look on her face. I'd like to think it's admiration but it's probably closer to horror. 'Tulip, in all my days I have never seen anything like this. Since when did you have an interest in bird-watching?' She starts to fiddle with a photo of a grouse that I've stuck to the wall, so I leap up to smack her hand away. Trouble is my legs get entangled with all the kit I have piled up on the floor, so I just start to topple.

'Woah there.' Kate catches me. 'I think you need to sit down and explain what's going on.'

'You two need to explain why you're waving loo roll at me.' I rub an elbow that I've caught on the corner of my drawers.

'It was a white flag, you know, the generally accepted symbol of peace in war situations,' Kate explains. 'I obviously didn't have a white flag on me. That would be weird. But when you sounded less than welcoming, I improvised.' We stare at each other, clearly bemused. Kate starts first, 'So, I've explained the whole tissue thing. Can you explain all this and why you've not answered anyone's messages and why you've not posted anything for so long?'

'I have posted…' I start. But then I think. Kate's right. Since getting involved in Operation Escotia (an old name for Scotland), I just haven't had time for anything else. Mum has bought this to my attention but somehow I've convinced her it was all part of my plan. 'I'm going dark now so when I get back, having created huge exposure for us, all my new stuff will really stand out. It will create anticipation,' I said to her and, amazingly, she fell for it.

I look round my room. 'Do you think it's a bit much then?' Suddenly, I see how it must look to them. Utter madness. On one wall, I've taken all the pictures down, put up a huge map of the area where I'm going to be camping and surrounded it with photos of animals and plants, each linked by a thread to the place it might be found. On another wall, I've printed out lots of selfies with a number underneath. To the untrained eye, I admit it all looks a bit weird.

Anjali takes a deep breath and taps the map. 'Please explain exhibit A then.'

'It's a map of where I'm going to be staying. It's part of the McManus family estate would you believe. Who has their own estate these days? Anyway, I've been visualising the terrain and looking for good places to shelter and learn what natural resources there are.' Sounds reasonable, I think.

'And these?' She points at the animals and plants.

'…are the natural resources,' I explain.

Kate looks in horror at the picture of a very cute rabbit. 'When you say natural resources, do you mean…?' Her words are left hanging.

'…things I can eat?' I say helpfully. 'In a word, yes.'

Kate squeals and grabs one of my teddies which unfortunately looks too like the photo of the bunny for my liking. 'You would eat this? You would really do that?'

'Maybe, if I was very hungry,' I start, but it's my turn to

stumble over my words. 'I mean, if I was starving I might.' Kate and Anjali exchange a look of horror.

'And these…' Anjali points at all the numbered selfies.

'Okay, well those are different looks for each day. I'm not supposed to take any make-up in but I've thought of how to braid or style my hair differently. I'm going to smuggle a few items in, so I can mix my look up a bit every day.'

Another look is exchanged. 'But some of them look the same,' Anjali ventures.

'Are you blind?' I go over to make my point. 'Look, this one has a braid running this way and the next day is the reverse. Ponytails can be high – low – side etc. This look has peach lip balm and this one has pink. Every look is unique.' I admit to the trained eye you have to look very hard to see the difference in some of them.

'Tulip, I hate to break this to you, but I don't think the camera is going to pick up all these tiny differences.'

I slump on my bed with defeat. 'I'll know though.' I think I'm trying to convince myself more than them, so I just hide myself behind my soft toys. Who am I trying to kid? Of course, I couldn't kill a rabbit. 'You're right. This has tipped me over the edge from organised to full-on weird. I need therapy.'

They sit on either side of me. 'You don't need therapy; you just need a bit of perspective. It really isn't that bad, you know. You're just camping for a bit. Lots of people go camping and they survive. Let's face your fears. What's the thing that you're dreading the most?'

I grab a list and give it to Kate. 'Here. I've prepared that too.'

'Of course, you have,' she says as she reads it. As she gets to the end of the list, her face drops and she passed the list over to Anjali.

'And that's what you're dreading the most?' Anjali says.

'Yes, I know it's pathetic but it's true. I've trained every day so I'm fitter, I know every detail of the process, the schedule, I researched how to make fire, how to make a shelter, how to weave clothes from leaves.'

'That's a thing?'

'Yes, you just need to find the right ... well, never mind. Yes, it's a thing.'

Anjali gives me a hug. 'You are awesome you know. Your level of preparation is like nothing I've ever seen before. No one else on this show will have gone into this much detail.'

It doesn't make me feel any better. 'But no one is going to be as plastic as me.' That word still hurts.

'You're not plastic.'

'No?' I say. 'But what other candidate's worst fear is going to be what they look like on camera? Who else is terrified of what their face really looks like naturally?'

They don't say anything because there's nothing to say.

'See,' I say with a triumph that hurts me. 'I'm right. I am the plastic candidate. And all the world is going to see that.'

I wish I liked myself a bit more. My friends hug me and tell me it will all be fine, so I smile to please them. But when they've gone, the room feels empty and cold. I hold Mr Snowy even closer. What am I going to do about the whole 'wearing no make-up' thing? This show is all about facing your fears. It's only now I'm beginning to realise the damage Jade and co did all those years ago. I thought I'd solved it by learning how to transform myself. And I cannot lie, that felt amazing. Like I'd opened a secret door to a better, more glamorous world. Then when I started to post images online, people started to follow me. Little old me from nowhere land. I got addicted. Yes, I still lived in a small town attached to some wet hills, but once I got home, I could get out my box of tricks and connect with the big, wide web through my phone and my computer and I felt like I'd found my place in life. People seemed to like me and like how I looked. More than that, I mattered. And looking back, that's the best I've ever felt about myself. I'm so scared of not feeling that way anymore.

Slowly I get out my make-up remover and cotton pads. I sigh deeply. Methodically I wipe all away every trace of all that I've so carefully applied. After a few minutes, a pile of grubby pads lies in front of me.

I pick up my phone and look straight into the camera. I don't smile or use any tricks like flattering angles. This just needs to be me. Plain, unfiltered – just me. I look at the results. My stomach clenches. Yes, the world keeps turning, there's no sudden total eclipse of the sun or plague of frogs.

But I don't like what stares back at me. My face is just too – uninteresting, too bland. My eyebrows have disappeared, my face just seems like a blob. My skin's all blotchy. My nose seems too big as my eyes have virtually vanished. That's me – the invisible girl. I try to tell myself it's not too bad but all I can hear is that old horrible word – ugly, ugly, ugly. And that's how I feel at this moment. Ugly on the outside and ugly on the inside because I know I should be able to say, 'Hey, what I look like doesn't matter.' I should be able to say, 'Looks are just superficial.' But I can't. And I hate the way I'm feeling now.

I stare at my sad selfie; my sad selfie twin stares back.

What am I going to do?

CHAPTER EIGHTEEN

Word: Tribulation (noun)

The days fly past in a blur of obsessive planning, list-making and hour after of hour research. I slowly become a walking encyclopaedia on Scotland. Every day, I count down to the day of departure.

Ten. Nine. Eight. Seven. Six. Five. Four. Three. Two…

I wake up, realising that this is the last full day in my house and then the fear kicks in. Tomorrow I will wake up in my cosy den of a room with my laptop, my toys and my row of dictionaries. But then I'll be ripped away from my Temple of Cosiness and taken to the edge of civilisation and just dumped there to face my fate. Okay, I might be getting just a teeny bit melodramatic.

To forget all this, I start to congratulate myself on the final step in my carefully formulated plan. Fear of my face? Sorted. I'm off to a smart make-up place in Manchester to get semi-permanent make-up applied. Whether I'm in this show for a few hours or the full ten days, the woman on the end of the phone in the salon has assured me that my eyebrows, eyelashes and liner will stay in place through storm, hurricane, tornado or whatever other meteorological event that might come my way. I asked her if it would survive a tsunami but then the line went a bit silent. Perhaps that was a bit weird on reflection. It's like wanting to be a perfect corpse, I suppose, which is too far even for me.

The whole thought of spending a day in an expensive salon puts a little bounce back in my step. Normally, all my beauty treatments are made from whatever ingredients I can forage from the kitchen. My oatmeal and honey face-scrub is very effective, cheap and one of my most popular skincare vlogs. After breakfast, I go to find Mum as I need the hard cash to pay for this. I know I earn lots of money for all the vlogs I do but I never get to see any of it. When challenged on this in the past, she's said it's to save me from the bother and that she doesn't want 'my innocence to be corrupted by money'. Hmmm.

Chanting reverberates from the pod this morning. Good, she's generally much calmer after she's been meditating. So I wait, sitting under an apple tree in the orchard until Mum falls silent, a rare phenomenon. In the early morning sun, shafts of light filter through the late spring leaves as they rustle in the wind. I lean back on the tree and feel the sun warm my face. There are worse places to spend time in on a Saturday morning.

Eventually the 'oms' and 'ahms' fall silent and I enter the pod. 'Hi, Mum, I'm off to Manchester in a bit. Can I have the money we talked about?'

She squints at me as if she barely recognises me. 'Money? Manchester? Have I missed something?'

Deep breath, Tulip. 'Mum, we discussed this. I've arranged to have semi-permanent make-up applied before I go tomorrow. You said you'd give me the money.' Panic is currently crawling all around my insides.

'Did I? My memory is shocking at the moment. How much do you need?'

I tell her. It is expensive, but I told her how much it was before.

Her reaction shows that she's completely forgotten all about it.

'Darling, I really don't think this is a good idea.'

She can't go back on this, she can't! I start to speak.

'No, let's just think this through.'

'But we already have. We talked about this and you agreed.' She can't backtrack on me now. My wonderful plan is starting to collapse around me.

'Maybe we did but the details are all hazy. You don't need all that silly semi-permanent nonsense. Think of all the chemicals going into your skin. I'm sure it's not a good idea. And the type of people who have it done. Well, they're really not our sort of person.'

Since when did she become such a snob? I open my mouth again, but she just keeps going. 'No, I think it would be the wrong look for you. You're all about glorious, temporary transformations. You're all about magic and fun. Having some strange person drawing permanent lines on your face with some kind of felt tip, no that's not you at all. And anyway, we can't afford it.'

'I told you how much it was, and you agreed.' I just about stop myself stamping my feet and screaming.

'Did I? Well, I'd forgotten about the twins' birthday. I'm spent up after getting them all the things they've asked for. So,

I'm afraid I just can't afford any treatments for you. And anyway, you're naturally lovely. A blank canvas. You don't need it.' Her phone goes, and she goes to pick it up.

'But Mum…'

Her hand goes up and she's launched into a full-on conversation.

That's it. I know she won't change her mind.

I don't know what to do with myself, so I just stand in the orchard, feeling lost. I can't think of what to do. I have no money. I can't think of how I can borrow any. I thought I had everything under control but as always Mum is the one thing that I just can't count on. Bit like Dad really. That, and us, are one thing they still have in common.

Then I realise that is exactly what is going to happen next. The cameras are probably already waiting for us in a Scottish glen. A car will be speeding down to whisk me away, away from my safe haven to a situation I can't control. I think seriously for the first time about quitting. Then it hits me. If Mum does go ahead with the whole cameras in the house/home-schooling, then home won't be safe either. I slump down and let myself have a little weep.

'Tulip…' It's Willow. She gallops past me at full unicorn speed.

'Willow, you'll have to wear clothes tomorrow, you know,' I point out to her as I wipe away my tears.

She trots up to me, looking concerned. 'Why are you crying and why do I have to wear clothes?'

'I'm not crying,' I lie. 'It's just a bit of hayfever. And you have to wear clothes because the people with cameras are coming tomorrow and you can't be filmed like this.' I gesture at her natural state.

Willow peers around, confused. 'There's no hay here. There are trees and grass. I know these things because I am the Chosen Unicorn.' She stamps her feet, tosses her imaginary mane and canters around to make the point.

'Okay, Chosen Unicorn, tomorrow you must wear clothes. Just for a bit. Aren't you cold anyway? It's not quite summer yet.'

She thinks about this. 'I don't care. My hooha likes to run free.'

She's lost me. 'Run that by me again?' I say.

'My hooha.' She points at the relevant body area.

'Your hooha,' I repeat, though still a bit lost.

'My hooha doesn't like pants. My hooha likes to be out. My hooha likes to run around.' She demonstrates by doing a cartwheel, showing off said body part in all its glory.

I start to giggle. 'Well, that's all fine but tomorrow, just for a bit, your hooha needs to be camouflaged. It needs to go undercover.'

'Never,' she squeals, heading off deeper into the orchard. 'Freeeeedooooooooom,' she calls as she disappears behind a tree.

'Oh, Willow,' I say to myself, 'don't let Mum see you.' She'd film this and upload it in a pica of a second if she saw her youngest daughter now.

Then there's a crash and a howl. 'Tuuuliiiiiiiip.'

'Yes, Willow?'

A sob. A silence. A hiccup.

'I fell.'

'Yes?'

'I've got a … I've got a … I'VE GOT A PRICKLE IN MY HOOHA!'

You would have to have a heart of stone to laugh at that.

I clearly have a heart of stone.

I snort. 'I'm coming,' I say, 'Tulip to the rescue.'

CHAPTER NINETEEN

Word: Chicanery (noun)

Next morning as I'm eating my breakfast of homemade muesli and oatmilk, I look at the slop and wonder whether I'll miss this. But it could be very good training for eating whatever comes my way. I see Willow, suitably but reluctantly dressed in her unicorn onesie, and Rowan is wearing a fairy top with Power Ranger bottoms. For a moment, it feels like something has grabbed hold of my heart. The orchard, my room, Willow and Rowan, even Mum. They are what makes home. I've never been away this long.

Mum gives me a pep talk. 'Now, be yourself. But remember that the cameras are on you. Look out for others. They'll all have their game faces on. Trust no one. Just go for it and make sure you win.'

'It's not that kind of thing,' I point out for what feels like the thousandth time. 'There's no prize. It's all about the experience and then someone – who isn't me – will win the title.'

Mum shakes her head. I think the word is sagely. 'Everything is a competition really. The others might want to steal your aura. Protect it at all times.'

I consider an actual facepalm.

At that moment, the doorbell goes. My stomach lurches. It's real. It is actually going to happen.

Mum leaps up to greet our guests. First there's a middle-aged man who looks a bit like a potato. He introduces himself as Maz. He's the director. Take a deep breath, Tulip. It starts now. There's a shiny camera on the other side of him. I'm introduced to the film crew by Maz who Mum immediately takes a shine to and starts to chat up. We do some shots in the house. The camera zones in on Rowan's fairy top. I feel like jumping between him and it. Rowan's so excited about going to big school. But I dread to think what the other kids will say to him if the whole princess thing gets out and about. I mean, not that there's anything wrong with it, but boys and girls can be horrid to anyone a bit different. Let's face it – both Willow and Rowan fall into that category.

The rest of the morning is spent filming little interviews with me and the rest of the family. Maz asks if it's okay to film in my room and I find myself agreeing. Why not? But when I'm sitting on my bed, full of my teddies, with a camera on me and Maz asking questions it feels all wrong. I mean, wasn't I trying to escape from the cameras? And then there's the way Maz stares at my stuff. He gives a nod to the camera guy and I hear the whirring of the camera as it zooms in on the boxes of make-up I have.

'So, Tulip, can you talk me through what's in your boxes? Remember to repeat my question as part of your answer so it makes sense when we broadcast. Oh, and always look at me, not at the camera. I know it's hard, but it gets easier.'

My heart is racing, and my hands get sweaty. Normally when I'm doing a vlog, I don't even get so much as a flutter in the stomach. It's as easy as breathing. So why is this making me so on edge? It's just the same, surely. I go into 'vlog' mode but having to stare at Maz's face puts me off. He's keeping his face neutral but there's a glint in his eye that I don't like. It's just weird to be having this much eye contact with an older man who I don't know. I stare at him, the cameraman and the sound guy, all standing in my room. I've been invaded. No, that's not the right word. I invited them in. There's nothing happening here that I didn't sign up for. But it still feels so wrong. I'm slowly losing my grip on the situation and I don't like it.

Maz asks me the question again so I go into full-on vlog mode. 'What's in my boxes? Well, this one is my go-to basics.' I see Maz's face react to the word 'basic' when the box is crammed full of things, so I smile broadly but nervously. 'It's stuff I use every day. I start with some primer...' I pick out each shiny object and describe it and its effects, all the time grinning like the Joker on helium. I know my face looks stupid and my voice is going all girly and high-pitched. My stomach lurches again as if I'm going to be sick. He gets me to talk about it as I rummage through box after box. Why is this so different to what I do normally? Then it hits me as I'm talking about how to create highlights to change the shape of your face. I'm not in control. If I don't like a vlog, I can delete and do it again until I'm happy with it. But now Maz is in control and not me.

'Sorry,' I say, 'I just need a moment.' I lurch out of the room and run to the bathroom as it's the only place I can think of where I might be safe.

Can I back out? Do I want to back out? Can I just stay in

here until they all go away? After a few deep breaths and running through my list of words a couple of times, I edge out of the room, still feeling sick. As I head back to my room, I hear voices around the corner of the stairs. 'Happy with the footage?' It's a man's voice I don't recognise.

'Fantastic. She really is as vacant as we thought. Like a lamb to the slaughter. It's going to be great TV seeing her fail and fail and fail again.' Big deep voices laugh, one of them is Maz and the other must be the camera guy.

Who are they talking about? Who's vacant and bleating?

That cold rush of fear runs through me again.

Me.

I'm vacant, clueless.

I think of everything about what I know of TV shows. There are always types. The leader. The one with a sob story. The joker. And there's always a stupid girl. That's me. My interest in make-up makes me stupid and helpless in their eyes and that's the role they want me to play.

I could cry.

I could give up.

I could throw myself into my teddies and barricade myself in and let the cameras film my door and the car drive away empty.

Or I could show them that they're wrong. Which one will I choose?

CHAPTER TWENTY

Word: Fortitude (noun)

If they thought I was going to cry when I said goodbye, then they miscalculated. I make my decision. I'm going. Outside, Mum might be blinking back tears, Willow might be howling, 'Don't leave us, Tulip,' but I just smile and hug. I'd rather look cold than be manipulated.

I flick a hard stare at the camera before I'm introduced to my chaperone who is disappointingly not wearing a crinoline or called something like Eleanor Moonbeam. Instead, she's an endlessly smiling young woman called Phoebe who seems determined to be made cheerful by everything around her. Everything is cool. Mum is cool. Willow is cool. Rowan is way cool. I smile like I'm finding it all cool when really I'm thinking of how to kill Maz with a pair of tweezers and a particularly sharp eyeliner pencil.

I thought that being whisked off in a black car with a chaperone might be fun. But, as it takes me away from home and all that I know, I feel very small in the back of the huge car. My phone is, of course, in my hands, so I decide to burn through my data allowance to make the journey go quicker. I do an update to explain what I'm up to while Phoebe watches on. 'So, guys, I'm in the car...' I show the interior. 'This is Phoebe.' She waves helpfully and mouths, 'I'm Phoebe.'

'As I told you guys, I'm heading to the true north for a while and I'm going offline. It might be for one day. It might be longer. All I really know is that it is taking me well and truly out of my comfort zone. I will be make-up free from tomorrow.' I do an exaggerated scared face here. 'Which is fine. It's totally fine.' Then I do a freaked-out face, mouthing 'no it's not'. 'And did I mention that there's no Wi-Fi and I can't have my phone.' Now I start to fake sob. 'So, to help me out on my last day in civilisation, let me know what the thing is that you've done that's scared you most.' I decide to go out on a dramatic note. 'If for any reason, this is my last post, then remember me like this.' I do a close-up of my face and braids. 'If nothing else, remember that Tulip Summer Acorn Taylor could braid. Whatever else in life she did, she could braid well. And blend. She was a mistress of blending.' I do a dramatic pause. 'This is Tulip. Signing out. I may, or may not, see you on the other side.' I pout and then stop filming.

Phoebe is about to explode. 'Oh my god. That was great. And you're going to upload that now?'

'I'll watch it back and edit it on my phone if need be but yes.' A few minutes later, I press 'share' and it's gone. Straightaway the pings start, showing that people are watching, liking and commenting, with lots of lovely messages, wishing me well and telling me about what crazy stuff they have been up to. For while it distracts me from whatever mess of feelings is swirling within me. But even as I read the comments supporting me, it can't shift the sense of dread. I am walking with my eyes right open into a trap and currently I am completely out of ideas about what to do.

What feels like several millennia later, the car finally turns off the little road that we've been driving down. Beyond are proper mountains, not like the hills we have at home. Even though it's June now, the sky is a foreboding grey. The drive takes us through a huge pair of gates with stags leaping on them. Then we drive down an avenue of trees that meander up to the biggest house I've ever seen. So this is what an ancestral home looks like, even after it's been changed into a hotel?

Bear in mind, we never go on holiday. We never stay anywhere nice. And this is where Harvey's family once lived? I feel a bit like Alice going through the looking glass into another world.

As we draw up to the front, I see that there's a welcoming committee. An actual doorman is going to open my car door for me. Which is rather nice. But as the phone call to Phoebe a few moments ago explained, there will also be a camera to film my every movement as I arrive. I take a quick selfie to check how I look before I get out of the car. As I open the door, I realise that of course that has just been filmed. I can imagine the voiceover at this point. 'Tulip, from Derbyshire, the queen of selfies.'

Out of the car, I'm trying to get used to the fact that my every move is being filmed. I know I'm not supposed to look at the camera but it's really hard. Generally, girls are told to avoid middle-aged men who stand too close to them and follow them around. But here I am, trying to pretend that Alan or whatever he's called, doesn't exist. An assistant director stands next to Alan and asks me questions, which I have to answer as I drag my bag into the rather swanky hotel lobby.

'Looks heavy, Tulip. What have you got in there? Just the essentials?'

'Just the essentials,' I repeat back. 'Lots of wet wipes, hand sanitiser, four different kinds of waterproof mascara and eyeliner. I've gone for the ones synchronised swimmers wear.'

'Right. Great,' says the director and I can hear the glee in her voice. 'How do you keep yourself fit?'

'I keep myself fit by shopping pretty much. So, I'm probably not as fit as some of the others but I'm sure I'll keep up with them.' By now the camera has zoomed in on the bulging bag that I'm slowly dragging over the floor. The voiceover in my head continues. 'How will the queen of selfies survive without her essentials? Can she drag something bigger than a twig? Will she survive her first encounter with a bug?' I smile my blandest smile.

There is a red carpet outside the hotel. How's that for bling? I can't help but do a little skip as I drag my case along. But then the wheels get stuck and then the case sort of explodes.

All my teddies and essential stuff suddenly burst out on to the red carpet. I can almost feel the scorn burning through the camera lens as I see how I must look to an outsider. There is not a hope in hell that they won't use this footage. I stuff down the shame I feel, as I stuff everything back inside the case. I have never been made to feel quite this bad about who I am before. It's stupid but tears aren't too far away. But I stand up tall, smile at the camera and strut down the red carpet like it's my natural home, Mr Snowy in one hand. 'This looks cool, I think we'll like it here,' I say to him. Yes, I'm talking to my toys while being filmed. I really don't care anymore, do I?

Inside the hotel, scores of people are there to sort me out and I feel that I'm caught up in a well-oiled machine. My stuff's taken off me, instructions are blasted at me and I'm whisked away to a room full of sofas, with other kids my age. I can't help but notice that I'm the smallest person here by some distance. Even the girls loom over me. One of these tall specimens, with white blonde hair, glares at me. A boy who has particularly well-defined arm muscles and a cool razor cut flashes a smile. I check he's not smiling at someone behind me. He's not. He smiles again. I return it. My churning stomach calms a bit. Okay, if I end up with him then things might not be so bad. The cameras start rolling and first we have to sit through the Health and Safety presentation. Just as it's about to start, I do a head count. Including me, there are only eight contestants.

'But there are supposed to be ten,' I mouth to Razor Cut, who shrugs and focuses on the talk.

After listening to this, I get the feeling that it is all part of our psychological torture. They might as well call it the Intimidation and Threats presentation. Another middle-aged man, this one thin as a scarecrow and with as much dress sense, stands up to warn us about things that might happen. He's called Stan and it's his job to 'make sure you don't die on national TV'. Great. Razor Cut and I exchange glances. I feel a bit of a bond developing between us, so I don't feel quite as alone as I did.

Apparently, we are safe if we do exactly what we're told but if we don't we might die. 'Obviously we won't broadcast the footage if you do die on national TV,' Stan assures us. The room falls silent. Stan looks confused. 'That was a joke.'

'You mean you will broadcast us falling to our deaths?' Razor Cut asks.

Stan laughs nervously. 'No one is going to die.' Then he checks his clipboard. 'But do tell us if you find any ticks on your bodies.'

I put my hand up though I really don't want to know. 'What can ticks do?' A boy who is approximately three metres tall rolls his eyes at my question.

'Lyme disease. If untreated, it can lead to inflammation of the brain and paralysis.'

'Oh,' I say. Great. How did I miss that in my research? Stupid Tulip.

Stan looks to see if there are any more follow-up questions but then he continues. We will be climbing, apparently. White Blonde nods her head, at this talk of belays and crampons. I slump in my sofa. Never in all my life have I felt so out of place.

Razor Cut smiles at me again. 'Hi, I'm Anton. This is quite the circus, isn't it?'

I nod but there's no time to talk as Maz now stands up and shushes us.

'And now, this is the moment you've all been waiting for. You're all here to meet one man. And here he is. Hugh McManus.' As there are cheers and whoops, I know the camera is zooming in on my face. I try to manage a little 'yay' but I don't think I'm fooling anyone. But then again perhaps I'm not even trying. I'm pretty sure Anton is clapping in a very ironic fashion. I think I'm warming to him.

But my mouth does drop a little when I do finally see Hugh.

The man's a mountain. He looks like he's been hewn from rock. His face is practically a sculpture and you can tell he's never heard of moisturising. Not only could he take on a whole posse of starving polar bears, but he could probably strangle two crocodiles with his hands and turn them into an origami unicorn. I find myself thinking of Harvey. What must it be like having that as a father?

'Welcome, welcome, one and all. Welcome to the McManus estate. I grew up on these lands. Here is where I learned to be an adventurer. Where I learned to be a man. I cannot tell you how excited I am about sharing this place with you. As you know, I've dedicated my life to challenging adults as far as they can go and then a bit further.' He stops for a reaction. There's some laughter. 'But this show is all about you. You are the future of this country.' I'm beginning to feel a bit like I've signed up to be part of a cult. 'You have all been hand selected. By me. You are all the very best at what you do. You will face eight different challenges, two for every element – earth, water, air and fire.' That sounds ... scary. I glance around the room. Every other person looks so capable. 'I've been carefully through your applications and hand selected you. We have a mountaineer, a fencing champion, a long-distance swimmer, a marksman or should I say markswoman, a decathlon competitor, a computer programmer, a chess player and even a make-up vlogger...' Suddenly, I know all eyes are on me. Is it that obvious? I could be the chess player, couldn't I? Hugh is stalking up and down the room, fixing us poor kids with his super-strong gaze and asking us a personal question. He's coming my way. I try to fall between the cushions but a) I'm not that small and b) I can imagine that he'd reach down with one of his spade-like hands and pull me back up again, squealing.

'Tulip, isn't it?'

I find myself nodding as words appear to be beyond me.

'Now, what's your greatest achievement in life to date?'

My brain now resembles the Artic, white and empty. Not even one tiny penguin of an idea to help me. But then I remember that there aren't any penguins there – they live in the Antarctic. This is not helping, Tulip.

'Er, I have 300,000 followers on my channel and once a celebrity copied my make-up look for the British Music Awards.'

As the very words tumble from my mouth, I feel the judgement. All eyes are on me. I mentioned make-up. I mentioned channels and vlogs. I am therefore clearly stupid. I'm back to where I was with Harvey all that time ago, still having to justify that liking make-up doesn't make me brain dead.

'Wow, that's inspiring, Tulip.' Is he trolling me?

With that he's gone. I can't edit this moment. I can't re-wind and do it better. Those words are out there like a genie out of a digital bottle and I can't get them back. As I'm processing this, Hugh has asked a few more probing questions and now he's back at the front again.

'My last job tonight is to introduce you to my team leaders. The observant among you will have noticed that there are only eight of you here, but you've been told that ten will be competing. I'm going to split you into two groups. Your leaders are very special to me. I've handpicked them for the role. Fancy meeting the guys who are going to guide you through the next ten days? You'll be living, sleeping, eating and working together 24-7.'

For some reason, my heart begins to pound at that moment. I'm beginning to have a bad feeling about this.

'Put your hands together. And meet the final two contestants, for they are contestants as much as you, my sons.'

I knew it.

'Meet Harvey and Hector. My boys. Your lives are in their hands.'

And in Harvey comes. With a slightly taller version of him, a smirkier, harder-faced version of himself, if that's possible. His brother scans the room, looking for someone. His eyes lock on me, then he scans me up and down, looking like I'm a piece of dirt on his shoe.

I look at Harvey.

He smiles, rather nervously.

I send him a death stare. Why didn't he tell me? He could have told me. He's been messing me about all along, treating me like a fool from the start. I will make you pay for this, Harvey McManus. I swear on my best mascara that you will pay. Let the competition begin.

CHAPTER TWENTY-ONE

Word: Nemesis (noun)

The cameras zoom in to get shots of my face. I try to make mine like a mask, but I know that they'll have got all my reactions. The 'no, no, no' to the 'bring it on then, Nature Boy'. I can feel myself being turned into a reaction gif.

'Now it's time to reveal who is in which team,' Hugh shouts and smiles so hard that I think his face is going to split in two. There's no need to ask. I know where this is going, and I know a set-up when I see one. Who exactly is behind the set-up, I'm not quite sure. But only an idiot would believe that coincidences happen in television. And whatever I am, I'm not an idiot.

Hugh starts with Team Hector first – he lists four names. Felicity, Cameron, Samir and Thomas. The chosen ones go up and the boys shake hands in a very manly way while the girl goes in for an awkward hug. I swear Hector and Cameron are the same person. Is there another brother that no one knows about?

Harvey stands alone to one side. If I didn't know better, I'd say he looked a bit lost.

'The rest of you – Anton, Jane, Freddie and Tulip – you are Team Harvey!'

The team is assembled. So, Razor Cut aka Anton, is still

with me, that's one good sign. There's the two of us, and then White Blonde or as I must now call her Jane, which leaves Freddie, a huge, silent boy who is currently winning the 'I'm not impressed face' competition. No one moves. This is tense to the extreme.

I embrace the moment, so to speak, and walk over to Harvey with a fake smile on my face. For a second, I think he's going to go in for a hug, but I stick my hand out instead. He doesn't realise so I semi-punch his stomach by mistake. What a great start! Harvey half-smiles, takes my hand and gives it a very firm squeeze. The only good thing I can find in this moment is that at least he doesn't have sweaty hands. But do I? Now I'm panicking but then Hugh looms up in front of me. 'I think you already know each other.'

'We do,' I say. The camera gets closer, but I don't say anything more.

Hugh puts out a huge paw of a hand and drags Harvey closer. Even Harvey seems a bit thrown by this. 'Tulip, Harvey. You are going to make a great team. You have so much to learn from each other.'

I concentrate very hard on a) not raising a sarcastic but perfectly formed eyebrow and b) not rolling my eyes while saying 'Really?' I smile a very bland smile that I'm sure stops well short of my eyes.

'Hi, Tulip,' Harvey says.

'What a surprise,' I reply, with maximum sarcasm.

He opens his mouth to say something. But then as the camera moves in a bit more, he stops himself and just looks at me. I can't quite read his expression. Is he enjoying this moment of having tricked me into applying and never telling me that he was part of the deal? Or is there something more going on that I don't get? I have a flashback to the library and how he said he wanted to tell me something. Was this it?

'Are you sure you're ready for this?' Is that concern or a threat?

Another tight-lipped little smile. 'Oh, you know me, Harvey, I'm ready for anything.'

Okay, now I'm being an idiot. I am so totally out of my depth someone should throw me a float and drag me back to safety. The camera is now practically on me, every tiny emotion recorded and analysed.

Harvey smiles at me. He's good at this because it does look like a real smile of warmth and dare I say friendship. 'Of course, you are.' Then he's off, to have a handshaking competition with Freddie.

One of the assistant directors touches me on the arm. 'Time to record your thoughts, Tulip.'

Really? My thoughts are currently squirming around like eels in a bucket. We're being told lots of information. What if I miss anything important?

I tap Anton on the shoulder. 'Tell me what they say when I get back?'

He nods and gives me a thumbs-up.

I'm taken to a room, sat on a tartan throne and told to talk straight to the camera this time.

'How are you feeling, Tulip?'

'Quietly confident,' I lie.

More questions come, each more leading than the next. 'How do you feel about seeing one of your school mates?'

'A bit surprised. But I don't know him very well. I suppose this is an opportunity to get to know him better.' More lies.

I'm quizzed about first impressions, but I hope I give nothing away. I sense some frustration in the questions, as if I'm not giving them what they want. Eventually, the director gives up on me and I'm allowed to re-join my team for our evening meal.

I feel sick as I walk into the restaurant. The walls are lined with the heads of dead animals. Apart from that, all I get is an impression of white tablecloths and a ridiculous amount of cutlery. At Harvey's table, there's a spare chair. I suppose that's for me, so I walk over, smile and sit down. Anton momentarily pauses from hacking his steak to pieces. 'Hi Tulip.' But then his focus moves on to Harvey. 'So what strategies do you have to make sure we win? Do you have some sneaky moves planned?' Harvey looks taken aback and Anton slaps him on the arm. 'Of course, stupid me.' He drops his voice to a stage whisper. 'You don't want to reveal them now do you? Anyone could be listening.'

'Something like that,' Harvey says.

I don't engage in any conversation. I just try to enjoy the food, despite my nerves. It's probably the last good food that I'll be having for a while. From now on, I'll probably be eating grass, seaweed and, if I'm lucky, raw, ungutted fish with my bare teeth. I will probably need therapy after this. But the food doesn't go down well. I can't relax as the cameras are still on us.

127

As I chase half-melted ice cream around my plate, I scan the room and think about how I'm the smallest, least fit, least skilled person there. I have never felt more inadequate in all my life.

'I thought you'd leap at the chance to eat something sweet.' Harvey leans over. 'Not hungry?'

'Something like that,' I say.

Anton asks, 'Are you on some kind of training regime then. A no-sugar diet?'

'No,' I say. 'My mum's a vegan without much time for cooking so I don't get much chance to eat food like this.'

'Vegan. That's full on. Do you find it enhances your performance?'

'Performance?' I say. 'No, I don't suddenly find I'm living faster or doing better at school.'

As Anton laughs, his whole body shakes. 'No, what sport do you do and does your diet make a difference?'

'I don't really do sport,' I say.

Now I have his full attention. 'No sport at all?'

I shake my head.

'What about a skill?'

Harvey wades in now. 'Tulip is very skilled at her chosen art form.'

'Art?' This concept clearly confuses Anton. 'How will art help you with your wilderness skills?'

Thanks, Harvey. 'I'm very artistic with make-up,' I say.

This time it's Jane who laughs. 'So, you're the vlogger. Make-up? How is that going to be useful?'

I keep my face blank.

Anton claps me on the shoulder. 'Never mind. We'll show you the ropes. I'll keep an eye out for you. I do ten different disciplines, more than enough for both of us.'

Jane seems to be laughing at me and even Anton, who I thought liked me, now seems to be patronising. I make my excuses. 'Time to get some rest, I think.'

Jane smirks, 'Do you want to get some beauty sleep to look good in your close-up tomorrow?' She guffaws at her own joke. Freddie, I think he's called, and so far, the only thing I've worked out about him is that he's silent, says nothing, but if his biceps are anything to go by, very strong. Maybe he's the swimmer or fencing champion.

I give Jane the death stare. She stops laughing. 'No, I want to be in the best shape I can be tomorrow. So, no sugar...' I gesture at the half-eaten ice cream, '...and plenty of sleep. Night, team.'

With that I'm gone. As I walk away from the table and the cameras, I feel the happiest I've been since I arrived. I've been putting all my efforts into hiding what I'm feeling. I can't wait to shut the door on all of this and just be myself. I'm almost running for my room by then.

I slam the door and throw myself on my bed. I think about tomorrow. That's when it all begins in earnest. I have never felt so unprepared for anything in my life. To calm myself down, I put on my comfiest clothes, get out my teddies and spend an hour or so distracting myself by reading all the comments under my last vlog.

My eyes are beginning to droop but there's a knock on the door. I ignore it. Then there's another knock, louder this time.

'This better be good,' I grumble as I open the door, expecting Phoebe there with some last instructions or words of comfort.

But it's not Phoebe. It's the last person in the world that I expected.

It's my nemesis.

Harvey.

And he looks worried.

CHAPTER TWENTY-TWO

Word: Parley (noun)

'And what exactly do you want?' I start off, leaning in what I hope is a semi-casual way against the door. Then it suddenly strikes me that I'm in my pyjamas (the ones with 'When I grow up, I want to be a unicorn' on – Willow's last Christmas present to me), I'm in a hotel unsupervised and I'm with an attractive though very annoying boy.

'Shush,' he whispers.

'Don't shush me,' I whisper as loudly as I can back. 'You knock on my door and then you and try shush me! How is that okay in any way possible?'

'Tulip, will you calm down?'

I raise a hand. 'Stop. Right. There. You don't get to tell me to calm down when you've manipulated me, pretty much lied to me and now you're going to get us both in trouble. You know we're not supposed to talk to each other until the morning.' The chaperones went through all of this before we came to bed. No unsupervised contact at any times. We are legally children and must be treated like that. Which is ridiculous but there you go.

A door bangs down the corridor. 'Listen, someone's coming.' Before I know what's going on, Harvey has grabbed me by the hand, pulled me out of my room and is now making me hide behind a rather large mannequin of a scary kilt-wearing

Scotsman. His beard is so large, I'm not actually bothered about being found. You could hide a whole hockey team back here and no one would notice. Despite that, I stay quiet as Phoebe and Alan walk past.

'I'll check on the kids.'

'Don't bother, I'll keep walking up and down for a bit. They'll be no trouble.'

Great. Now, how am I supposed to get back? I'm going to blame Harvey no matter what.

The footsteps fade away on the thick, tartan carpet. I wonder if I stay here for much longer whether I'll start developing a checked pattern too and become part of the Scottish-themed upholstery. I'm about to start protesting when Harvey checks the view and pulls me again, this time in direction of the stairs.

'Harvey,' I start.

He pulls me along again.

'Harvey!'

'Shush!'

I think I might have to punch him soon. But I manage to keep that under control. I stop. I pull my hand from his. 'Just tell me where we're going and why and I might go willingly. But stop pulling me along like I'm a dog on a lead. And stop telling me to shush.'

'Okay, I want to talk to you. There are a few things I need to tell you before tomorrow. I didn't think going in your room was such a great idea if we got caught. There's a snug downstairs which seems to be empty, so I thought we'd go there.'

'That's all I needed,' I say. 'It's generally considered good manners to ask and explain rather than drag and shush.'

He bows down as low as he can. 'Miss Tulip, I would be most awfully honoured if you would deign to accompany me downstairs to converse upon a number of diverse topics. As our discovery would be disadvantageous to us both, perhaps it would be most beneficial if conversation were kept to a minimum for a brief time.' Then he puts out his hand.

I almost smile but I don't take his hand.

'Lead the way, oh loquacious one.' He looks confused for a second. 'It means someone who talks a lot.' I can see he's about to say something, but I go 'Shush' at him and now I think we're quits. In fact, I realise that this is the first time since I've arrived at this gothic pile that I'm actually enjoying myself. Not a lot. But a bit. Creeping round using big words with Harvey is certainly more fun than listening to everyone else's sporting achievements.

But then I have to check myself. This is Harvey. I need to be angry with him. I add random shushing to his list of crimes.

After creeping down a small staircase, hiding behind a few pillars, we eventually find ourselves in a small room, full of equipment all packed away in squat black boxes. Harvey shuts the door behind us.

'Right,' I say, settling down on a box and trying to make myself comfortable. 'You have got some explaining to do.'

'I know. That's why I wanted to talk to you. I want to explain about everything.'

'Everything? You mean how you've treated me. You post a link to the show. You get all your buddies and hangers on to have a go at me until I apply.' I keep my eyes on him all the time though he's shifting around as if he's sitting on hot coals. 'But what don't you do?' I wait for dramatic effect. Harvey is getting a bit smaller as I speak. 'You don't tell me that you're going to be on the show too. And somehow, magically, you're my leader.' Now it's my turn to bow and scrape before him. 'Oh Harvey, my great and good leader. Do lead me and make sure this silly little, fluffy-headed girl doesn't get into trouble.'

I stop. He doesn't say anything, just fiddles with his fingers for a bit. 'The reason I didn't say anything…' He stops. 'This is so hard.' I stare at him in confusion. Where is cocky Harvey? Who even is this person?

'Okay, here goes. But hear me out before you say anything, can you just do that?'

'Er, I reserve the right to express myself as I see fit.'

'Of course, but can you give me a chance?' The gorgeous eyes are used to good effect.

I say nothing and gesture with my hand for him to go on. I might as well hear what he's got to say for himself. It's not like I'm going to sleep tonight anyway.

'Okay. I suppose it all starts with school. My original school. I hated it there. Dad went there and was Head Boy and then Hector went and he's now Head Boy, of course. But it wasn't for me. It was all petty rules and long hours. I'm not that great academically and I never felt I fitted in.'

This is all unexpected and I'm not quite seeing what this has to do with harassing me, but I'll give him a bit longer.

'I did really badly in some exams. Dad and I had a row and I said I hated school. That I felt trapped there. He said I could go to a school near his new activity centre if I wanted and live with Mum while she sets it up. The school hours were shorter, it meant I could do what I wanted in the evening. Go for walks in the hills wherever and whenever I wanted. Take photos. It seemed like a good idea. I'd have time to do my own thing in a way I never could at boarding school.'

He pauses. I think of him on his first day. It's like he's another boy.

'I was so nervous on my first day. I really regretted my decision by then, but I was too proud to back out. McManuses never fail at a challenge. Stupidly, I talked to my brother the night before who persuaded me that no one would like the real Harvey and that I should pretend to be more like him. Be More Hector was his mantra.'

I can't help myself. 'You kept repeating that on your first day. I saw you.'

He nods weakly. 'I'm such an idiot. I get really nervous before things like that, so I just imagined I was Hector and behaved like him.'

'Is he an obnoxious snob?'

'He has his moments.'

'Then you did well because that's how you came across.'

'I know. When you came in with your eyebrow missing, I thought you were some airhead. I'm sorry. You soon proved me wrong. But by then it was too late.'

'Okay, but what about tagging me on that post?'

'It wasn't me.'

'Come on, of course it was you. It was your account. It was your photo.'

'I don't have any social media. I just message people.'

'Then who called me a chicken and tagged me?'

'Guess.'

I think for a minute and then remember a look from earlier on today. 'Your brother?'

'See, you're smart.'

'But why didn't you tell me?'

'Well, this is where it gets bad. I'm not quite sure how to tell you.'

'Tell me. Now.'

He takes a deep breath. 'I don't know if you've realised yet, but Hector is really competitive. And he's always going on about how he's the better son. I know it shouldn't bother me, but it really does.'

'What's that got to do with anything?'

'He said that if I got you to apply to the show, then he'd admit that I was better than him.'

'What?' So, I'm part of a bet between two competitive brothers – not cool.

'I know. I didn't tell you that it was him, I called you a chicken, I kept on at you to go on the show to get you to apply.'

'At the library, you said you wanted to tell me something. Was this it?'

'No, by this time, I'd found out that Dad wanted Hector and me involved with the show. At first, we weren't going to be, I promise. But then Dad thought it would be a good idea to test me and Hector against each other. I was going to tell you that if you did go on the show, I'd be on it too.'

'But you didn't.'

'No.'

'Why?'

'First because you never talked to me.'

'That's pathetic. There was nothing to stop you talking to me at any time.'

'I know but there are other reasons. I get nervous. And also…'

'What?'

'I really wanted you to come on the show.'

'I don't see why.' The more he says, the more confused I get.

'Because I thought you'd like it. I began to see how what you do is all about beauty and art and I thought you might begin to see the natural world like I do.'

'Very altruistic of you.' I feel I'm still missing something.

'But there was another reason. I've messed everything up since we met. I pretended to be someone I wasn't. I know now that I just need to be me. That's what I'm going to do on the show, just be myself for once. I need you to know that.'

'You're babbling now. Why should I care what the real Harvey is like?'

'Because… Because… God, going to a boys' school did not prepare me for this.' He just looks at me with a wounded expression. Then he leans in. Is he going to kiss me? No. He can't. I won't let him.

I leap away and squeal. 'What in holy heck are you doing?'

Harvey leaps up as if burned. 'Sorry, I'm so sorry.'

'What. Was. That?' I say.

'Um…'

'Were you going to kiss me?'

'Um…'

I gaze at him. 'But you don't like me. Why would you like someone like me? Aren't I supposed to be the epitome of things you hate?'

'That's what I thought too. But I've been a total idiot.' He sighs. 'The truth is there's something about you. Things always seem to happen around you. Fun things. Life's never dull with you around. The other reason I didn't tell you was because I thought you'd drop out. And I really wanted to spend time with you. But Tulip, there's something else about the show that you need to know. I think you should drop out.'

'Oh, now I should drop out, after you've gone to all this trouble to get me here.'

'Yes, it's the director, Maz…'

'What? That Maz is about to make me look like a fool. I know that already.'

'Oh.'

For the first time, I feel something positive bubble up in me. And something else. Something like control. 'See – I know things.'

Harvey smiles at me. 'I should have guessed. I keep underestimating you.'

'Yes, you do.'

He laughs. 'Well, if you will sit there in unicorn pyjamas.'

No one has a go at the unicorns. Everyone has a line that mustn't be crossed, and he marched straight across it. 'So, you're unicornist, are you? Can't deal with people who have imaginations and find mythical creatures inspiring and magical?'

He raises an eyebrow. 'Unicornist?'

'You said it.' Now my hand finds itself pointing itself at Harvey's nose in a very dramatic and jabby kind of way.

'Now you listen to me. I may wear unicorn slippers and pyjamas, I might not have wrestled polar bears and run up Mount Everest in record times. But I am as good as every other person on this show. Whatever challenge or task I am set, I will give it everything. I will prove to you and everyone else that I, Tulip Summer Acorn Taylor, can do this. Now let's see who's the last person standing.' I start to go, and Harvey begins to speak. 'And just so you know. I don't care who the real Harvey is. You're weak, you're easily led, and you agreed to use me as part of some stupid bet with your brother. That is not the kind of person I like. I would not kiss you if you were the last boy left on the internet.' Harvey seems to jump at every accusation. 'I have just one last word – Shush!' I put my fingers to my lips and sweep out.

Then me, my unicorn slippers and my racing heart march down the corridor and back to my room.

CHAPTER TWENTY-THREE

Word: Eosophobia (noun)

It's hard to sleep when your heart is pounding. It's hard to sleep when you're angry and scared all at the same time. Is it possible to explode from too much emotion? Pacing round my room doesn't seem to do much good. I move on to my normal calming technique by going through my list of favourite words. Mellifluous. Anti-disestablishmentarianism. Waffle. Toffee. Cirrus. It takes quite a few goes but eventually the feelings start to lose their edge, if not fade away. I replay everything Harvey said. Was he telling the truth about everything or is it just another game to confuse me? He used me as some kind of bet with his brother but then started to like me and just wanted to spend time with me? On one level, it all makes some kind of sense and then on the other, it's just as confusing as before.

At some point, I drift off to sleep with my phone in my hand, quietly flashing away to itself as the comments to my last upload come through. They stay unread.

Knocking on my door wakes me up far too soon.

It's all dark. I reach around, confused, for something familiar to grab on to. Like a huge teddy or something. But there's nothing. I sit up, bolt upright.

'Morning, Tulip. Time to rise and shine.'

I try to speak. Words don't come out but what I think I'm trying to articulate is 'Holy heck, what time is it?' The clock next to the bed tells me the horrible truth.

It's 4.30.

4.30! There is only one activity that someone should ever be doing at 4.30. Sleeping. Anything else is child cruelty. But clearly Phoebe doesn't think so because she continues to bang away at the door. 'Tulip, time to get going.'

I drag myself to the door and somehow manage to fumble it open.

Phoebe is there, as super cheerful as yesterday. 'What a day you have ahead of you. It's going to be wonderful.'

'Yay' is about all I can manage.

'Now, here are your things for today. Put them on and be down in fifteen minutes.' I find myself holding a huge bundle of shiny material. After closing the door, I shake them out and hang them up to myself. Really? My eyes hurt from the complete absence of any attempt at fashionable design. I mean, yes, I get that we have to wear the right clothes for the landscape, but do they all have to be this dull and badly fitting? This stuff is unisex, for goodness sake. I'm going to be in front of the cameras shortly in a set of very expensive clothes that appear to have been constructed from plastic bags.

Another bang on the door. 'Five minutes.'

I mutter quietly to myself while I drag the clothes on. Under layer, fleece, waterproofs and then the world's biggest boots. I feel like I'm ready for the moon landing. And, to be honest, the wilds of Scotland might as well be the moon as far as I'm concerned. I braid my hair into something that looks presentable and, as the door bangs yet again, I apply some extra waterproof make-up before hiding an eyeliner. We're not supposed to take anything with us, but you really can't expect me to give up without a fight.

The banging continues until I answer the door and the fun begins.

By fun, I mean, being laughed at when I ask about breakfast. By fun, I mean being put in the back of a Land Rover and driven off into the dark. It feels like the start of a horror movie. We've been split into our two teams obviously, though the atmosphere in our vehicle makes the dank outside look tropical. Harvey keeps looking at me, but I won't catch his eye. Of course, there's Alan, filming again, and I'm not saying or doing anything on camera to suggest I have any feelings towards Harvey. Jane is muttering to herself in a very annoying way and Anton keeps trying to talk about how he's already done a hundred press-ups. Freddie gives his best impression of a statue by not moving or speaking. Which is pretty much what he does all the time. I'm half tempted to touch his hair just to see if that's as immobile as his face.

But that would be weird, so to distract myself I stare out of the muddy windows. I would like to say that the natural landscape made some kind of impression on me. It might. If I could see it. The air is grey and wet with mist and so it feels like we're bouncing down something that aspires to be the road to nowhere.

'Are you enjoying this?' A voice from nowhere booms. I leap

back in surprise. Hugh has arrived on the back of a moving vehicle. Did he leap out of the bracken? Did he drop out of the mist? I'm sure he wasn't here a minute ago and now he's here, grinning and hanging on to the edge of the open door at the back of the Land Rover.

Hugh leans down over me. 'What do you make of all this?' He gestures at what I'm wearing.

'I think that there must be a fortune to be made in designing clothes for the outdoors that actually fit and look good.'

He slaps me on the shoulder. 'Quite the entrepreneur, aren't you?'

I sniff. 'Aesthetics are important to me.'

'And this?' Hugh points to the grey. 'Isn't nature the ultimate aesthetic experience?'

'If you could see it, it might be.'

Jane tuts. 'It's there. You have to feel it.'

Have I been kidnapped by some kind of nature cult?

'You'll soon be able to see it and feel it. Look over there.' I do as I'm told but again all I can see is grey. It's like someone has stolen Scotland and replaced it with soggy air.

The Land Rover slows to a halt and we tumble out of the back. Beneath my huge boots, the ground squelches and mud sucks up round my feet. If I'm feeling disgust, I hide it. Alan is showing far too much interest in me, almost as if he's been told to track my every move. I know Mum told me that all exposure is good exposure. But I don't want to be edited into a fussy girl who faints at the sight of mud.

We have to stand in a semi-circle around Hugh. As he

begins to speak, the air slowly gets a bit brighter. As the minutes pass, the grey begins to thin, and I can see that we're standing in a clearing, surrounded by ragged pine trees that reach up into the remaining mist.

We're not alone in the clearing. There's us, the Land Rover and a camera crew. And something else. Keep your face straight, Tulip. Do. Not. React.

Gasps from all around. Anton exults, 'Yes, man. Yes. It's been a while since I've been in the back of one of these bad boys. This must be the first air task.'

'As you can see, ladies and gentlemen, this is how you will be arriving at your destination today. You will be taken to your rendezvous point and there you will jump into the sea and swim to the nearest beach for your camp. Due to the water element, this first task has been designated a water task.'

Hugh points to the red helicopter which by now is gleaming in the early morning sun.

The fear, which I'd about managed to push away, is back.

'You don't have to do it. But if you fail, then you will be going straight back to the hotel.'

Did I tell you that I really hate heights? And water. I really really hate water. And now I have to jump from a moving helicopter into the sea.

Time to girl up, Tulip, and show them what you're made of.

CHAPTER TWENTY-FOUR

Word: Gyroscope (noun)

I wait in the clearing for my moment of doom. Only a few hours ago, I was complaining about having to wear stupid amounts of technical fabric. Now I'm wearing a wetsuit, accessorised by a rather large life jacket and some neoprene boots. I'd give a year's supply of waterproof mascara to get back into my fleece and assorted layers. Changing into a wetsuit while hiding behind a tree in a Scottish forest was not quite how I imagined I'd be spending today. I may have a new career ahead of me as a contortionist.

The others have changed and gone into the bowels of the helicopter and have been whisked up into the now slightly less murky air. The helicopter returns after about half an hour – empty. Sitting here, my hands don't know what to do with themselves without a phone to hold so I find myself twiddling air. Then I see that I'm being filmed so stop. Because, seriously, who twiddles air?

The sun climbs but the day doesn't get any warmer. Huddled in my unflattering wetsuit, the cold air matches the feeling in my stomach. Heights are bad. Jumping into water is worse. And it's not any old ordinary water, it's the sea. Sea equals salt and not being able to see what's below you, which I absolutely hate. By now, I'm breathing heavily and, before I know it, I'm running to find a tree to throw up behind. For the first time in my life, I'm glad I've not had breakfast.

But as I stumble back through the wet ferns that cling to my legs, I see the camera on me. Yup, I'm confirming every one of their prejudices about me. I bet no one else was sick before this. I also bet I know why I'm the one to wait the longest – it gives me more time to torture myself about what's going to happen next.

I find a rough log to sit on and wait. I could run away. I could ask to be taken back to the hotel. I could have a full cooked breakfast, then get myself nice and toasty in bed and sleep. Later I could get back online and post a video about how it was all a terrible mistake and wait for the love to roll in. But then I'd have to go back home, having proved nothing to anybody, having achieved nothing. No, that's not happening, I decide. I have to keep sitting here, with my bum now solid with cold, and wait for the distant hum.

All too soon, I hear the steady beat of the helicopter's blades. As it comes nearer, I see Hugh hanging out from the side of it. This guy has no limits! He's like a proper action hero, swinging out the open side of the helicopter as it comes into land.

The fear that has never really gone away comes back in a wave. Focus, Tulip, I tell myself. List your words and keep calm. Follow the instructions. Shut off all the craziness that's inside.

He's showing off now is our Hugh as he jumps the few feet when the 'copter hovers over the ground before landing. 'And now time for Tulip. How are you feeling?'

'On top of the world,' I lie. I really wish he'd stop asking me that. The last thing I want is to be reminded that I am capable of having feelings, especially when I'm experiencing every single, horrible feeling in the world.

'Great.' He grabs my hand and gazes at me with an intensity that is more than a bit awkward. 'Are you ready to face your greatest challenge to date?'

'Well,' I say, 'mastering the art of water-marbling nails took me three years of hard work. This is a little jump, isn't it?'

Hugh just guffaws. I think that's the right word. Anyway, his whole body shakes with laughter. I didn't think it was that funny.

'Oh, Tulip,' he says, 'you are very refreshing. Come with me and let's see how you get on with the little jump as you call it.' With that, he pulls me into the helicopter. What is it with this family and their need to touch you?

I climb into the black seat of the helicopter. It's open on both sides but Hugh shows me how to strap myself in. Next, I have to put headphones on to drown out the noise of the blades.

And then we're off.

I've not been in the air much. For one thing, we can't afford to go abroad and for another Mum says it's not environmentally friendly. As we lurch up into the sky, I can't help but scream a bit. Hugh smirks, and I'm pretty sure I saw the lens glitter at me in a particularly knowing way. I cling on to the belt and close my eyes. I don't want to see the land move below me. I chant through some particularly calming em words. Em words are always good in an emergency.

I keep my eyes closed. Reassuringly, I don't appear to have

died yet. I feel someone tapping me on my arm and see Hugh right in my face. He indicates that I should remove my headphones and points out of the 'copter. I can see the dark grey sea topped with waves below us. I'm not good at judging heights but the gap below us is huge.

Hugh is now hanging back out of the side, holding on. He's standing on the runner of the helicopter and beckoning me to follow.

'You mean take the belt off?' I squeal.

He nods.

That's not possible.

'Come on, you can do this.'

Slowly, I unbuckle the belt but I can't move. If I stand up, I'll fall out, I know it.

'Stand up and hold on to the edge.'

Somehow, I manage to do this.

'Now keep holding on, but move your hand down until you're sitting on the edge.'

And there I am. On my bum, legs dangling out of a 'copter. Above me, blades are spinning round which is good because if they stopped we'd be dead. But they are also very scary as they look like they could take off my head. Below is the cold, cold sea. I can see the beach a little way off. Beneath us, the air from the blades forces the waves to turn on themselves.

'Okay, give me your hand. On the count of three, you're going to stand up and then jump.'

It sounds easy. All I have to do is follow a few simple instructions. I must cross my arms over my chest and step out.

I can see the safety boat to one side, so I know it will come and get me if need be. But my body is still going into meltdown.

'You can do this, Tulip. But say the word and we'll take you back to the hotel. The choice is yours.'

But I don't have a choice.

I look down. It's too far. I think I'm going to be sick again.

'Tulip, do you want to do this?'

I sort of nod.

'Do you trust me?'

Er, no, but there's a camera on me which means I have to lie. 'Yes,' I squeak.

'Then brace yourself.'

Then he lifts me with one massive arm and – I think the word is unceremoniously – drops me off the side of the helicopter.

CHAPTER TWENTY-FIVE

Word: Squaloid (adjective)

I'm falling, falling, out of control. Someone is screaming and it's probably me.

My first thought is – I did it. I really did it. Go, Tulip. My second thought is – okay, I had to be dropped in. Stupid Tulip. My third thought is – but now I'm going to die.

My arms and legs are flailing as if I can claw my way back up to the helicopter. Getting closer and closer to me is something worse than heights.

Water.

I'm in

Down

Under

Water is over my head, the salt stinging my eyes and nose.

Don't breathe, Tulip, I tell myself. Remember that bit. Just don't breathe. Aim for the light then, when your head is above water, you can breathe.

I breathe anyway.

Bad mistake. Mermaids can breathe under water but not me. Because I'm not a mermaid. Curse those stupid, mythical creatures for confusing me.

By the time I'm gasping at the surface, I probably resemble a whale or some huge floating object. Fortunately, my life jacket keeps my head up while I try to cough out the oceans of water that I've accidently swallowed.

Any attempt to look like I'm in control or create a certain impression for the cameras is out of the window. Sorry Mum, but whatever brand Tulip stands for, I've forgotten. In a case of life, death or brand awareness, I'm all about living.

I cough, I'm sick, I flounder around like an electric eel that's got itself into a tangle and is shocking itself for fun. In short, I'm a mess but I'm alive, which is always a bonus.

'Tulip, hang on to the boat.' A hum of an engine buzzes near as the rubber safety boat comes close.

I'm on my back now, floating. For a glorious moment, I've stopped coughing and normal breathing is resumed. Until that is, a huge wave crashes over me and I'm breathing in seawater again. I'm reminded that I don't even like salt and vinegar crisps so actual seawater is beyond vile.

'Tulip. The boat.' Stan, the health and safety guy, is holding out his hand. Despite his blatant disregard for manicuring, the hand looks very tempting. It is slightly reassuring that he's not really going to let me die.

I splash half-heartedly towards the boat and reach out to grab Stan. Our fingers meet and then I'm dashed away by the waves. Far away but tantalisingly near, I can see the shore and a few figures on the shore that I assume are my 'team'.

'I'm coming in, Tulip. Grab harder this time. You can do it.'

But I don't. I don't even try.

'Come on, lass, you must be getting cold in there. Let's be having you.'

'Stan, did you have to pull anyone else out?'

He looks down at me with an odd expression. 'What does that matter? I need to get you out of there PDQ.'

I start to splash out away from the boat and to the shore. 'I'm doing it on my own,' I think, with a grim determination. 'If they swam, then I can swim. It's not that far really. It just looks it.'

Stan positions the boat alongside me. 'You want to re-think this plan? It's cold in there and it will start to affect your performance soon.'

I wish he'd stop telling me that it's cold. I mean it's not exactly escaped my notice. My feet are currently masquerading as icebergs and I think that my blood has been swopped for ice-water. I think Harvey has done this to me somehow. I'm don't know quite how but I'm sure he's done it.

'Tulip, you're babbling.'

'Was I talking?'

'There was something about icebergs, but the rest was you foaming at the mouth.'

'That's what I like about you, Stan. Your warm, comforting presence. You're a real motivator.'

He's almost smiling. 'Stop talking and try not to drown.'

'I'm relying on you for that bit. I'll keep swimming but if I go under can you fish me out?'

'Not sure I've got my big net with me.'

'Stan!'

'What?'

'Why do you need a big net for me? I'm only little.'

He pauses. 'It's not for you, Tulip. It's for your mouth, that never seems to shut up.'

'There was me thinking this was the beginning of a great friendship.' I gasp for breath.

'Do you have a problem with girls who talk? Are you at heart a misogynist?'

'Just shut up and swim. No one's drowned on my watch and I'm not about to let you to be the first, though if you keep talking I might let you drown anyway.'

And do you know what, we're nearly at the shore. It's slow progress but what passes for a beach is getting closer. I can see Harvey, standing with his arms crossed.

Stan starts to shout. 'Watch out!'

My heart leaps. 'What?' I spin round but all there is grey, cold water all around. Below me, my legs flap but what's beneath them … who knows?

'Something over there. Looked like a fin.'

'A fin? Like a shark fin?' I'm squealing now. 'Get me out. Stan! It's time for the little net. The big net. I don't care about the size of the net, just get me out.' I grab on to the boat. 'Stan, I don't want to die. I'll stop talking, I promise.'

'Tulip, shush. Watch and listen.'

Okay now he's trolling me. 'You want me to watch a shark devour me? Am I supposed to listen to my own agonising screams as my blood drains away?'

'TULIP. Just look and stop screaming.'

I follow the line of his pointing finger. My heart goes cold as my very blood seems to congeal with fear. A dark triangle breaks the surface. Then an eye peers at me through the water. I'm screaming, grabbing on the boat, babbling about the net.

'Stan, it's going to eat me.'

'It will, if you don't be quiet. Talking annoys them.'

'Are they related to you, by any chance?'

'Are you half grumpy northern man and half shark?'

'How many times do I have to tell you, it's not a…'

I'm nearly at the shore. If I can just get there, I might not end up as shark bait. Stan's not helping me, there's no net coming my way, I've just got to get out of the water, so I surge forwards as best I can, one hundred per cent fuelled by fear.

And with that, I finally feel a few stones under my feet. A few more strokes and I can stand. Though it's hard to walk when you're exhausted, cold and very wet.

I make a wobbly turn back to the sea. 'Ha, shark. You didn't get me, now did you?' I'm about to say 'I laugh in the face of peril' but I don't. I throw up some seawater instead.

That's when I trip and fall at Harvey's feet.

CHAPTER TWENTY-SIX

Word: Prostrate (noun)

I think the word is spreadeagled. Basically, I'm sprawled out like an out-of-control starfish, spitting sand while lying at the feet of someone I have sworn to despise.

But at least I didn't get eaten.

'What are you talking about?' Harvey looks at me in confusion. I realise that I've been talking out loud again.

'The shark … I outswam it,' I boast.

He shakes his head. 'You know when you were in the library, did you bother to look at the differences between a shark and a dolphin?'

'Dolphin?' I stare back out to sea. A fin dances around Stan's boat. 'It was a dolphin?'

'Yes. Not a girl-eating shark. Which you should probably know are not native to Scotland's seas.'

'Yes, but there are seven different kinds of shark indigenous to this area,' I begin.

'But that wasn't one of them. You need a hand?'

'I don't need any help from you,' I say, half choking on sand as I do so, though in reality I'm so tired, I need a fork-lift to drag me up.

'Fine.' He shrugs and walks away. Then he turns back. 'There's a fire and dry clothes to change back into at the camp.

Not that it matters in any way at all, but you've got seaweed in your hair.'

My hand moves up to my head. He's right. I've turned into a Medusa creature, half human, half seaweed. He only said that to make it look like I care about my appearance. Okay, I do care about how I look but he didn't have to tell everyone in front of the cameras, I fume. Yet another moment when he's making me look bad. A tiny part of me thinks that I'm glad he did say something. I mean, it would be worse to arrive in camp with a full wig of sea foliage. But … but … I'm too tired to think this through. I just lie there, being angry takes up the last remaining bit of energy. If I stay here, they might build a shelter over me and then I can spend the rest of my time here lying on the beach. But then again, dry clothes do sound appealing.

'Tulip. Come on. We need to have a team meeting.' It's Jane. 'We can't do it without you apparently.'

'I feel so special.' I slowly push myself to my feet. Then something sharp jabs into a rather private place and I squeal.

Jane looks me up and down. 'What's the matter?'

'Er, nothing,' I lie. I can see why she's confused as from the outside there's nothing to see. What I can't tell her is that the eyeliner that I've hidden in my knickers has been dislodged and just poked me in a very delicate area. I try to take another step forward but again it stabs me. I manage to contain the squeal and grimace instead. I try to turn that into a very unconvincing smile.

Jane shakes her head in despair and walks away, leaving me trailing in her wake. I grab the bag of clothes that have 'Tulip' emblazoned on them and look around for somewhere to change. Nothing. There's a kind of tent-like cloak a bit like you get at the hairdresser's which I assume I'm supposed to put over me to protect my modesty. My modesty might be protected but my dignity certainly isn't. The removal of a wetsuit and then the putting on of clean clothes is challenging when you're pretty sure that there might be a camera near by. The fact that you've hidden an eyeliner in your pants is an added bonus.

I do a weird sort of shimmy to try to dislodge the eyeliner. I must look deranged as I shuffle, jump, wiggle my bum and generally contort myself until finally the tiny weapon of destruction finds its way down my leg. It slides down until it's trapped between my trousers and my ankle. I look around. A camera, of course, is trained on me. All my graceful gyrations have been captured. I can't rescue the eyeliner now – they'll just take it off me, so if I leave it here, hopefully I can find it in a quiet moment. That's if I get a quiet moment.

Now unimpeded in the knicker area, I can walk freely so I stride over to where I assume is the camp area, after clipping on my radio-mic. There's a fire. That's a start. They've given us fire, water and food for the first day. After that we're on our own.

'Finally,' Jane complains but I just smile at her.

'Some things are worth waiting for,' I say but she just rolls her eyes at me.

'Right.' Harvey stands up, resolutely not looking at me. 'Our next challenge is to establish a camp. We've been given fire today and we just have to heat up our rations. We need to build a shelter, dig a latrine and we need to find a clean water source.

First of all, let's go around the team and say what our skills or strengths are. So, I'm Harvey and I've been involved in wilderness training for some years. This is my seventeenth expedition, though the first one where I've not been supervised. I have camped on the estate before but I'm not familiar with this part.' Imagine being part of a family that owns so much land that you don't really know it that well. Our orchard suddenly feels very small.

He nods at Jane who hardly needs any encouragement. 'I'm Jane and I'm on Team GB's under 17 elite shooting squad.'

'You're the markswoman,' I say in awe.

'I am. I could kill if I wanted to.'

Right, Tulip, you need to start being nicer to her. She doesn't have a gun here as far as I know but maybe she can kill me with her bare hands.

'I'm Anton, as I think I've already said, I'm a decathlete so that means I have ten disciplines. Strength and speed are my key assets.'

Me? Harvey nods at me, with a slight smile. Is it patronising or not? If this is new Harvey I'm not really noticing a big difference.

'I'm Tulip and I would say my assets are planning, research and organising. I am very creative…'

'You're a make-up vlogger,' Jane says, as if this ends the conversation.

'I am.' I leave it at that.

Harvey nods at Freddie who takes in a deep breath and just says, 'Chess.'

I look at him in surprise. That was not what I was expecting. But that's all he says, 'Chess'.

'Okay,' Harvey says, 'so maybe you'll be good on strategy.'

No reaction from chess boy. Maybe he should start playing poker. No one would ever guess what he was thinking. 'Right,' Harvey continues. 'Dad will choose someone to leave tonight based on their contribution and performance today so we all need to work together.'

'Or lack of contribution,' Jane says, with a meaningful glance in my direction. Ignoring her, I put my hand up like an excited Year Seven, jiggling around on my log. I have something to contribute. I have studied the location. I know where the nearest stream is. I will show them and prove to them that there's more to me than smuggling contraband make-up into the wilderness. I can contribute!

Harvey ignores me and my hyperactive hand. 'Freddie and I will build a shelter. Jane, you prepare the food and then you look for water. Anton and Tulip, you can locate and dig the latrine.'

'But…' I start.

Jane interrupts. 'A latrine is a toilet, you know.'

I purse my lips at the thought that I, Tulip, queen of the dictionary, does not know what a latrine is. 'Thank you for that, Jane. I think you'll find it's derived from the Latin "lavare", meaning to wash.'

Jane does a double take. Freddie's mouth opens a bit though he doesn't say anything. Harvey's mouth quivers with something. Is he laughing at me or their reaction? He clears his throat. 'For those of you who don't know Tulip well, I think you need to know that she has quite an extensive vocabulary.'

Which is quite a nice thing to say but I'm still cross about the water thing. I try again to explain about my local knowledge. I need him to know that I can do this, but he just stares at me. 'As part of the application process didn't you say that you would give any task all your energy?'

I stare daggers at him. If I argue with him, I'll just look like I'm cross about my duty which I am but not for the reason he thinks. So, if I try to get out of latrine duty, I'll look like a princess. Whether he means it or not, he's got me. If this is him being himself, then I don't like him.

'I did. And I'm a girl of my word. I will dig you the best latrine this particular part of Scotland has ever seen.'

Now a full-on grin has spread across his face. 'I have every faith in you, Tulip. I look forward to seeing your handiwork later.'

'Come on, Tulip.' Anton stands up and then pulls me to my feet. 'The team has got to pull together so let's go and do our duty.'

'I know that but...' No one is listening to me. Anton strides off with a spade, Jane smirks at me and starts to put the pans ready and Harvey and Freddie grab axes and start to slash at trees. I want to tell them which kinds of branches will weave together best but it's clear that no one is listening to me.

I walk after Anton, full of emotions. None of them are positive. Now I have to dig a toilet. Let's just say I'm not feeling the joy. Can this day get worse?

CHAPTER TWENTY-SEVEN

Word: Pierglass (noun)

'So, we need to dig it at least fifty metres away from open water,' Anton says.

'I know.' I stumble over a root. Why does everything have to be so higgledy?

'Careful.' He puts out a hand to grab me.

'Thank you,' I reply. At least someone likes me.

I notice the air ahead has gone grey. Which is odd. And it buzzes. Which is even odder.

'We'd best avoid those.' Anton changes direction to the left. 'Nasty critters when they decide that they like the taste of you.'

I've read about these. It's the number one irritant for tourist to Scotland: the dreaded midge. They are particularly bad in the early summer and as it's now June I guess that counts. They're one part of the Scottish experience that I'd like to avoid if at all possible, so I follow Anton away from them.

But instead of getting quieter the buzzing gets louder. And then it happens. I am engulfed by a mass of tiny, biting monsters. They assail my face and eyes, so I start waving around in an attempt to bat them away. But they're in my eyes and ears.

'Keep walking and they'll go away,' I just about hear Anton advise. 'You might want to stop the arm gestures, they're not going to help.'

But I can't stop myself. I know I must look like an out of control robot, but I don't care.

'They're biting me,' I squeal.

'They like you,' Anton laughs.

'It's not funny,' I reply, wiping my lips after I've spoken as around three billion of them fly into my mouth. I try to spit them out. I know I'm hungry, but I was looking for a more substantial protein source than this.

'It is a bit.'

'Anyway, abusive behaviour is not a compliment. Being nasty to someone is not a good way to show them that you like them.' Yes, Harvey, I am thinking of you!

I'm going off Anton quickly, as he just smirks at that. Eventually the midges depart to bother someone else. It would be great if you could control them with your mind. I imagine them now pursuing Harvey and Jane into the loch. I find a few more on my hands so I swat at them. They turn to black smudges in a very satisfying way.

'That's the first time I've seen you smile,' Anton comments.

'People keep telling me about the great outdoors. So far, I'm not impressed,' I say. 'I'm wet, cold, hungry. I've been attacked by blood-sucking monsters, terrorised by a dolphin masquerading as a shark and now I'm about to dig a toilet. I don't really think I've got much to smile about.'

'You are funny,' he says and slaps me on the back. 'You're loving it really.'

No, I think, no, I am not. My hands go to my face and hair. I have no idea what I look like. This is a strange feeling for me.

I check my braids. They're still in though they do feel a bit like fuzzy caterpillars. I pat at them but then realise this is pointless. I can feel tiny, itchy bumps on my skin that I'm sure weren't there before. I've either got the plague or those midges have taken chunks of flesh with them. What must I look like?

I glance around. There must be something shiny here somewhere. All I can see is dirt, fir trees and damp air. Nothing that even remotely glitters, glistens or shines so there's zero chance of me seeing myself. It's driving me crazy – it's even worse than the midges.

By now Anton has stopped and is assessing the situation. I see something and suddenly have an idea. I congratulate myself on my ingenuity. I really do have the capacity to solve all of these little problems.

'Here's good I think,' he says, looking around.

'Good?' I repeat. 'I'm not sure that's the word that leaps to mind. We dig a hole, we put in a bucket, so we can take it all away. It's gross but I get that. But what about a shelter? No one seems to have mentioned that.'

Anton looks at me oddly. 'There's no shelter. You just come here and do your thing.'

'But … but … but…' For once words fail me. I gesture around at the widely spaced out trees. 'Anyone could see you!' My voice drops to a dramatic whisper. 'The cameras.'

'It'll just be a few birds or rabbits. No one is going to be watching.'

I am speechless. The thought of baring my lower regions to the world, even the very sparsely populated part of the world that I am currently residing in, is beyond horrific. I had presumed that our modesty would be protected in some kind of way. I am just going to have to think about a way to solve this too.

'Damn,' Anton says. 'We've forgotten the chemical drum.' We look at each other.

I yawn very loudly and expressively. 'I really could do with a rest.' Now is my opportunity. This could be my only chance. I smile as sweetly as I know how.

'It's a good job I like you, Tulip,' Anton mutters. 'I'll go back. I won't be long. You could make yourself useful and start digging. That'll wake you up.'

'Sure,' I lie. 'I'll get right on it.' I grab the spade as if I'm going to do as he says but I have another plan in mind.

He's out of sight. But are there any cameras? I peer around. I can't see anyone. Might I finally have a few moments without anyone looking?

I take my chance. I peer at the spade. The blade itself is quite dull but the metal of the handle is shiny. Very shiny. So shiny that I might be able to see myself in it. I polish it as best I can with my sleeve, spit on it to clean it and then polish it again.

Then I bring it close to my face. Yes, that's me though I'm a bit distorted. Now, if I pull it even closer, I should be able to see the state of my skin.

'Tulip. What on earth are you doing?'

Busted.

CHAPTER TWENTY-EIGHT

Word: Frivolous (adjective)

It's Harvey, of course. With a camera behind him. I imagine what I look like – a bedraggled girl staring at a spade a few centimetres from her face. Weird. Very, very weird. He stares at me. He looks at the spade. Then he realises what I'm doing and laughs.

I draw myself up to my haughtiest. 'I am inspecting the manufacturing quality of this implement.'

'Hmm' is Harvey's amused response.

'Look.' I wave the spade in his general direction as I lie. 'There's a flaw here. As I am someone who gives her all to every task I didn't want less than satisfactory implements to impede our progress.'

'A flaw, eh?'

Our eyes lock. 'Yes,' I repeat, 'a flaw. Now unless you've got anything useful to contribute, I have a hole to dig.' I pause. 'A great team leader might want to lead by example. Or are you lord of the manor and above getting your hands dirty?' It's worth a try. I smile brightly at him.

He shakes his head but he's still laughing. I mean I must look ridiculous. I'm beginning to conclude that I am the most ridiculous person in the world.

'You look like you've got the situation under control, Tulip.

You are a completely competent person after all who doesn't need any help from anyone, so I'll just leave you to it.'

I glare at his retreating back. Okay, he got me. Again. I'm not sure which is more annoying – when he gets me wrong or when he completely and utterly outmanoeuvres me because he totally understands me. The spade and the ground beneath the spade feel the full force of all my many feelings.

Then it starts to rain.

But I keep on going. Cold bullets of water might rake my face. Rivulets might find a way down my neck and begin to soak me more. But I have been set the task of digging this latrine and dig it, I shall. I am the most ridiculous girl in the world in the most ridiculous of situations, but I will just keep going for as long as I can. I will give this my all.

A while later, Anton lopes back, carrying the chemical bin with ease, a huge grin across his face. Rain just makes him look good. I, on the other hand, am now dripping with a combination of sweat, water and dirt. The mud has splattered up my legs, arms and hands. I'm learning to keep my mouth shut after the midge incident. I've consumed insects against my will today. I draw a line at eating earth.

He grabs the spade from me and I don't protest. 'I'll finish off. You've done okay.' For once, I don't argue. Soon the hole is big enough for the chemical barrel to fit it. We have to 'go' in it so we don't contaminate the area. As I read the rules about using it, I just get sicker. Toilet paper must go in a bag. The contents need to be bagged up and changed every day. I have to face the fact that I'm going to have to use this. I think of my bathroom back at the hotel. It was shiny and white and all mine. It was not a bucket.

'I still think we need a shelter. It's not right just to go here,' I say.

'Why don't you see if there's anything left over at the camp? Harvey and Freddie might have finished by now,' Anton grunts. 'I'll finish off here.'

It seems like a plan, so I drift back to camp, feeling a bit woozy from the cold, the hard work and lack of food. Surely, they need to feed us soon? I walk up to the fire and put my hands out to warm them. Immediately, my shoulders drop a little. It's amazing how the snap and crackle of wood, the colour and warmth of the flames can transform my spirits. I can see why ancient mankind worshipped fire. I'd give it a hug if I thought I could. Jane gives me a tin container full of brown slop. It's warm, it's allegedly food and I wolf it down. Mum's lentil Bolognese was good preparation for this. After her cooking, I think I can eat anything.

'What do you think of the shelter?' Harvey says.

'What shelter?' I rub my hands over the fire, looking for a tent or some other suitable construction.

'That shelter,' Jane says. 'Are you blind?'

'Oh,' I say. 'Right.'

Between two trees, a piece of grey material has been strung to create something a toddler would only be partially proud of. Beneath it, five sleeping bags are stretched out on a waterproof mat on the stony ground.

'Is it up to your standards, Tulip?' Jane mocks. 'Or were you looking for the en suite?'

Inspecting the shelter closely, I stand under the tarpaulin and try to imagine sleeping here. How is it even possible? For a while, I just stand there and look in horror.

'Well, say something? What do you think?' Harvey asks again.

'What do I think? Since when is anyone interested in what I think? For the record, I think it's lacking in flair and imagination.'

Harvey stares at me as if I've got two heads. 'What are you on about? It's a shelter. It's supposed to keep wind and rain off us. I can alter it depending on the direction of the wind. I've chosen the most sheltered spot. It's not a bad job, even if I say so myself.'

'Perhaps,' I say, 'but it's all a bit utilitarian.'

Now Freddie is staring at me too. 'You know, boring?' I elaborate. 'But thanks for the contribution, Freddie, it's always good to talk.'

'And exactly what do you suggest we do about that then?' Harvey says.

'Well, just watch me,' I say, as I stride off into the forest.

'But we need a team meeting. We've got things to decide,' Harvey yells. 'We need you to be there.'

I spin on my heels to yell back. 'That's okay. You never listen to me anyway. So just decide what to do and I'll just give my all as directed, glorious leader.' With that, I march off, with a plan in mind. I start to hum a little tune as I do so. For the first time, today I almost feel happy. I'm going to do something I like, for me, which may or may not be ridiculous. But it will be fun. And fun is always good.

CHAPTER TWENTY-NINE

Word: Contraband (noun)

In the forest, the sun comes out, casting fingers of light through the trees. It's beautifully quiet. I stand for a moment and take it all in as mist rises from the damp, pine-covered ground. A bird calls in the distance as wind rustles the branches together. It's like being in an Instagram post, only it suddenly strikes me, it's real. No filter is required. The soundtrack of wind, leaves and birdsong would be top seller on some mindfulness website and I'm getting it all for free. I'm not turning into a hippy like Mum and Dad but, for the first time, for a few minutes, away from everyone else and out on my own, this feels okay. So, Tulip, I tell myself, you need to do more of this. Go off on your own and find a little slice of happiness. If you can do that, then you might be able to survive putting up with everyone else.

I potter around, filling my arms with things that I can find to take back to camp. I think I hear a woodpecker and some pigeons. I'm not sure about the rest. I didn't research birdsong as I didn't see why it would be useful. I make another mental note to google birdsong when I get home. I like listening to it. I hum along with the birds as I look for things that might be useful. My feet make a soft crunching sound as I saunter along. I just need to start singing and then it'll be like I'm in a Disney cartoon.

'Tuuuliiiip.' My name reverberates through the trees. I shake myself out of this moment, sigh deeply, consider whether I can make my own shelter in the woods away from them all but then turn and track back to camp. I grab all my treasures and pick my way over the tree roots that lie like snakes in front of me.

It was Anton who came to find me. 'You okay?' he says as he eyes up the finds that I'm carrying.

'Absolutely fine,' I say. I decide not to explain my stuff. Hopefully, all will be revealed soon. We walk together in silence back to the camp where Harvey, Jane and Freddie are huddled round the fire.

'Finally,' Jane says. 'What on earth…' she starts when she sees what I'm carrying. 'We need to go foraging for food. What are you doing wasting your time on rubbish like that?'

I pick up a perfectly formed pine cone. 'I think it's aesthetically pleasing, myself.' I turn to Freddie. 'What do you think?'

He just shrugs.

'Ah, I see, you are stunned into silence by the sheer perfection of its symmetry.' He stares at me.

'I'll take that as a yes.' I begin my work as the rest of the team stares at me as if I'm deranged. I suppose it does look like that.

'Tulip,' Harvey says evenly, as if trying to control something. I'm not sure if he's cross with me or not but I don't really care.

'Yes, glorious leader who can do no wrong?' I answer.

'How much longer will you be? Jane suggests that we forage for food to gain points. Are you coming?'

'Just give me a moment,' I say and then I whistle a happy song. This seems to send Jane over the edge.

'She's wasting time.' Jane turns to Harvey. 'Do something. You're the leader. Shouldn't you – well – do some leading?' I roll my eyes. So, it's not just me she doesn't like. Harvey's now in for it.

To be fair to Harvey, he does keep whatever he's feeling under control. 'Thanks, Jane, for that reminder. Yes, I'm in charge. Tulip, you have half an hour with whatever you're doing and then you need to join the rest of us.' I don't say anything, I just nod. Harvey seems about to say something else but then he heads off towards the sea.

'Not that way,' I say and point towards where I know there is a spring. 'Go over there. You should be able to find some edible berries.'

Jane snorts. 'As if you'd know.'

'Try me,' I suggest. Harvey looks between me and Jane as if deciding who to believe. Jane is looking strong, competent and cross. I'm looking wet, and I'm standing in a pile of foliage with pine cones in each hand.

'Let's go, Jane,' he says and follows my direction.

I'm stunned. He believed me. Is this another of his little tricks?

It takes a while longer until I'm happy and then I stand back to survey my work. I've woven long twigs into coils, so I can put ferns in them to decorate the trees that form the shelter. Every piece of rope has pine cones attached so they hang like lanterns to create a party feel. I've put soft pine needles under

171

everyone's pillows for comfort. All in all, I've added a touch of beauty and softness to the camp. I sigh with satisfaction. It might not be particularly useful, but it's given it personality.

That's what this place needs. More fun. The Tulip Touch.

But there's only so much fun you can have on your own in a forest. I could go and help forage. I could sit by the fire. My hands keep twitching and grabbing for a phone that's not there. I don't know what time it is. I don't know what's happening with Kate and Anjali. I have no idea if anyone cares that I'm here. Mum could be transmitting live from our house with Willow showing her hooha to the world and I wouldn't know a thing. I don't like it. I don't like it at all.

I need something to do or someone to talk to. I lever myself up to go and find the foragers when the crunch of footsteps and mutter of voices tells me I don't need to go anywhere to find them.

'We found berries,' Harvey says, 'just as you said!'

I grin at him and then stop, reminding myself that he is Not The Kind of Boy I Like. Jane ignores us both.

'What is this?' Jane says, lifting up a pine cone. 'What is the point?'

'The point,' I say, 'is that it didn't feel like a home or as if anyone cared about it. Now it's been given some attention.'

'A makeover?' Harvey asks.

I purse my lips. 'You can think of it like that, I suppose. It's just…' I find it hard to explain why I did it. My hands were bored, my mind was whirring with ideas. Making the decorations gave me something to do and made me feel like I was contributing. I also felt that I was being me for a bit. Whatever that is.

Jane peers at each of my alterations, touching the ferns and poking at the stones. 'I just don't get it.' She's not angry with me for once, which makes a change.

I show her the pine needles that I've found to make pillows and for a split second I think she might be impressed. But then something rolls out of the bottom of my trousers. The eyeliner from before.

The little stick drops at her feet. As she picks it up, she stares at it like she's never seen make-up before. Though I don't think I've got anything to be ashamed off, I do feel a bit silly. Her expression makes me feel even more stupid. 'Yours, I think,' she says as she hands it to me.

Another hand grabs it. 'No, that's contraband. We're not allowed anything like that in camp.'

Harvey. Now his true colours show, and he grabs the eyeliner, breaks it in half and throws the bits into the fire. 'What are you doing?' I yell. 'That was my personal property.'

'Do you want to be thrown out for breaking the rules?' His eyes meet mine, soft brown and seemingly sincere. 'I'm doing it for the best. I'm doing it for you.'

'Don't expect any thanks,' I mutter. 'You owe me £19 for that.'

With that, I'm sulking. I don't react when Harvey seems impressed at what I've done.

That little eyeliner was like a talisman for me. Another bit of me. And he just threw it in the fire. I wonder if any of it survived?

I try to stir through the fire but feel Harvey watching me. I blush, he knows exactly what I'm doing. Before this, I felt he was laughing with me. Now he's back to laughing at me. He never did like me, I think. It was all some sort of game between him and his brother.

'Time for the eviction announcement,' a voice calls through the dusk. 'You'll get your evening meal at the shoreline where Hugh will decide on the first person to leave.'

It's probably me; I know it. I mean who else has had to be thrown from a helicopter, got a dolphin and shark confused and then been caught trying to use a spade as a mirror. I know I'm the most pathetic person here, but I don't want to go yet. I need a bit more time to show them all what I can do.

CHAPTER THIRTY

Word: Hubristic (adjective)

We march back to the dunes, where a huge fire is burning. Of course, Hugh has to have a bigger fire than anyone else. It's an inferno. I'd like to say it's impressive (which of course it is) but it scares me, as branches hiss in the heat, spitting and popping as the sap burns. I jump, and Anton puts a hand on my arm. 'It's just the sap,' he says reassuringly, moving over to sit down before I can tell him that I know.

The other team is there. Hector comes over to give Harvey a man-hug, then he punches him and then they wrestle in a really weird way. It's like a constant battle to be the alpha. It all feels like a performance for us, the cameras and, most importantly, Hugh.

After a while, Harvey shoves Hector off. 'Have you admitted that I'm the best son?'

'That,' Hector shrugs, and then finds me out. 'The infamous Tulip? Getting ready to leave? Bags all packed to go home? Bet you'll be glad to get back to the hotel.'

'Let's just see, shall we?' I reply. He rolls his eyes and heads back to his team. From close observation of the opposition, I would say that Felicity, with amazing braids and wide shoulders, is the climber. Cameron is tall with huge feet and hands which suggests that he might be the swimmer. I'm left choosing between Thomas and Samir for the computer programmer and the fencer. Given Samir has much more defined muscles, I decide that he must be the fencing champion.

We're given bowls of warm slop. It might be stew, it might not.

I take a mouthful. 'What in holy heck is this?' I splutter though grey sludge.

'I think it's shepherd's pie,' Harvey says though a mouthful.

'I don't like eating shepherds. I think mine is an old and smelly one.' I think about objecting on grounds of being a vegan but a) I'm not a vegan, that's Mum, and b) this looks marginally more exciting than the tree bark or the few berries that we found.

Then I sit and await my fate. I suppose I can eat something nicer at the hotel when I get back. I need to mentally prepare for my ignominious ejection. I like the word 'ignominious' in general but I'm not at all happy that it can be used to describe what's about to happen to me.

Hugh paces around the fire, like some ancient god. Then it begins. 'I have reviewed the footage filmed in both camps today. I have seen some leadership. I have seen some team work.' He pauses. 'I have also seen some people who have not pulled their weight.'

If it's me then it's just not fair. I did try. I might have made some mistakes, but I have contributed, I tell myself.

'So, after careful consideration, I have decided that the person who is leaving their camp tonight…' A pause. The waves sigh, the wood crackles, no one breathes out. 'Is…' Hugh rakes

176

us with his gaze. His eyes stop on me. I'm about to say, 'Now hang on here, I dug a toilet.'

'Thomas.'

Thomas! On Hector's team. He looks confused. He stares at me. As does everyone else. They all thought that I should be the one to go and yet here I am. I can breathe again. I might not be having a lovely meal back at the hotel, but I've survived. Despite all appearances to the contrary, I wasn't the worst. Go, Tulip. I give myself a metaphorical hug and slap on the back. I have survived Day One. That is beyond huge.

Hugh goes over and shakes Thomas's hand. 'A hard decision, Thomas. You're a good lad, but you need to be more of a team player. Get out from behind your computer screen from time to time.' Ouch, that's harsh.

'That is just weird,' Jane says quietly.

'We didn't see what happened in their camp,' Harvey says, 'so we don't know what he did or didn't do.'

'Maybe.' But she's not convinced.

'Shouldn't we be glad that we're still a team and that we've not lost anyone?' he says. All he gets in return is a 'hmmm'. All I get is a dirty look from her which I see clearly in the firelight.

Back at camp, the glow of still being here keeps me warm for a while but then it's time for bed. This is the most awkward thing ever. We pull ourselves into our sleeping bags, and then lie inches away from each other, out in the open, under the 'shelter' of the tarpaulin. I can't see my cosy touches in the dark. I'm a long way from home.

It's probably the worst night's sleep anyone has ever had in the history of the known world. Sleep deprivation is a well-known form of torture and now I know why. For a start, you might think that the wild is quiet but it's not. The clue is in the name – it's full of fluffing wildlife who have no consideration for the needs of others. The leaves rustling is fine for the first hour but then it just gets repetitive. Pouring rain on tarpaulin is not quite the same as raindrops tapping on glass. It's hard to sleep when there's a gale blowing round you and branches from the tree above begin to fall on you with monotonous regularity. Okay, they are twigs rather than branches, but they are still made from wood and hurt when they fall on you from a great height. Did I mention the cold? It's cold.

I know there are chaperones somewhere to make sure we're all okay. I know that we are never alone. But I've seen horror movies. If a maniac with a knife wants to turn us into kebabs, then Phoebe with her endless smile or even Safe and Healthy Stan won't be able to help. I don't think Stan's big net will be much use in the face of a homicidal psychopath. I toss, I turn, I list every word I can think of to do with sleep. I drift off for a while but it's no good. The first hint of a step out there and I'm wide awake. I almost cry when I think of my lovely room back home, warm, full of soft things, fully equipped with life's luxuries such as a bed and – hey – here's an idea for you – a roof!

Eventually, I see part of the sky get lighter. Dawn is coming. In a few hours, we'll be up and out. I think about moving me and my sleeping bag towards the fire, so I might feel a bit cosier. I think of the eyeliner. Maybe now would be a good time to look. If the Goddess of Make-up is smiling on me, then I might be able to find a bit. I know that it's crazy, but it would remind me of home. It would remind me of who I am.

I get up and hop like a huge caterpillar over to the fire, hoping that no one wakes up. I probably look like someone's nightmare at the moment – a large insect leaping through the forest. The fire still glows. Someone must have kept it going through the night. I glance around. I can see the odd light in the distance that means someone's close at hand but there's no one near at the moment.

I take a stick and start to rummage about. Nothing. Just ashes.

It's all long gone. Okay, I know I'll just have to go on as I am, but I hate being defeated by a situation. I like to think that I can always discover a way through a problem.

I look at the ash on my finger. I look at a small stick burned in the fire.

And then I have an idea. Clever Tulip, you always manage to find a way.

CHAPTER THIRTY-ONE

Word: Folly (noun)

Five minutes later, I'm biting on my hand to contain my screams. But it's hard to be quiet when you've just stuck a stick in your eye. I once stuck a mascara wand in my eye before but that was nothing like this pain. Imagine the most painful thing you've ever done and then turn the dial up to 99. Why do I do this? I think I'm being so clever and really, I do something monumentally ignorant. Tears stream down my face as the burning sensation gets worse. I bite on my hand even harder.

At least there are no camera guys on me. I don't think I could bear it if anyone saw it. The shame. I'm not sure which is worse – the stabbing pain in my eye or the thought of being revealed on TV as clearly the most ridiculous girl who has ever lived.

'Tulip?' Harvey stands next to me, his hair ruffled, and his face concerned. 'Are you okay?'

I sit before him, still sobbing and biting on my hand to stop my screams. 'Do I look okay?'

'To be honest, no.'

He doesn't say anything else – we just sit for a while as I wipe away the tears and hope that I've not blinded myself. At least I'm hoping that all my tears will wash away any evidence of my world-class idiot behaviour.

'Are you missing home?' he asks quietly.

I shake my head.

'I miss my mum sometimes,' he says unexpectedly.

I hiccup but then find my voice. 'I thought you loved it here. I thought you were all about the outdoor life.'

'I am. Well, maybe not this.' He gestures at where the chaperones are sleeping.

'You didn't want to do the TV show?' I find myself asking.

He shrugs. 'You don't say no to Hugh McManus.' All I can do is nod in agreement. Though frankly there is a weird dynamic in their family.

'My mum is totally nuts,' I say. We look at each other and laugh, though my laughter is mixed with tears. We do have one small thing in common after all though, I'm here to escape my mum and Harvey is here because he can't escape his father.

Harvey peers at my face. 'Is your eye okay? It looks really red.' He takes my face and gently turns it, so he can see it better. 'It looks like you've been poked in the eye.'

I don't reply. He wipes a finger on my face and looks at his finger tip. Black with tell-tale ash. For a second, I think I can hide the small stick that I used but as I move my foot to cover it up, he sees what I'm up to and the flash of revelation on his face shows that he has just worked out what happened.

Shame floods through me and I have to fight back more tears.

'Oh,' is all Harvey says.

'Go on,' I say, 'you can say what you're really thinking. That you were right about me all along. I am plastic and ridiculous. I really am.'

'Why did you do it?' he asks.

For a while, I sit and think about that. 'That's the annoying thing. I don't even know. Yes, I'm bothered about being filmed without any make-up. But it's more than that. I think it's that I always like to do my own thing. I don't like being told what to do. So, the more that I'm not supposed to have make-up, the more I try to break the rules.'

'So, it's a control thing?'

'I think so. Something like that.' I take a deep breath. 'This is all about learning about yourself then? Isn't that Hugh's big thing? So maybe I've learned that I'm a control freak who would poke herself in the eye rather than not have eyeliner.' But I hate that those words are even out there. I feel exposed by anyone knowing the real, stupid truth about how weird I am. 'At least only you know about it.'

Harvey stares at me. 'What do you mean?'

I gesture with my head at the empty woods. 'No camera guys are up yet. I don't think I could cope if that had been filmed.'

He sighs, shaking his head. 'Did you listen in the talk?'

'What?' I missed a bit when I was being interviewed. I remember asking Anton and he said I'd not missed anything. But maybe I did. I gaze at Harvey, with mounting horror.

'There are unmanned cameras on the camp. Look.' He points to a tree next to the camp and I see a box attached to it that I'd not noticed. A box with a lens pointing straight at us. My heart lurches as if it's a lift in freefall.

'So, everything is filmed? All the time?' I say, wrenching the words out.

He nods. 'By the sea is safe. But that's the only place that I know of.'

'Right, the sea.' I stand up, and my feet start to take me in the direction of the sea.

'Do you want me to...' Harvey starts.

I put my hand up. 'I just want to be on my own for a while. Completely, properly on my own.'

He nods in understanding. 'For what it's worth ... I know it doesn't matter ... but just so you know...'

His words trail away but I don't fill the silence. If I say something now, then I really will lose it and I need a bit of time to get myself back together.

'You look great all the time. Make-up, no make-up. I just thought I'd say.' He looks so sad and I'm not sure why. Can he be properly upset that I'm upset? If so, then maybe the real Harvey is a lot nicer than I thought. But now I just need to be on my own.

Ripping off the radio mic, I don't say anything. At first, I don't know where my feet are taking me. They seem to have some purpose, but I don't feel that I'm guiding them. All I can do is focus on the sobs that are welling up in me. I'm walking on stones, which then turn to sand. I climb over dunes where sand pours into my boots, dragging me down and back but I keep fighting to stay upright. The murmur and crash of the sea pulls me forward as I dash away tears, rubbing grit into my eyes as I do so. Another mistake. Another stupid decision. Now I wish that I'd been sent home. At least failure would be better than total stupidity.

Once I reach the top of the dunes, I take a moment to draw in the cold air that blasts in my face. Just now it helps. It feels right. It distracts me from all that's churning up inside. Then I start to slide down the steep slope to the beach and I don't stop myself from falling. Why would I? Even if cameras can see me, then I'm just giving them more of what they want. I'm just a stupid idiot.

As I sit on the beach, I take it all in. In the early morning light, the waves look grey and cold. Maybe I should swim out there, to the huge expanse of the horizon, and find a friendly (or not so friendly) shark to eat me. RIP Tulip Taylor, who died of shame due to her own stupidity.

My cheeks blaze at the thought of the last two days. In my head, it's like a loop of shame. All on camera.

But what did you expect, Tulip, when you agreed to go on a TV programme? That's the bit that gets me. I walked into this with my eyes wide open. I thought I was being so clever, coming up with my wonderful plan. I think about the last night in the hotel. How can that even be two days ago? My words come back to haunt me. How I, Tulip Summer Acorn Taylor, was going to prove everyone wrong. Well, I seem to be the only one sitting on a beach with one eye in agony, having a breakdown.

Twenty-four hours. That's all I've managed. And in each of those few hours, I seem to have made myself into an increasingly cartoon-like parody of a plastic girl.

I have no one to blame but myself. My head rests on my hands and I just let the sobs come out. If they film me, then so what? This is real. This is true. This is me realising what a worthless person I am. I have no idea how much time is passing, I just listen to the waves and think of all the different words I could use to describe them. My breathing starts to match the rhythm of the waves. Eventually, I find the energy to lift my head. The sun behind me throws my long shadow forward, making a dark twin that stretches out to sea. The sky has changed from dove grey, to soft green with tinges of purple before expanding out into blue. I think of eyeshadow colours that look like this and how they could combine to make a beautiful look. If I had my phone, I could take a photo or jot down some notes. But as my hands are empty, I decide I'll have to try to remember it. I stare at the colours, trying to fix them in my mind so I can do something with them when I get back.

My thoughts wander as my fingers reach up to my face. I've never been this long without seeing my face. It feels the same as normal with my lips, eyes and mouth exactly as they should be. Why am I tormenting myself with what I look like when I can't even see myself and it feels just the same? Is it because I'm facing a situation that I can't control or do anything about?

I think about how Harvey has been kind. He's been gentle. He could have laughed at me, but he didn't. Like he understood me. Unless it was all for the cameras.

My thoughts ramble around. I take in the grains of sand blowing up in a tiny hurricane, how a crab scuttles across the sand bars before me, how the frothy waves are creeping closer to me. It occurs to me that I'll have to move at some point or just let the sea take me away like – what do you call rubbish that floats up on the beach – flotsam and jetsam. If I have my dictionary I could see where those words come from but as I can't I just repeat them over and over again in a weird sort of mantra. I notice all the colourful scraps, bits of plastic that really shouldn't be here in such a beautiful place. It shakes me out of myself. When I get back to my normal world, I'm going to get Mum to make sure we're a lot more eco-friendly. I start to pick plastic up but then I don't know what to do with it.

Flotsam. Jetsam. Flotsam. Jetsam. I'm muttering as I scour the shoreline.

Suddenly, I see myself as a camera might. A wild-haired girl wanders on a deserted beach, muttering weird words that no self-respecting teenager would ever use, picking up plastic that has nothing to do with her

You are so ridiculous, Tulip.

But instead of crying, it strikes me that it's very funny. So now I'm a wild-haired, rocking, beach-dwelling plastic-picking teenager who is laughing hysterically.

In fact, I wish I was being filmed now. This is me. This is what I'm like. Yes, I'm self-obsessed. Yes, I'm a control freak. Yes, I do stupid things.

But I'm me. I think I make the world a funner place, possibly even a better place. I probably can think of another word than funner but that's all I've got for now.

I've made a fool of myself. That's what everyone thought I'd do and I did.

I've got nothing else to lose. I need to embrace my ridiculousness and just go for it.

Maybe we all need a bit more ridiculousness.

I walk for a while longer, not really thinking much, just contemplating how lovely this beach is and how I'm the only person in the world who's seeing it just now. That's pretty cool.

The lightening of the sky tells me that time has passed. I'm not quitting yet.

If I go down, if I get kicked out, I will do it in true Tulip style and be true to my ridiculous self.

CHAPTER THIRTY-TWO

Word: Bludgeon (verb)

Back at camp, I put the rubbish in my pack as the others are starting to stir. Harvey looks dejectedly at what was, when I left, a fully functioning fire. He shoots me a smile but I pretend this morning never happened, adopting a cheery tone. 'Have the fire thieves been? Did Prometheus just run through and steal it from us?' Only ridiculous people reference Greek mythology in times of crisis, but I don't care.

'If Prometheus is a middle-aged man, then possibly,' Harvey replies. 'Today's challenge is to find our own food and light our own fire.' He gestures at the ashes. 'So, this beauty has just been put out. I think we can all guess the theme of today's challenge.'

Immediately I miss the warmth of the fire, but Harvey's in full leadership mode.

'Right, Jane, you look for berries, mushrooms and leaves. Anything that looks edible. I'll check it when I get back. Anton and Freddie, you make the fire. Tulip, you come with me to do a light spot of fishing.' Then he strides off.

'Right, we're going to tickle trout,' says Harvey when I finally catch up with him. 'Now I know that sounds weird but...'

'No, I get it,' I reply, 'we lie with our hands in a stream and lure trout to their death by lulling them into a false sense of security and then flicking them up to their death.'

Harvey's doing the fish mouth thing. I get a little glow inside despite the cold. I like it when I surprise him.

'You look like a stunned trout. Are you wondering how I know?'

He nods.

'How do I know anything? I googled it.'

'Of course, you are indeed Queen of Google.'

'Why I thank you, kind sir. Okay, but I'm not hot on whereabouts to look.' I spin around aimlessly. 'Any local knowledge?'

'If I remember rightly there are good spots a bit further up.' As we walk, he tells me the fish like sunny, shallow water. Which makes sense. If I were a fish that's exactly what I'd like. Soon we're in a sun-dappled clearing, next to a gurgling brook. I can't help but sigh at the beauty of it all. It's almost perfect, if you can forget about the cameraman following us. 'Nice place for a picnic.'

'You can picnic on trout if you can catch it.' His face clouds. 'Are you okay with this? Or do you want to leave it to me?'

He's making me mad again. 'Do you think I'm incapable…'

Harvey puts his hands up in peace. 'I was referring to your vegetarian or vegan tendencies. And, also, it takes years of skill to perfect. Are you an experienced trout tickler?'

'That is the weirdest thing anyone has ever said to me,' I can't help laughing. For once it's not me who is ridiculous but the whole situation. 'Perhaps not but I'll give it a go,' I say more confidently than I feel.

Harvey points to a dark fish swimming in the sunlit stream. 'That's what we're going for.'

'What do I do?'

'Tickle.'

'Yes. And then?'

'Flick.'

'Yes. And then?'

'Bludgeon.'

'Bludgeon?'

'Bludgeon,' Harvey repeats. 'Heavy blow in other words.'

'I know what bludgeon means,' I hiss. 'It's a bit harsh on the poor fish after tickle and flick.'

'You can't tickle a fish to death. Well, maybe you can out of water, but then technically that's drowning,' he muses. 'Whatever, do you want to eat or starve?'

My insides say eat. My heart says, you can't kill something. But if I don't contribute, we won't impress Hugh and then I'll have to go. Which I really don't want to do.

'You try this spot,' Harvey suggests, 'and I'll try that one and we'll see who gets a trout first.' I nod my agreement.

The sun is beautifully hot, warming me and my horrible waterproofs up. It's the first time I've felt warm since I arrived. We don't talk but it's still nice. I put my hand in the water – it's cool and refreshing. Fish swim past my fingers but never come to rest in my hand. All I can think of is bludgeoning.

'Would a slight tap do?' I whisper.

He nods.

'I mean there's no need for excessive force is there.'

He shushes me, and his face goes rigid with concentration. There's a splash and a flash as a shiny fish flies through the air and then lands on the ground.

'Help me!' Harvey yells as it flops around on the grass.

I fly to my feet, grab a stone that I've put to one side for moments that require bludgeoning, but when I see the fish gasping for breath, I drop the stone. Harvey swiftly picks it up.

'Close your eyes.'

For once I do as I'm told. When I open them, a fish lies still on the ground.

That's when I wail, 'I'm an accomplice to fish murder!'

Harvey responds, 'I think you mean you're an accom-plaice.'

I stare at him.

'Fish. Plaice? Get it.'

'You've bludgeoned a fish to death and you think you can mark its passing with a joke. A bad joke?'

'Er, yes and it wasn't that bad as fish jokes go.'

I silently wipe tears from my eyes. I'm tired, cold and hungry and I've just aided and abetted in an innocent fish's death. I am officially a bad person.

Then Harvey does something surprising. He doesn't talk. He doesn't tell me I'm stupid or try to reason with me. He takes my hand and holds it until I stop crying. The fish is still dead, but I feel a bit better.

After a while he says, 'Do you want me to throw it back in?' It lies, all sad and wobbly at our feet. The sun shines on its scales turning it into gold.

'No,' I say, 'That would make its death completely pointless. Might as well take it back. But I don't think I'll be eating it.'

'Okay, well we need to try and catch some more. Are you up for that?'

I nod. 'I'll kill it next time. It was just all a bit of a shock.'

We spend the next few hours lying next to the stream, mostly in silence. It's the calmest I've felt since I've been here. Apart from being complicit in the slaughter of my piscine friends.

'Come on, let's hope the others have found something worth eating.' He picks up the shiny, dead trout and wraps them gently in leaves. We walk back to the camp to find the others talking round the campfire.

'Any luck?'

'A few fish,' I say glumly.

Jane looks at them dismissively. 'That won't feed us all.'

'It's okay,' I say. 'You can have my share.'

Anton is looking over our offerings. 'Gave him a good battering, then? Fish? Battering? I thought you'd like it, man.'

'It's a good one, you got me,' Harvey replies but his face doesn't smile.

'Well, all the more for us then,' Jane says.

'Did you find anything?' I ask. Hoping against hope that perhaps she found a random portion of my mum's lentil Bolognese floating about. Well, maybe not floating, more like being used as a doorstop.

'Only this.' She gestures at a few fruits and leaves. 'They've all been cleared to eat so we should be okay. But I'll happily swop your fish for some berries.'

'Sure,' I say. It's like some faddy dieter's food blog. The ones who go on about how natural raw food is and how we should eat like our ancestors. But then they get cross if you point out our ancestors died young, due to lack of antibiotics and marauding sabre-toothed tigers.

'Right, so that's the first part of the challenge over. Well done team,' Harvey says.

Freddie and Anton look grimy and sad. 'No luck yet?' I say, taking in the general lack of fire.

I get a vicious hard stare from Freddie and even Anton seems annoyed by my questions.

'Right,' says Harvey, 'I'll help out. I'm generally good at this. Tulip, can you find more firewood. We'll need it later.'

'Okay but...' I stare at the fire-lighting situation. They're trying to start heat through pulling a stick that fits in a small hole on a branch back and forth very fast with a rope. 'I'm not sure...' I start.

'Quit whining,' Jane says. 'Think you're going to break a nail?'

I try to ignore her. 'No, but can I say...'

Harvey holds up a hand. 'No time for discussion. We need to get on and I've lit lots of fires before. You've all got your tasks, let's get going. We work together now, then we can face whatever challenges come our way.'

And his face makes it clear that that is that. Nice, hand-holding Harvey has gone. Right. I'll have to accept my role as log girl. For now.

CHAPTER THIRTY-THREE

Word: Conflagration (noun)

I trudge through the muddy forest looking for things to burn.

I might start with my teammates. For a moment, I thought Harvey was actually okay and then he just ignores me and sends me off to find wood. Any idiot can find wood in a forest. How can I show them all my patiently rehearsed skills if he won't give me a chance? I wanted them – I wanted him – to listen to me, and not ignore me. I kick a root. It hurts. I jump around for a minute yelling because my foot hurts. Then I remember that I'm being filmed. All the time. Even the nice, hand-holding moment. I stop jumping and yelling and get on with the job in hand.

Which is – find smallish twigs for kindling and then bigger bits we can snap and keep the fire going. That's if the allotted fire team can get it alight. I peer over in the direction of the camp. No sign of smoke. No sign of fire. 'You'd think with all that hot air that they'd get fire going pretty quickly,' I say to a tree. It doesn't answer back.

I get on, less yelling, more singing. I feel like a lost princess in a wood, doing a mundane task to win her freedom. That makes me think of Rowan and that keeps me going for a while. After getting quite a pile, I stop for a minute to look round. I get a pang for home, for Willow and Rowan. Are they missing me? Has Mum uploaded any more stupid videos about them? I dread to think what kind of mayhem she's causing without me to stop her. I miss my phone, my room, I miss every soft thing in the world. And my accounts – all those likes, and retweets are going to waste. My internet life is going on without me and I'm not sure how I feel about it.

Well, enough introspection. I dust my hands on my damp clothes. We need fire. I need fire. It would be amazing to be able to feel my fingers again. Any warmth I felt in the sun by the stream is a distant memory. I carry as much wood as I can back to camp. Innocently, I drift over to the fire pit. Or the non-fire pit if we're going to be accurate.

'How are things?' I start as blandly as I can.

Jane leans back on her heels, black smudges on her angry face. 'Are you being sarcastic?'

I keep my face neutral. 'I'm trying to find out what's going on to see if I can help.'

'It's not working. That's all you need to know.' She gestures at the fire-starting kit. We've got kindling, a stick to spin round, a piece of twine to pull it and a smooth plane of wood with a circle drilled in. 'We're never going to get it done.'

Harvey looks frustrated. 'I've done this so many times. I don't know why it's not working. I must be missing something.' He blows on his hands which are red raw from pulling the twine back and forth. 'We can get smoke but never enough friction to get the kindling actually on fire.'

'Can I look?' I lean down.

Anton jokes. 'Are you going to use the ash for eyeliner or

something like that?' I recoil. Does he know? I glance at Harvey to see if he's told him, but a slight shake of the head tells me that he has kept this morning's stupidity to himself. Until the world finds out when the show gets broadcast. My shoulders slump at the thought but I'm here now so I might as well try to contribute.

'The Egyptians used kohl which is a kind of ash so actually that's not a bad idea,' I say. 'But no.'

I pick up each bit of equipment and consider it carefully.

'Stick, meet Tulip, Tulip meet stick. Oh, look she's still not made any fire,' Jane observes. Freddie just sits there and adds to the overall awkward atmosphere.

I ignore her and re-play the videos in my head from my intense period of research. There's something wrong here – I can't quite see it. What was the stick and the hole exactly like in the examples I saw?

And then I have it.

'Right,' I say. 'I think I know what we need to do.'

'What – make a huge fuss about a small jump, get scared by a non-existent shark and then struggle to swim a few metres. You are going home, Tulip, and you know it.'

Deep breath. That girl is really getting on my nerves. Has she not heard of female solidarity? 'Does anyone have a knife? And no, I'm not going to stab Jane.'

'Here,' Harvey hands over his rather sharp-looking blade. I'm a bit nervous about handling it but I'm going to try not to let it show. I take the smooth plank of wood and start to dig into the hole that's already there and make it deeper.

'And what exactly do you think that will achieve?' Jane says.

'Well,' I say, 'you've not been able to generate enough heat. We need more friction. If we increase the surface area between the stick and the wood, then we could increase the amount of friction and therefore heat.'

Silence.

'What do you think, Harvey?' I say.

'It makes sense. That could be it.'

'Let's go. This is going to be the one, I know it.'

'Kindling ready?'

'Ready.'

'Okay, Freddie and I will pull, Jane, you keep the wood steady. Tulip, get ready with the kindling when you see any sparks. Anton, you have more kindling ready in case we need it.'

For the first time, we feel like a team.

The boys pull the twine back and forth furiously. Sweat beads on their brows. This is the first time I've seen any sense that Freddie is really a human being. Smoke soon starts to rise. 'Keep going.'

But it's not enough. Still not enough heat.

But they don't give up. They keep going. And then I see it. A spark and then another.

I put the kindling at the base of the stick and then I keep it loose around the heat. I blow gently on it.

Smoke, but no fire.

Failed again.

But I don't give up, I keep blowing.

'Look, there's a flame.'

And there is.

Something small but yellow and hot is flickering in the kindling.

'Get some twigs.' I have twigs, I know all about that. I am log girl.

And that's it. We have made fire together. And suddenly I feel warm in all sorts of ways.

CHAPTER THIRTY-FOUR

Word: Ascendancy (noun)

There's shouting. There's screaming. Because we have fire and I did it. Is that enough of a contribution to mean that I get to stay? Or does all the ridiculousness of this morning mean I go home?

I don't have time to think about it. 'Good work,' Harvey says, and he's about to hug me when Anton grabs me. 'You only went and bloody did it. Amazing, amazing. I'm not sure how someone so small can be so awesome but clearly I've got some learning to do.'

Jane is finding it harder to process and her mouth is flapping open and shut. 'But how…'

Freddie has gone back to his default look – impassive – but I think he might give me a thumbs-up. That or he flicks away a midge. I decide to take the positive interpretation.

With Anton standing next to me with his arm still around me, Harvey changes his mind about the hug. 'You did good.' I get a smile. Suddenly I feel warm inside again. Him being clearly and openly nice about me is lovely. I find myself grinning and wishing for a moment that Anton wasn't standing quite so close. 'But how did you know what to do?' he asks.

'Well,' I say, 'I don't know if you've heard of it but there's this thing called Google.'

He still looks confused.

'I did research, you know,' I explain. 'You know survival skills. I don't. So, I watched videos on how to do things.'

'Well, it paid off. You really do have an eye for detail. I completely missed that.'

I nod and agree. Now all the good stuff can happen. We can cook the fish and we have heat for the night. But best of all I, Tulip Taylor, have made fire from a few bits of wood and twine and that feels okay. Maybe I'll get sent home. Maybe I won't. However long I've got, I'm going to make the most of it.

I'm sat next to the fire, slowly feeding it to make it grow. In front of the fire, I'm scorching, and I love it. I love the crackle of the wood as it burns, I love the smoky smell. I love the way the flames leap around, bringing colour to the dark brown forest. But most of all, I'm warm. I will never say I'm freezing again. And I will never say I'm starving again.

'Is food an option now?' I say. 'I suggest killing and eating Anton as he's the biggest.'

Anton swipes a friendly cuff at me, but I dodge it and then he falls over.

'Cannibalism is not happening,' says Harvey, 'yet. Let's see how much food we've got.'

Some fish, some berries and few leaves. Not much to feed five people.

After gutting the fish, Harvey spits the fish on a stick and puts it over the flames. It smells good. I know it's stupid and I might get sent home for refusing good food, but I decide not to eat it. It's just not me.

When Jane dishes it up, I shake my head when she offers me some. 'Are you sure?' She almost looks worried for me. 'You'll be starving.'

But I just shake my head again. Then she offers it to Harvey. Who also shakes his head.

She looks stunned. 'Really?'

'It was a beautiful fish,' Harvey says. 'You enjoy it but count me out.'

In the dusk, I don't know how to think. It feels like that was an act of solidarity with me. And he was nice to me when I got upset. What kind of boy is he really? A cocky snob? A nervous boy who's awkward around girls? Or someone who is really quite sweet if you give him a chance.

There's no time to over-analyse this moment because it's time. We have to go down to the shore, to find out who's going. I don't want to go. I really don't. I'm literally starving but I don't want to go. Last night I didn't want to because of the shame of being first. Now, I don't want to go because I've actually enjoyed myself today and, for the first time, I feel that I'm being useful. I'm not dreading tomorrow; I'm looking forward to what might come.

Tonight, there's no huge fire. We're given some cereal bars to keep us going. Hugh stands there, with the sun setting behind him. Tonight, I decide he looks like a Viking, someone who would tear a monster to pieces with his bare hands. Hector's team arrive, one short from last time. We have no idea if they have been more successful in the whole fire and food thing than we have. Anyone of us could be going home. I made the fire. Surely that's enough to save me.

Hugh starts to speak, his voice resonating in the dark. He goes through our various achievements and failures in the task.

'The person who is leaving camp tonight … is the person who is not fully part of their team.' Okay, that's me then. My stomach lurches and I await my name. 'This person has not communicated well with their team. Strength is an asset, but good communication skills are worth so much more.' That doesn't sound like me. I look at Hector's team. Maybe it's one of them. They'll struggle if they lose another person.

'The person leaving is … Freddie.'

Wow. I did not see that coming. Neither, it appears, did Freddie. Like a mutinous mountain, he stands up, refuses the Hugh hug and walks off into the dark.

My heart starts to slow down. I'm still here. I've lasted another day. Wow. I don't hear what we're told after that and follow the others back to camp. Day three here we come.

Back at our fire, we sit in silence, perhaps we're honouring the silence of Freddie. I realise that we're in the only spot of light for miles. Darkness stretches around us. It should be terrifying but in a strange way, it's liberating. Sparks from the fire lift up like fireflies; they drift and crackle in the dust. The sky beyond us is deep blue but streaked with gold and pink. A few stars hang in the sky.

I sit between Anton and Harvey. Harvey's hand is just next to mine. I think about how nice it was when he held my hand this afternoon. I think about giving it a squeeze to say thank you. Our eyes meet, and he smiles at me.

But then I think back to our last night in the hotel. I

remember telling him about all his crimes and how he denied it. I think that he used me in a bet with his brother. Maybe I've got a way to be quits with him after all.

I take my hand away from Harvey's and deliberately place my head on Anton's huge shoulder. I don't look at Harvey. I don't see if he's sad, amused or shocked. I do know that he stands up and walks away.

I should triumph now, at making him feel bad.

But I don't. Despite the fire and the stars, I feel just about as bad as I can. That was not well done, Tulip. That was not ridiculous. No, it was something far worse. That was cruel. That was not okay.

CHAPTER THIRTY-FIVE

Word: Ligature (noun)

I don't sleep much for all kinds of reasons. I'm full of regret. And the forest doesn't get any quieter. It's still grey when I open my eyes. I try snuggling back to sleep but I can't. A flash of movement makes me sit upright.

At first I'm scared, but then I see what it is. A couple of bunnies dash through the camp, all brown with white tails showing up in the gloom. I sit up to see where they've gone. They're sitting on the edge of the camp, almost blending in with dull light. I hold my breath as a few more dash around, nibble at the grass and then disappear. I breathe out. Okay, that was cool. Bunnies are not such a bad way to start the day.

I sit in the quiet, listening to the trees creak and sigh, and wait for the day to begin. At some point, as if by magic, something creeps into me. A sense of calm. I breathe in and out. I can't change what I did last night. I just have to accept it and move on. I trick my mind into forgetting about it, by staring at the branches dancing in the morning light.

Suddenly, I see a shadow. Fear grabs me. My mind goes blank on whether there are any real predators in Scotland. I'm not in the water so the Loch Ness Monster can't get me. Then I remember that there's no such thing as the Loch Ness Monster.

But it's only a deer. A small one, with a red coat that shines like glossy lipstick in the shaft of sunlight. It looks at me with its huge dark eyes, rimmed with eyelashes I might kill for. But I don't want to hurt it; I just want to gaze. The deer bolts. Then I'm all alone again. For a few moments, I just sit there and think about it. I mean, it's not that I've got anything else much to do. It was so lovely and so near. I'm not quite sure what I'm feeling so I search around for the best word.

'Privileged,' I find myself saying. It's true. Despite my soggy clothes (Why – oh why – are we only allowed one set? Nothing ever dries.), my hunger, my cold hands and my messy braids, and even though it's been challenging in so many ways, I feel lucky. It was an honour, just for those seconds, to share this wood with that deer. Okay, Tulip. This moment has to count. I need to make sure that when I get back home, I never use make-up that even goes near a bunny, let alone is tested on them.

A while later, happy that I've made a positive decision, I hum, rummaging through the embers of the fire to create a new one as the others shuffle awake. Then I heat some water for tea and some sad excuse for porridge that's been left overnight over the embers. In the night, a few supplies have been left for us – mainly oats – so that we don't really starve to death. I pass Harvey the first bowl as some sort of peace offering. But he blanks me. I don't blame him. I'd blank me too under the circumstances. The mood in camp is bleak until it's time for today's challenge.

We're led to a sort of track not far from the camp and put into the back of our old friend, the Land Rover. We bump and jump along the track until we come to a wide loch. The sun is up but not yet over the mountains. Wisps of mist drift over the loch that's as smooth as a mirror, reflecting the sky back on itself. If I had a phone, I'd take a photo of this and it wouldn't even need a filter.

We're given wetsuits to put on again. I look at the suit; I look at the loch. I think I can see where this one is going. Hugh bounces up, ruffling Harvey and Hector's hair but I feel it's all for the cameras. He never really interacts with them. I can't help thinking that it's all a bit weird, the way he's setting one son up against the other as part of a TV show. Maybe there's a reason why Harvey was so keen to put me down when we first met, maybe that's what he thinks is normal. They might own beaches, dunes, forests and their own personal loch but they don't seem to know how to talk to each other like humans.

'Morning. Today's challenge is to create a craft capable of crossing the loch. The first team to raise their flag on the other side of the loch is the winner and all of them will be safe from elimination.'

We stare at Hugh, waiting for more information.

'That's it. Off you go and may the best team win.'

'Right, team, go,' Harvey commands, and we follow him down to the edge of the loch.

'For a start, can we do well at this because I really don't want to get wet again,' I say. Which is honest but then as the others exchange looks, I realise it also makes me look pathetic.

Harvey looks at me. Does that mean I'm forgiven? 'So, did you research how to make rafts before coming here?'

I shake my head. 'I didn't see that one coming. But I'm your girl if you need a tourniquet, or snake venom removing.'

He laughs. 'I'll bear that in mind. Let's get going.' I smile back, hoping that somehow this exchange means that he knows that I'm sorry. Harvey and Jane sort through the pile of apparent junk that's next to the loch, shouting at each other what to do. Anton joins in and I'm left to one side like an unwanted scrap. I try to get involved but get, 'Leave it to me, Tulip.' Have they all forgotten about the fire? I keep myself busy by gathering pretty things by the shore.

Eventually, a raft emerges but looks a bit like something Year Three would make.

'Is it seaworthy?' I ask.

'We're not going in the sea. It's a loch. Just get on,' Jane says.

'Okay but I have made no contribution at all. Which is good if it goes down, cos then it's not my fault. But bad if this is about team-building because we've not worked as a team.' I have learned something so far. The people who go are the ones who aren't at the heart of the team.

'She's right,' says Harvey. 'Sorry. I was thinking about the task, not you. What would you like to contribute now?'

'Styling,' I say.

'Okay. Be quick though, we need to get on the water and across, so we don't lose.'

'I am renowned for my nimble fingers, I'll have you know.' I reach over to the raft and start to place ferns in all the ropes and weave some pretty flowers I've found too. 'These knots are a bit rustic. Are you sure they'll hold?'

'They are good knots,' Jane says, 'don't mess with the knots.'

'I'm just tightening them up. Look they're symmetrical now.'

Jane is now jumping up and down with frustration. 'I don't care about symmetrical knots. I care about losing. We need to get on the water now.'

'Let me help.' Anton gives me his broad huge smile and leans down towards the knots at the back. 'Right, launch time.'

'How do I get on?' I begin to panic at the thought of climbing up on to the raft which is moving away from the shore at a startling rate. Anton's leapt on of course but because of his size the raft is beginning to go down on his side.

'Harvey, get on this side, then Jane, then Tulip.' Anton is right. Harvey's got to balance out Anton's weight or it will go down. The other team are now in the water too and the race is on.

Harvey leaps on and the raft tips from side to side in a rather frantic fashion. I know that the TV crew won't let us come to any harm and that Stan is there with his net. But still … it's water. It's deep. You can drown in a puddle remember.

'Don't you dare go without me,' Jane says as she wades out towards the raft leaving me in the shallows.

'Jump and we'll pull you. Tulip, come on or you'll get left behind.'

Jane launches herself forward with a yelp. Anton and Harvey haul her up, all long rubber clad arms and legs. She lands with a bump in the middle and nearly falls into the water.

'Tulip,' she cries. 'Just do it. We all have to get on.'

The raft drifts further from the shore.

'Tulip!' Jane's shouting now and Harvey's paddling back to the shore as hard as he can.

'You've got to come now.'

It's now or never.

Harvey's still holding out his hand – if I can get out there…

And that's when I jump.

Leap forward, into the air, into the water.

And fall.

But then a strong hand grabs on to me and I feel myself being dragged forward. Then another hand grabs me and I'm hauled up through the air and dumped like a landed fish over one of the barrels.

I'm on the raft. Face down, bum in the air, spitting out mouthfuls of hair. But I did it.

Harvey pulls me up. 'You okay?' he says, looking down at me with concern.

'Never better,' I say. 'Is it me or are we getting lower in the water?'

Jane looks round in panic. 'What do you mean?'

'I mean that a minute ago the water only came up to the planks. But now it's over them.' I point to where the wood runs down the side of the barrels, now well below the water line.

'That's because all of us are on now,' Anton says. 'I'm not going to be rude enough to say it's because of your weight but…'

I glare at him. But then I stare around. We're drifting in on a tiny homemade raft toward the middle of a deep, dark, cold loch. I do not have a good feeling about this at all.

Harvey takes charge. 'Whatever, talking isn't going to sort this out. Get rowing everyone.'

He passes me a paddle. We sit, two on each side, legs in the water and paddle for dear life.

'Row harder,' yells Anton. We're ploughing through the water with grim determination.

But I know that the water's higher than it was. Before it was around my shins, now it's up to my thighs. We're barely making any progress now. The far side of the loch is a long way away. I feel like we're some small insect on the surface of a huge sea. The loch seemed quite small before. Now, on the surface, it seems huge and terrifying.

We row in silence. I can hear birds calling, the slap of the waves on the plastic of the raft, the shouts from the other team. They're pulling away from us.

'Does anyone else feel that the raft feels funny?' Jane says.

'It's a homemade raft put together without much planning by four arguing teenagers. What is it supposed to feel like?' Anton says.

But then I get what she means. Everything feels suddenly looser. I lurch down in the water so that I'm up to my waist now.

'The ropes!' I cry. And at that moment the raft decides to get its own back on us and self-destructs. The ropes pull loose as the barrels make a bid for freedom. My knots are coming undone. I grab at them to try to re-tie them but it's too late.

First, I'm on the water, then I'm in the water, then I'm under the water.

It all goes murky over my head.

And then it goes black.

CHAPTER THIRTY-SIX

Word: Ignominy (noun)

Here I am again, spluttering up to the light.

The good news, again, is that I'm not dead.

Jane is very much alive and furious. 'Tulip. You had one job. You didn't even have one job. Your only job was to leave the ropes alone but no, you had to make them pretty and you messed it up.'

She's right. I'll be going home. At least if I cry, no one will notice a few drops of water in a loch. I stare up at the sky. It's cloudless and perfect. If this is my last day, then it couldn't be prettier. I mean, I've got to Day Three so that's cool. I just wish... No, it's too late for wishes.

'Yes, Jane, I completely agree. I am pathetic, rubbish and have sabotaged the team. Now if it helps you feel any better, vent away. But I'm going to enjoy the moment.'

'Enjoy? We failed. What is there to enjoy?'

I float around and gesture at the scene around us. 'If you can't see it, then me pointing it out is hardly going to help, now is it?'

Jane gets more and more annoyed. 'Harvey. You're the leader. Do something about her.'

Harvey's floating on his back, looking at the birds scudding across the sky. 'What do you suggest, Jane? Drowning her?'

211

I think Jane might agree but she splutters. 'Will someone get me out of here?' She waves furiously at the safety boat. My friend, Stan, will come to the rescue of course.

Just drifting about on the loch, taking in the view, I suddenly feel like a weight has been lifted from me. There's no point trying to contribute or worry if I'm going to be evicted. Because now I know that I am. But I'm in a beautiful place and I'm going to appreciate every last moment that I have.

By now, Anton and Jane are on the safety boat, leaving Harvey and me alone. I wave the boat away when it comes for us. 'I'm happy here for a bit,' I say.

'I'm with her,' Harvey replies.

'Okay, I'll leave you for a bit, but you'll need to come out soon,' Stan shouts as he zooms off to drop the others on the shore.

'I'm sorry I messed up,' I say. Which is true. In so many ways.

Harvey sighs. 'It doesn't really matter. You helped us win yesterday. It all balances out.' He spins himself around. 'In a way, it makes things easier.'

'How?'

'If I keep winning, then Hector will never forgive me.'

'And your family use a TV show to sort all this stuff out? I thought my family were a bit weird but seriously!' I think and float for a bit. 'Do you think you'll go back to your other school?'

'I don't know. Your school – our school – it's a bit more normal. The boarding school is like living in some fake world. No link to reality.'

'Whatever that is.'

'Are we beginning to have a deep conversation?' He grins at me.

'Maybe. Why would that be so surprising?'

'I think we got off to a bad start.'

'And whose fault was that?' I say, but then regret it. I'm beginning to see why he was like that at the start. It must have been so hard just to walk into a new school like that, especially if you get nervous. I mean, he was massively out of order that first day, I know that, but if he sees that now then surely that's a good thing, a sign that he is okay underneath.

'And one thing I've learned about you?'

'What?' Let's see if he has learned anything.

'You're more than capable of looking after yourself. You're determined. You're competent. You're pretty awesome.' I turn away to hide my smile. That is the nicest thing a boy has ever said to me. I've been told I'm pretty. I've been told I'm nice. But no boy has ever told me I'm capable, competent, determined and awesome. And I am. Despite the cold water, I have a lovely glow inside.

'Shall I tell you something?' It's full-on confession time from Harvey. Now he's started there's no stopping him. 'I don't like leading the group. I don't like responsibility.'

'You're mostly okay at it. You get things done.'

Harvey swims closer to me. 'That's the nicest thing you've ever said to me.' We're in a loch. We're close to each other, our heads bobbing centimetres apart. Is this a moment? Again, I think of last night, me and Anton and what a stupid, nasty thing that was to do.

A speedboat whizzes over, the wake hitting us and making us splutter. I swim a few strokes away from Harvey. Hugh is looking very serious and solemn. 'You two, out of the water now.'

'That's a shame,' I say. 'I was enjoying it.'

'Maybe, but there are other things we need to do today.'

I am hauled out of the water like a particularly large and ungainly seal and land face first in the bottom of the boat. Great. Not quite the elegant impression I wanted. With that we're off.

I stare around me and take it all in. I was supposed to hate it but I'm going to miss it when I'm gone. At least I can imagine it here. It can be my happy place. When I'm stressed, I can think about it. I really don't want to go.

Then it hits me. The real reason I don't want to go. I'm getting to know Harvey. He's nice. He's more than nice. Newsflash: perhaps I was wrong about him, just as much as he was about me.

I'm not ready for this to be over.

CHAPTER THIRTY-SEVEN

Word: Volte-face (noun)

Back at shore, we're allowed clean dry clothes at last and we're fed while Hugh makes his decision about eviction. As if there's any debate to be had about who's going home. It takes a long time though.

Time to pay the price for failure. Harvey smiles his sweet, fleeting smile and Jane radiates scorn. Anton gives me a fist bump. 'You gave it a good shot.' My fate's sealed then. That's that. I'm sick to my stomach and I think I'm going to throw up.

It's Hector's turn to look smug. I can't help but feel that Harvey dealt with winning with much more grace. They might look alike but from what I've seen, they are so different on the inside. If Hector has a softer side, it's locked up in a huge safe with a thousand locked chains on it.

'It's the losers,' he says, 'led by the biggest loser of them all.' What I don't get is that Hugh seems to love this competition between his boys.

I put on my best calm face, with a hint of 'Yes, it was my time'. That's the dignified way to go, you say, 'Thank you for the opportunity' and then wish everyone else good luck. Hugh takes one huge bound into the centre of the circle.

'You've survived another twenty-four hours. You've provided

for yourselves for the first time in your lives.' It's true. And I'm proud of that to be honest. I never thought I could but apparently I can. Go me.

'But now it's time for one of you to go. One of you has to be left behind.'

I feel like putting my hand up and saying, 'I'll go now and save all the theatre.'

But, of course, this thing's all about the theatre. It suddenly strikes me that while we might be standing next to a loch, with Scottish mud between our toes, this whole experience is as fake as anything you see on the internet. The scenery might be real, but the set-up is fake. None of this really proves who is the best at anything. I think I've done well, far better than I ever thought. My heart leaps, despite my imminent eviction. I don't need these people's approval. I can go with my head held high. The only person whose approval I need is mine.

Chin up, smile and wait for your name.

'I've thought long and hard about who's leaving today. There were a couple of you who didn't quite make the grade. And then I thought about what this experience is all about. Teamwork.'

Get on with it. Hugh does like his moments of power.

'Trust.'

Oh, for goodness sake, I don't see what either of those have got to do with me, but I might as well get my pack and go.

'At first, I chose one person who made a mistake.'

Whose name is Tulip. My calm, preparing-for-a-dignified-exit face is getting tired now. My face wants to adopt a more normal expression.

'But then when we reviewed the evidence from today's footage I came to a different conclusion.'

Okay, now that is interesting. We've all gone from vague indifference to keen meerkat expressions. What does he mean?

'When the editing team looked back at today's footage, we saw that all was not what it seemed. And of course, the camera never lies.'

Just tell us, Hugh. I can feel a bit of an eyeroll coming on.

'Tulip…'

'Thank you for the opportunity,' I blurt out.

'It's not you.'

Okay, I'm halfway out of the clearing by now.

'Tulip, I said it's not you.'

I stop and turn.

'Come back. I'm sending someone else home.'

Mouths are gaping wide-open all round. I walk back. Am I supposed to strut? Can I rewind the last few seconds, so I don't walk off at the wrong moment and make myself look like a noob? I was aiming for calm and dignified under fire but instead have made myself the class-A idiot. I'm half expecting Hugh to send me back anyway for this. But of course the one thing that I want to know more than anything else is … who is out and why?

I'm back. And still feeling stupid.

'So, why not Tulip? She made a big mistake on her challenge and that's what lead to her team failing.'

A pause. Yes, we know, get on with it.

'Or did she?'

This is getting ridiculous. 'I did though. I mean, I'm not saying I want to go home because I don't. But the ropes untied because of me. You all saw it.'

Hugh has this strange look on his face. 'That's what we thought we saw. But that isn't quite what happened now. Is it, Anton?'

What?

Heads and cameras swivel to Anton, who suddenly looks nervous, shifting from one foot to the other.

'Anton. When we reviewed the tape, we saw that it wasn't Tulip who was last to fix the ropes but you. You deliberately untied them when you thought no one was watching.'

Anton clears his throat.

'Anything to say?'

Silence. But Anton – I thought he liked me. He flirted with me a bit. Didn't he?

'No? This experience is all about teamwork. And all you were about was yourself and trying to win. This is not the place for you. Anton. Goodbye.'

And with that he's gone, walking off, hands slightly shaking, through the clearing and into the shadows. A camera guy tries to get a shot of his face, but Anton shoves it away.

Ouch.

Suddenly, I realise that walking off halfway and having to come back again isn't as bad as being caught cheating on a TV show. He is never going to live that down. What was he even thinking?

'And so, you all remain.'

Harvey, Jane and I take a collective deep breath and exhale. Hector and Cameron whoop at exactly the same moment, Felicity almost smiles, and Samir tries to high five her, but she leaves him hanging. Cameron stares at me. 'Close call, make-up girl. Bet it's you next time.'

I'm safe. I do an internal jig while keeping my face poker straight.

'Well,' says Jane, 'that was unexpected.'

'I'm like that annoying bit of tissue on your shoes. You'll never get rid of me.'

She turns to me. 'What Anton did was not okay. You've done well this far.' For a moment, I think she might hug me. I panic. Is this a hugging moment or not? But her arms stay down. 'He was a bit stupid, too, to think that he could get away with it.'

I don't say anything.

'Did you think there was something odd about him?' she says to me. 'No, you liked him, didn't you? Weren't the two of you snuggling up in front of the fire?'

Harvey now looks sad. I burn with embarrassment. Why does she have to bring this up now?

'I guess I was wrong about him,' I mutter. It crosses my mind now about the whole 'have I missed anything' moment back at the hotel. Did he accidentally forget to mention that we were being filmed the whole time or was that deliberate to make a fool of me? Short of tracking him down (and possibly torturing him) I suppose I'll never know. One thing I do know is that I never want to see him again.

Harvey says. 'Funny how you can get people wrong. You know, you make a first judgement and then realise later how mistaken you were.'

'Yes,' I say. 'I suppose everyone does it.'

'You mean even the infallible Tulip makes mistakes?' Okay, he's enjoying himself far too much, but I can hardly blame him.

'Are we even now?' I say.

Jane looks at us as if we're talking another language.

'Yes,' says Harvey, 'I think we are.' He holds out his hand. What am I supposed to do with that? I shrug and shake it.

'You two are weird,' Jane mutters and strides ahead. Harvey and I walk on in silence. I might be tempted to say more if there weren't a camera crew behind us. Will we ever get a moment alone together to sort things out?

CHAPTER THIRTY-EIGHT

Word: Stalemate (noun)

'Well, this is different,' I comment. We'd been told that today's task was an earth challenge so I had visions of us pretending to be moles and digging huge holes. Instead, the three remaining members of Team Harvey stand in a line facing what's left of Team Hector: himself, Samir, Cameron and Felicity. It's blatantly obvious that we are the smaller group. It's also blatantly obvious that they think that they are so much better than us.

Obviously, Hector has to make a comment. 'Ready to lose again, baby bro? You'll be down to two after this. And let's face it, maybe it's time for you to go.' Which is true. I've never thought about Harvey getting eliminated because I know my mother would never take me off her TV show. But Hugh is clearly made of tougher stuff than Raven.

'Or maybe it's time for you to go,' I say, before Harvey has a chance.

'You need girls to fight your battle do you, little bro?' Hector's face doesn't look so good when he's cross. Which, let's face it, seems to be most of the time. 'Fighting talk from Make-Up Girl. Or should I call you by your real name, Tulip Summer Acorn Taylor. Acorn suits you, small, round and brown.'

'She may be small but she is fierce,' Harvey says. 'Know where that's from, big bro?'

'Does it matter?' Hector says. 'This is an outdoor competition not a literature love-in.'

'Just a bit of Shakespeare,' Harvey says.

I can see Hector struggling to keep control before he says something crude in front of the cameras. 'Shakespeare. Great. Just what this situation needs.'

'Don't underestimate her,' Jane says unexpectedly. 'I did. But she's still here.'

I flash a smile of gratitude at her. 'Team Harvey,' she says and we bump fists. 'Team Harvey,' I say to our leader and we bump fists too. I get the most glorious smile in return. We might be fewer in number than them but at least we are now well and truly a team. I never thought that would happen.

'Not for much longer,' Cameron throws back as Hector is still struggling for words. Hugh strides up, beaming as he always does.

'Morning, Team Harvey. Morning, Team Hector. Today's activity will take a different form. This is not about any particular physical skill or courage. Today's task will test your resolution. What would you do to preserve your life?'

We stare at each other blankly. This sounds scary.

Hugh laughs, the glade echoing with the boom. 'I mean, if you were starving or dehydrated, what would you eat or drink to stay alive?'

Right.

Here we go.

I always knew that this was going to come our way at some point. We have to eat and drink something utterly disgusting.

And I have a really bad idea about what at least one of these things might be. I keep my face as neutral as possible.

'First, you need to find your food and then you'll need to eat it. You'll be taken off individually under supervision and return, hopefully, with something to eat. Anyone returning empty handed will certainly be under consideration for elimination.'

With that, a number of camouflaged rangers step forward and I'm led away by a short, stocky woman called Helen who is very serious about everything.

About an hour later, I'm back with my contribution, my stomach in complete rebellion at what I'm going to have to do shortly.

Harvey and Jane are already back. 'Good hunting?' Harvey says, looking at what I'm carrying.

'No hunting was involved,' I say.

'Yes, but you didn't get that from a supermarket,' Jane gestures at the large, bedraggled pheasant that I'm reluctantly carrying.

'No, I did not.'

Realisation spreads across Harvey's face. 'Road kill!'

I nod. 'Apparently if it's still warm then it should be okay to eat. You two?'

Jane looks happy. 'I bagged us some pigeon. They let me shoot it.'

Harvey pulls out two small, furry things from a bag.

'Oh.'

He purses his lips. 'Sorry, Tulip, but I made sure that they didn't suffer.'

A rabbit and a squirrel lie on the ground before us. I might be just about okay with the pigeon and pheasant but these two? They just remind me of my toys at home. How can I do this?'

'Right, guys, while you're waiting for the others to get back, just pop behind those trees and give us a sample.' We've been given small plastic pots.

'Is this for what I think it is?' I squeal.

'It's wee time, Dad's favourite,' Harvey sighs. 'I wish he'd go for something more original.'

Can I back out of this? Am I ready to go home? Jane and Harvey head off straight away as if there's nothing odd about it. At Hugh's house they probably drink each other's wee for breakfast.

'Am I the only normal person here?' I ask of the trees. 'Is it just you and me who can see that this is not right?' The trees rustle in support.

Sighing, I find a quiet spot and do … well … what needs to be done. There is screeching though, and complaining, and requests for hand sanitiser. But no one appears to be listening. I am allowed to rinse my hands afterwards so at least some semblance of hygiene is followed.

A short while later, we've made a fire, Harvey has skinned and gutted all the animals with a tiny bit of help from me and now Jane is frying assorted cuts of them for us to try. Think of it like a forest version of an all-you-can-eat buffet. Just with more feathers, fur and feet.

Hugh inspects our plates. 'So, everyone has something they've caught? Excellent. You all need to eat everything on your plate.' I think I can do this. Now it's cooked and cut up, it just looks like small bits of brown stuff. I can do this.

'And just for fun, I'm adding an extra element to your dishes to add choice.'

He walks down the line of us and the other team, dropping something on each of our plates. It lands with a wet slop which is particularly unappetising.

'Raw deer heart. Caught it myself just now. Great for vitamins.'

I'm about to ask if I can have a vitamin tablet instead but just about stop myself.

On one side, Jane whispers, 'You can do it. Don't think, just swallow it. Don't chew.'

Harvey suggests, 'Eat it with the pigeon. That will drown out the taste a bit.'

I smile thanks at both of them but my stomach is not easily convinced. Years of my mum's cooking might have prepared me for many things but badly cooked meat is not one of them.

Hugh says, 'Okay, lunchtime. Let's see clear plates all round.'

Hector finishes first of course and then belches loudly. One by one, everyone else has eaten.

'Tulip?'

The raw heart is defeating me. The texture is alien. It's bleeding. I swear it's still warm.

Harvey says quietly, 'If you don't want to, don't. But I know you can do it if you want to.'

I nod.

'Count of three?' Jane suggests.

They count me down. I close my eyes, grab the morsel, shove it in, chew ten times and then swallow. They both pat me on the back and congratulate me. It stays down. You know, I do continually surprise myself. I sigh a meaty, bloody sigh of relief.

But I'd forgotten…

'Now pick up your pot of urine. And, in your own time, drink.'

One by one everyone does it. Samir swears but it goes down, Felicity holds her nose but she does it.

Until it's just me.

I look at it. I sniff it. I retch.

Hugh comes over to me. 'It's just a natural product – part of the great cycle of life. It could save your life if you couldn't find a water source.'

I don't reply. I put it to my lips again and then put it down.

'She's a chicken,' Hector says and starts to squawk. He begins the whole routine just like Harvey did in the bad old days.

'You can stop that right now,' I say.

Hugh continues, 'Just think of how it could save your life.'

I realise at this point how much I hate being pressured into doing something I really, really don't want to do.

'Yes, but I'm not dying,' I point out. 'We're in the north west of Scotland where there's a particularly high rainfall. I'm not likely to run out of water.'

'I know but imagine…'

'No. I won't. If I had to choose between living or dying, then yes, I probably would. But that isn't the situation. I'm on a TV show. You can't let me die or my mum will sue you. So no point is being made here apart from the fact that you are using your power over us to make us do things we don't want to do.'

I take a breath. Am I actually going to do this? Am I really going to refuse Hugh and get eliminated?

'This is a waste product of my body. It's been excreted to take toxins out. So, there are no benefits to me in drinking this at this particular point in my life. Or have I missed something?'

Hugh is regarding me with a new look. 'No, it's more…'

'I know why you're saying that. But unless you can give me one good reason for why I should do this now, apart from being eliminated, then I don't see why I should drink it. Because I don't want to. The only reason you are asking me to do this is to create good TV out of our reactions.'

Our eyes lock. If I didn't know better, I'd say that Hugh doesn't know what to do or say to me.

I'm right. Hugh looks away first. 'If that's your choice, then I respect it. You're refusing to drink it?'

'I am,' I say with a confidence I don't really feel.

Hector says, 'At last. We'll get to see the end of the acorn. No one disrespects a McManus and gets away with it. Just chuck out the rubbish, Dad. You've humoured her long enough.' Hugh looks at him closely and then back to me. What is going on in that man's mind?

Jane hugs me. Harvey hugs me. I don't want to let go because this time it is clearly the end. I'll be gone by the evening.

227

CHAPTER THIRTY-NINE

Word: Zenith (noun)

I feel like crying. I don't want to go now. Despite everything I said only five days ago, I'm not quite ready to spend my days with no Harvey in them. I don't know what there is between us but there is something. Every time we talk, every time we're together. Stuff happens. But I've just made sure that I'll be kicked off the show. No more excitement and challenge. Just back to my normal life. Who knows if he'll stay at our school. It's not as if it's his natural environment.

Standing waiting for elimination, I blink tears away. It's been the best of times and the worst. It's going to take me a long time to process all I've learned.

Hugh strides in. His face looks different. Rather than his normal beaming smile, he seems quieter. I'd say he was contemplative if I was pushed to choose an adjective.

'This has been a difficult decision. It's not one I take lightly. I've thought long and hard about who should leave. You are all proving to be excellent, resilient people. You are teaching me so much about young people today and how you work together in tough situations.'

'Yawn. Get on with it,' Hector says.

'I have deliberated. I have decided to take one of the most difficult decisions of my life.' Come on, Hugh, don't pretend that I matter to you. It's all about the TV show. 'You are now two strong teams. When I started this, I thought that I would be teaching you about the world. But perhaps it is I who have had to learn a few things. A few difficult things.' He almost looks emotional. This is beyond strange.

'It's so difficult to decide. But I have to remove the person who has gone as far as they can. I have to choose the person who is not taking this seriously. The person who thinks that they have nothing to learn.' I just don't get this.

'One of you is not respectful of your opposition. And therefore, even though this is such a hard thing for me to say, Hector, it's time for you to leave.'

'What?' Hector and Harvey shout both at the same time.

Hugh moves in. 'Sorry, son, but there are lots of ways to succeed. Perhaps you need to think more about how you succeed than how to put people down.'

Hugh offers a handshake but Hector bashes his hand away. He starts to walk away, his face a mask of fury. He turns back for a moment as if to say something but he changes his mind. And then he's gone, storming away to beyond the camera.

And I'm still here.

It's three versus three. Samir's mouth is wide open, watching where Hector has gone. Cameron and Felicity exchange glances and then stare at me with the same contempt that Hector always did. They will not forgive me for somehow still being here. I'm not quite sure how that happened and I'm not the only one.

'I can't believe it,' Harvey mutters. 'But why…'

'Stop filming,' Hugh commands. He walks over to Harvey and talks to him quietly. I don't hear much but I pick up a few things. 'Bully' is one. 'Seeing things more clearly now.' It still doesn't quite make sense. Either Hugh has thrown his eldest son off his TV show to shock the viewers or he's just taught his son one of the hardest lessons of all. That Hugh has been paying attention to who Hector is and doesn't like what he sees. Their house will have an atmosphere like Antarctica after this.

Hugh leaves and Harvey comes back to us.

'Tulip made a moral stand. Your brother is a bully. Maybe your dad is finally acknowledging that. I know who I'd choose if I were him,' Jane offers. She puts her hand out. 'I'd like to keep in touch after this is all over. Friends?'

'Yes,' I say, still in shock. 'I'd like that.'

She says the same to Harvey. 'Friends?' and he shakes her hand. Harvey and I look at each other. I don't want to say 'Friends' to him because I want to be more than friends. I know that now. But how can I say it?

He puts out his hand. 'So, we're friends now, are we?' Is he hinting at more? I don't know. My heart sinks but I reach for his hand.

'Friends,' I lie.

The next two days offer many experiences. Mostly involving me being terrified but each time just about rising to the challenge. Somehow, I manage to stay in, though only by the tips of my by now badly damaged nails. Day Five's challenge involves descending into the deepest, darkest cave, following ropes in the dark and squeezing through tiny spaces. I just close my eyes – it's so dark, I can't see anything anyway – and recite the longest list ever of favourite words. If I ever get out of here alive, I expect to be sponsored by the Oxford English Dictionary. Felicity from Hector's team freaks out when she thinks she's got a bat in her hair and they have to give her oxygen before she can get out of the cave. She clearly didn't do her research otherwise she'd have known that's an urban myth. That was the end of her.

Day Six involves the longest zip wire in Europe. For once, this isn't on land owned by Hugh. We're allowed off the estate for a few hours. The zip wire is the first air challenge. I cry at the prospect of doing it. I weep when they attach me to the harness. I scream all the way down.

When Jane comes down after me, with a quietly smug expression on her face, it's clear to both of us who's going home. So, I'm not sure who's more astonished when her name gets called as the person leaving.

Jane looks at Hugh. 'Are you sure?' Everyone else gasps at this. No one has dared challenge Hugh McManus's decisions so far.

'Jane, you are fantastic. You don't seem to have a fear in the world. So today wasn't hard for you. I choose to keep in the ones who have overcome their deepest fears.'

She turns to look at me. This is awkward. 'I don't like losing. But you did do well. Again.' And with that, she walks off. Team Harvey is now Team Harvey and Tulip.

It's two against two. Cameron whispers to me, 'You might not be outnumbered, but you are outclassed in every way. They might as well just give us the trophy now.' Team Hector might have lost its leader but his spirit lives on. But Cameron makes sure Hugh doesn't hear him. He's smart this one, nasty but smart.

The Land Rover drops us back near camp, and we trudge through the forest. You'd think that I'd be overjoyed to be in camp with just Harvey. Yes, we're together. But we're not alone. Chaperones and camera crews watch our every move. It's possibly the strangest, most awkward experience of my life. There's so much I want to talk to him about but every time a camera zooms in on us I fall silent.

We spend the evening mostly in silence. It's like when I realised out on the loch how fake the whole situation is. If it really were just the two of us, learning about how to live out there then that would be amazing. But it's not. And despite what I've been told over and over again, you never forget that the cameras are watching you.

It's not until the next morning that we begin to talk to each other properly.

'What do we have to do today?' I ask. 'Do you know?' This is our second to last challenge. If I can get through this, then I'm through to the final challenge. If I fail, then it's Harvey versus the two of them. Samir seems okay but Cameron? He's just like Hector but in a different body. I can't let them win. I have a thought. What if Hugh chooses to get rid of Harvey? He wouldn't. He couldn't. But he did it to Hector. And then I'd be on my own. I have to face it but how could I take on the two of them on my own? We both need to get through this and take on the final challenge together. I can't fail at this one.

'Today we are taking on the Klettersteig,' Harvey replies with a particularly dramatic flourish of his hands.

'What's that when it's at home?'

'You don't like heights, do you?'

Experiencing a sudden sinking feeling, I shake my head.

'Then you're really not going to like this.'

'What does it mean then?' I say.

'I'm going to enjoy this moment,' Harvey says, throwing a bit of fern at me.

'And why exactly?' I take up the fern and weave it into my hair. 'Is this a good look?'

'Of course it is. Well, for once you don't know what some words mean and for seconds, you can't look it up on the internet. How does that feel, Web Girl?'

'Web Girl? That's all you've got? That is lame.' I look, I hope dismissively, at him.

'Lame or not, for once I know something and you don't.'

Am I going to ask him? Is he going to tell me? But I do need to know.

It means a climbing path. It's German, don't you know?'

'But what is a Klettersteig and don't say a climbing path because I've got that bit?'

'Okay, in the Second World War, the Swiss used to cross the mountains and smuggle things across the borders. You see?'

'I'm not stupid.' But I don't really see. 'And?'

'And they put iron rungs, ladders and cables along the mountains so that they could climb up high safely.'

'Okay.'

'You're not fully visualising this, are you?' Harvey says.

'Well, maybe you've not explained it well enough.'

'Imagine the Swiss Alps. Imagine a huge gap between the mountains. Now imagine a tiny, thin ladder reaching horizontally across the abyss. You're edging forward over the gap. There's a fall of hundreds of feet below you if you put a step wrong. And after surviving the ladder climb, you have to edge along a crumbling rocky ledge with only an ancient iron rope to hold on to which may or may not come out of its pins at any time.'

I struggle to get a few words out. 'But we're in Scotland. Not Switzerland.' Then another thought strikes me. 'And why would anyone want to smuggle anything in or out of Scotland?'

'My great-grandfather had one built into the mountains here decades ago. For fun.'

'Fun?' The word hangs in the air and, I hope, is dripping with sarcasm. There are lots of things that are fun but clambering on ladders in mid-air is not one of them.

'You do realise that your family are and have always been a bit weird.'

'Maybe but no one outside the family has ever used it. So, it's a real honour. Unless you want to back out,' Harvey says.

'Never.'

'That's the spirit. It's lunch and then we're off.'

Lunch is a pathetic affair. A few berries and nettles, bulked up with the porridge which is all they'll give us. It's a strange state of affairs when the best, most plentiful thing on offer is the seaweed that we discovered on the beach a few days ago. Ah the joys of kelp. I would never have considered that that was a thought that would go through my starved, confused brain.

We're off again in our Land Rover, winding through the forest on a tiny track. Harvey and I get jolted around in the back for what seems like hours. Eventually we break out of the trees and the sky opens above us.

And then I see something that makes me lose my breath completely.

I see what must be the Klettersteig.

Whatever I imagined, this is far, far worse.

This is not jumping a few feet out of a helicopter.

This is not flicking a fish out of a stream.

This is not making a raft and then collapsing.

This is a whole different experience.

And this time, I can feel only one thing.

I really don't think I can do this one. Team Hector might as well win now.

Out of the vehicle, we stand, looking up at a chasm in the mountain. A great split widens in the side of it as if a giant has got angry and split it from top to bottom. Across the huge split I can see a tiny crossing point, as thin as a spider's silk. Then I notice that an even thinner thread leads up to it along the side of an ever increasingly high ledge. The other team arrive just then. Cameron leaps out of the back and takes in the view.

'Shouldn't be too bad. Mummy and I did a number of these last summer. This will be child's play in comparison. Have you spent much time in Zurich, Tulip? Or is Blackpool more your scene?' Cameron sniggers. I decide he's not worth my words. I stare up at the mountain with increased determination. I need to do this with confidence and courage if I'm to stay in.

'So that's it.'

'That's it.'

'Right.' There doesn't seem much more to say.

I try to think this through. I don't want to do this.

But I don't want to go home either.

We have the Health and Safety briefing while we get kitted up. After he's finished presenting to both teams, Stan comes up to offer some words of wisdom to us.

I look at the Klettersteig. 'We're really attached at all times to a cable?' I decide now is the time to interrogate him. If Stan tells me it's safe, then I'll do it. And, of course, I must keep telling myself, the TV company aren't about to let me die in front of the cameras. I hope.

'Yes.'

'And we can't fall?'

Stan's face is rather conflicted. 'Yes, you can fall off but you can't fall far as you're attached by a safety line to the cable.' This is not as reassuring as I'd like. 'And I really wouldn't recommend that you fall as it's quite tricky at that point.'

Great, so the health and safety guy is telling me not to fall off.

But the key point that I need to tell myself is that I can't die. Well, not today anyway. 'What's your advice on what to do?'

'Just put one hand in front of the other and let your feet follow. Keep going and you'll soon be there.'

Harvey looks green. It's not like he's exactly loving this either. Perhaps it's not such an honour to be allowed to do this. We are united in fear.

'You're not going to let us die, are you?' I say, desperate for reassurance. 'Seriously, what if someone freaks out or gets stuck?'

'I've been over it twice to prepare. It's old but it's well-constructed. But you do need to know this. You start this. You finish this. It's that simple. If you have any second thoughts, then don't even put your foot on the first rung. You have to be able to see it through.' Thanks Stan, I feel so much better now.

Teams ready, we toss a coin to see who goes first. Cameron wins. Of course. He winks at me – yuk. 'We'll go first and show you how it's done.' Double yuk. But how can he be so confident? It looks like a fate worse than death. Stan takes them away, makes sure that they are clipped on and they start their trial.

Up bounces Hugh. 'All ready then, Tulip? It's a bit windy up there, do you think that you can handle this bad boy? They seem to be coping.'

You can see the ladder bouncing in the wind. Actual metal is bending above me and that's what we've got to cross. As my heart is now digging a hole to Australia in an attempt to escape, I distract myself by noticing that he doesn't ask Harvey if he's up for it and he's looking greener than me. This small detail really, really annoys me. I am as capable as Harvey. Okay I've not wrestled a polar bear to the ground with nothing but my hands but hey, I'd give it a go if I had to.

In fact, I would give anything a go if I had to. And currently I have to do this.

'I think you'll find that I'm up to it, just as I have been on every other occasion.' I lock gazes with Hugh. Which is probably foolish as it's like being caught in the full beam of the sun. But I don't back down.

'Indeed, Miss Taylor. Well, let's hope that this is not the experience where you finally wilt. As soon as Team Hector are over, you can begin. With that he's gone to watch the other team on the monitors in the van.

I whisper to Harvey, 'I'm not being funny, but your dad's jokes are probably some of the worst I've ever had to experience.'

But Harvey doesn't reply. We sit and wait in silence until it's time for us to start. This means the other team are across. Presumably Hugh will judge who shows the most courage, teamwork and communication skills to decide who leaves. But then again, who knows? Hugh's decisions have been unpredictable so far. Maybe he'll declare himself the winner!

After an age, we get the go-ahead. The crew point out the cameras that will be watching us. We have our helmet camera GoPros on as ever. There's the ground crew looking up. A line has been put across the crevasse so that the camera can track our every move and there's a drone above for good measure.

In short, everything is in place. Even Mum would be impressed by the attention to detail and how our every move is to be constantly monitored. If I freak out, then it's there for the world to see. I am freaking out already, but I have to keep it inside. Another thing spurs me on though – only a few days ago I was being set up as the stupid girl, the make-up girl, the girl who only knows about eyeliner. And yet I'm still here. Still rocking my braids but make-up free. Others have left, cheated, not met the grade. And I'm still here. Go me.

'Right,' I say to no one but myself. Oh yes and to however many people watch this programme. 'It's Tulip time.'

CHAPTER FORTY

Word: Apogee (noun)

Harvey's already started ahead of me, clipping himself to the safety line. We have two clips, one of which must be on the safety line at all times. As long as we do that, then we're safe. But it is completely up to us to make sure that we put the clip on. Otherwise we could fall. Completely fall. And we're only safe as long, of course, as the safety clip or the line don't break. I consider if this is possible.

Deep breath. 'Here's where I clip it?' I ask Stan.

'Yes, remember the golden rule. You must always be clipped on at any time. This is quite an old-fashioned design. When you transfer from one line to the next, you put your new clip on before you take the old one off. If you do that, then you can't come to any harm.'

If. My brain must not freeze or make any stupid mistakes. Because gravity will kill me if I fall. It's as simple as that. I can't quite remember all the equations from school now, but I know enough. It's not like a cartoon where you bounce up again.

I step up to the slate-grey cliff face that looms over me. Harvey is ahead of me, slowly stepping his way along the iron cable that is pinned to its oozing face. Grimly, I clip myself to the safety line that runs along at shoulder height. I can hold this and use it to pull myself along while my feet follow the bottom line.

I begin.

So far so good. It's not hard but the cable is as cold as ice even through the very unattractive gloves that they made me wear. Finding footholds is not easy though, that's the hardest bit. Sometimes the cable is right next to the stone and there's barely a toehold. Sometimes it's further out, pushed by the steel pins that attach to the rock, and then my feet can slip off.

I'm getting higher though. I don't look down, but I know I must be higher than when I did the helicopter jump. My breath is coming faster now, and not because it's hard work. I need to concentrate on this. I just need to endure the next few hours.

I have my first corner to deal with. I can't see Harvey. All I can see is that the cables disappear around a corner and I have to follow them, even though I can't see where they are going. It feels like a leap of faith. I edge my way along until I can't see any further. How do I get around? Small stones scutter from below my feet and then bounce below. They fall and fall. I mustn't watch them. I watch them. They tumble down the sides of the mountain and I freeze.

A distant voice calls, 'Keep going Tulip. Just follow the cable.'

I take a few breaths and practise a bit of mindful breathing. Clear the mind. Live in the moment. I'm aware of my body and how it feels. Then I go through my favourite list of words. I mentally edit out any that refer to danger and make sure I add in a few extras that are to do with bravery.

Then I push my safety cable as far forward as I can, reach around the corner and tiptoe along.

The toehold is tiny. My feet slip. I lurch downwards and find myself hanging by my ice-cold hands from the top cable. Someone is screaming. Oh, that would be me again. My feet cartwheel until I find the cable again and I'm safe. Relatively speaking.

My heart has never beaten so fast. No PE session has even made my heart pound like this. I need to calm down.

Breathe in, and out. Breathe in, and out.

I look ahead. The next section doesn't look too bad. It's the ladder that I'm dreading though. But when I go around the next corner, I see Harvey ahead of me. He's not moving. He's got to the next 'experience'.

Instead of walking along a cable attached to a mountain to get to the ladder, there are three cables that reach high over the valley floor. One to walk on and then two at shoulder height to hold, one of which is the safety cable.

I catch up with Harvey. I see the drone come in closer to film us. Even up here there's no privacy.

'What do you think?'

Harvey puts a foot tentatively on the bottom cable. It wobbles in a way that doesn't encourage any confidence. 'You think it will bear our weight?'

'It's been tested. We've got the safety cable. It's fine.' He sighs. 'It just feels wrong.'

Below us the valley stretches away, and I can see the loch sparkling in the afternoon sun.

'Not a bad view. Might be even better further on.'

Harvey's face reveals turmoil. I try to think of something comforting to say but my mind too has gone blank. The cables sing in the wind, making a strange crying sound as they vibrate. I know the word 'keening' is an old word for sobbing and now I understand what it means.

'Right,' he nods. I know how hard he's finding it, but he can't say. He can't let his dad down and he can't show him how frightened he is. We're a hundred feet up in the air. We're all alone but he's still trapped by other people's expectations.

One foot on the cable, he ekes himself along. 'You're the bravest person I know,' I yell after him. I don't care who hears. I've gone beyond caring what people think of me.

When he's further on, I start after him.

It is the most beautiful and terrifying thing that I have ever done.

The cable beneath our feet bounces and sways in the most alarming way. The ones on either side for our hands do the same. Concentrate on breathing, I tell myself. Look around. Okay maybe that's a bad idea. I mean this is utterly beautiful – the sun hits the distant hills turning them gold. Clouds scud across a blue sky, so intense that my eyes hurt. But if the cables snap, then the distance between me and the beautiful scenery will kill me.

I find that my feet have stopped. The drone is over me, filming my lack of progress. That's enough to get me going – I will not be seen to be a loser.

Eventually, I'm over. I hated dragging myself along the cliff earlier but now I'm connected to this new cable, it gives me a sense of security after being out in the open air.

Then I see our final challenge.

The horizontal ladder that reaches across the gap.

I finally realise why this is the most horrific thing we've been asked to do so far. For a start, there's the crawling. You have to lie on the ladder and somehow crawl over it. In order to see where you're going, you have to look down. It's pure psychological torture.

Harvey starts. He moves himself down slowly so he's kneeling down. Waiting for my chance to start all I can think of is how tired I am. But I fight back those feelings. If I keep going, then I can get off this mountain and I will never go on an escalator again. I won't wear a pair of high heels. In fact, I'm going to give up standing. I will approach the world from the point of view of an earthworm and spend the rest of my life wiggling along the ground.

It seems so unnatural to lower myself down. I'm not even sure how to do it. I mean, I'm not going to let go of the link between my harness and the safety cable. Otherwise I'll just be standing on the ladder, not holding on to anything. I know I can't fall – the line will still be there – but I like holding it. It makes me feel safe. But I don't see how I can get low enough to grab the ladder until I do.

I look at one hand holding the line that links to the safety cable. And the other reaching out for the ladder. I try to pull my arms out of their sockets. It doesn't work.

'Harvey? How did you reach it?' Then I realise that his arms are longer than mine. This wasn't designed for small people with appropriately proportioned, but short, arms.

I'm stuck. I can't go ahead unless I let go of the line and let myself fall on to the ladder. It goes against every survival instinct I've ever had.

I let go.

I fall.

I grab on to the ladder. I am going to die. Not from the fall as now I've stopped falling. But from cardiac arrest.

'Tulip.'

'Yes.'

'Don't come any further.'

'Why?' My voice quivers.

Silence.

'Harvey. Why?'

Silence.

'Harvey, you're frightening me. Why not?'

'I'm trying to think of a way of saying it without frightening you. And me.' I've never heard him sound like this.

'Just say it.'

'Okay. I think that there's something wrong with the ladder.'

CHAPTER FORTY-ONE

Word: Trepidation (noun)

At that point, there's an ominous creak.

'Okay, for the record, what makes you think that there's something wrong with it?'

'Because…'

And then it happens. The thin ladder beneath us wobbles furiously, ripples like it's a duvet cover being shaken out and then it tilts suddenly to one side. We both tilt too and are left holding on to the dangling ladder, the only thing between us and falling is the tiny line linking our safety harnesses to the cable. For now.

By now we're both screaming. This continues for a time.

But then nothing else happens.

The safety cable above us stays intact.

My hands and feet are entwined around the metal, as I cling on, sobbing for dear life.

Still nothing happens. The drones whirr around us and Maz starts to shout instructions in our headsets. The idea of being told not to panic brings me round. 'Of course, I'm flipping panicking,' I scream. 'That's an entirely rational reaction to this.'

'Tulip.' Harvey's voice sounds odd.

'I'm here. Can you move forward?'

'I'm not sure how.' He's all wavery.

'I think that's what we have to do. We have to get off this as quickly as we can.'

Silence, apart from the wind moaning and the distant voices in my headset.

I try again. 'How far to the edge?'

'Not too bad. We're – I'm nearly there. About four metres.'

'That doesn't sound so much.'

'I suppose not.' He's not convinced.

'Can you get it down to three?'

'I don't know. I want to move but my body isn't listening.'

'It's okay to be frightened,' I reassure him.

'No. It's not allowed.'

'That's ridiculous.' I'd laugh if this were even remotely funny. It's not.

'No. That's how it is in our family.'

'You don't know what to do with being frightened?'

'Maybe.'

'Well, it's a good job I'm here because I'm an expert at being frightened.' My bluster covers the utter terror that's bubbling up inside me.

'You? Don't make me laugh.'

'What's funny about that? I mean we're hanging off a broken ladder. I'm not really in the mood for jokes.'

'You say you're an expert at getting frightened. But you never back down.'

'But I'm still frightened,' I say. Which is true.

'And what would you do now?' I'm reassured that his tone of voice seems a bit more normal now.

'Well, I generally do my breathing exercises.'

'And then what?'

'I go through my list of favourite words.'

'You have a list of favourite words?' That's better. He's almost laughing at me.

'Doesn't any sane person?'

'Er – by that definition I'm not sane.' The ladder creaks again.

To distract us, I try to joke. 'Tell me something new. Now think of your favourite word?'

'Pebble.'

Is that the best he's got? Well, now is not the time to judge. 'Now yell it,' I say.

'Yell it?'

'Let's make the mountain sing! Not too hard just in case we cause an avalanche. I really don't think that an avalanche would add much to the situation.'

And then we say 'Pebble' as hard as we can.

'Right. Keep saying pebble and edge forward,' I say.

And he does. I can see his feet moving slightly away from me. 'Keep talking.'

Cry after cry of 'pebble' rings round the mountain. The voices in my head are approving.

And finally, he makes it. 'I did it.' He's standing up, clipped to the safety cable. 'Come on.'

And now I realise exactly how hard it is.

'My legs seem to be like jelly.'

'Remember. You're competent. More than competent. You're

… what's another word for competent… I'd say that you are highly proficient at this. I can't think of another. Tulip, can you think of another word?'

Really? This is not the time but my brain can never give up on a challenge. 'What about adept or even … even … adroit?'

'That's it, you are proficiently competent at this, adroitly adept at this task. You just keep going. There you go.' Once I start I keep going and finally I find myself within grabbing distance of the cliff face with its safety cable firmly attached to rock for a change.

Harvey's holding out his hand for me. For once, I'm so grateful. My heart is lurching – I'm almost safe. The edge of the ladder is wobbling under my weight. I tell myself that the safety cable above me has me, and I can't die. That's my mantra, 'Today is not the day I will die. Today is not the day I will die.'

The second I'm close enough, I reach and grab Harvey's hand.

'That's it, just edge a few more centimetres, then you can get up. Hand me your second clip and I'll secure you.'

So I do and the sound of the clip falling into place is the best thing I've ever heard. Then I pull myself to standing with Harvey's help and finally we're safe. We turn to each other, feet on the ledge, faces on fire with joy. Of their own accord, our arms go around each other, and we pull each other close. It's the safest I've ever felt.

'Thank God. Thank God.' The voices in our helmets go crazy. 'You had us worried then. Take a minute to compose yourselves and then get your sorry asses off that mountain.'

I don't want to let go and clearly Harvey doesn't either. Our helmets bash so we can't get our heads close but it's enough to be alive. All I know is this – whatever feelings I'll ever have for another person in my life, I'll never have a moment like this with anyone again.

After a while, feeling begins to return to my legs.

'Should we move soon?'

'Probably a good idea.'

'I mean we've got warm beds and lots of food to look forward to. Oh, silly me, it's berries again for dinner.'

'Thanks, Tulip.'

'For what?'

'You know what. I would never have got down without you.' His eyes are centimetres away from me and the most beautiful thing I've ever seen. But they are also very sad eyes.

'What's the matter?' I ask.

'I've made a fool of myself in front of the world.'

'Er, we faced death and came through it. I think we've won at life in every possible way.'

He nods in a sort of agreement then we unentangle ourselves and Harvey's off. This cable malarkey is easy after everything we've been through. Whatever this experience was supposed to teach us, I think I've learned it all now. Whatever happens to me in the future, I know that I rock when things get tough. I can be Bad Ass when required. That is what I've learned – my inner core of steel.

I pull myself along, and eventually I'm back on solid ground.

Harvey is being pummelled by Hugh who seems for once

to have lost his composure. Stan is white and shaking. 'I can't believe this happened on my watch.'

'Where was your big net when I needed it?' I ask.

Suddenly, I'm shaking and crying. He pulls a silver sheet round me. 'I'm not sure I'm allowed to hug you. I'll find someone who can.'

Phoebe is there and hugs me like a mum would do. Then the crying really begins.

Everyone's crying, me, Phoebe, Stan, Harvey and – would you believe it – Hugh. He's holding on to him like he's a drowning man. Harvey is whispering something to him that I can't hear. The cameras are still on them. This is not okay – no one should be filmed like this without their permission. Stuff like this is private. I wipe away my tears and stare around for Maz. This needs to stop.

But then Hugh pushes Harvey away slightly and wipes his eyes. 'Camera on me, please. I've got something to say.'

Phoebe and I glance at each other. What's going on?

'Right,' Hugh stands up as tall as he can. 'We ready?'

'We're still rolling, Hugh, so go when you're ready.'

'This competition was all about testing our young people to see what they are made of. This generation comes under so much criticism. People say that they are lazy, spend too much time inside and on computers, that they don't know the meaning of hard work, that they are too soft – that this is the snowflake generation. Well, today, I saw and you saw what these young people are made of. My son, Harvey, faced his greatest fear. You saw how the ladder broke. I nearly saw my child fall to his death

before my eyes. But he came through. Son, I'm so proud of you.'
They hug. I cry again, Phoebe's full on sobbing. Stan keeps
muttering, 'There's something in my eye.'

Hugh calls out, 'Tulip, can you come here?'

'Me?' I mouth at him.

'Yes, you Tulip.' Like a zombie, I walk towards him. What
is he up to?

Now I get a bear hug. 'This young woman also showed true
grit in the face of adversity. Working together, they supported
each other, they communicated, they helped each other face
their fears and they got themselves out of a very difficult
situation.' He pauses. 'I'm stopping the competition. There's no
point in going on. There's no other task that I could set them
that would test them the way that they have been tested today.
I give you your winners – Tulip and Harvey.'

'What?' we say in unison.

'This is my show and I can do what I want. There is no way
I'm sending my son out again. You have passed every test.
Together. You are worthy winners.' Hugh steps back and starts
to applaud. 'Tulip and Harvey.'

Then the noise starts. The crew are all on their feet
applauding, stamping their feet and shouting our names. 'Tulip
and Harvey.'

On the edge of the group, I see Cameron and Samir. Samir
is applauding loudly. As for Cameron, he's looking at me with a
new expression. It looks a lot like respect but I must be mistaken.

I turn to Harvey to see his reaction to find that he's already
looking at me and only me.

'You did it,' he says. 'I always knew that you would. Right from the first time I saw you I knew that there was a girl who would go far.'

'Liar,' I smile at him, 'just like I saw that you were a kind, thoughtful, artistic soul.'

He leans in a bit but then a cheer makes him jump and he dodges back. 'We'll talk later.'

And then it hits. Yes, I've won. But I've also lost. I've lost the chance to be with Harvey all day. All of a sudden, I want to go back to our little camp, take the mics off and for it just to be the two of us.

But Phoebe hugs me and leads me away to my car.

The Tulip and Harvey show is over. Where do we go from here?

CHAPTER FORTY-TWO

Word: Matriarch (noun)

The journey passes in a blur. Back at the hotel, Phoebe takes me up to a room which feels too small, clean and claustrophobic after my time outdoors. But the bath calls to me. Soon, bubbles are reaching up to the ceiling as I run hot water, after tipping small bottle after small bottle in. Then the pile of empty plastic ruins the moment for me. I can't help but think of all the plastic washed up on my beautiful beach. From now on, I vow I'm going to think more about the natural world. Perhaps SuperMakeOver Girl should become EcoQueen. The steam makes me slightly lightheaded, so I imagine what my life might be like as EcoQueen. Certainly, long hot baths would have to be limited. Realising that my recent life has all been about just needing a bit more time, I decide to take all the time in the world in my scorching bath because EcoQueen might renounce hot baths soon, so I should enjoy this one while I can. I need to think of the fish, and my best friend – the deer!

But that's for later, now I need to think about how smelly I am and the hot bath is heaven.

Eventually I rise up. Absentmindedly, I wipe away the condensation on the mirror. Then I jump – there's a ghost in the bathroom! A strange-looking creature, which looks like it's just crept from the depths of the ocean. As I squeal, I realise it's me.

Oh. I step closer, wiping the mirror clean with a towel so that I can see myself fully.

Right.

Who is this girl? Her face is tanned, her hair dark and curly, her eyes seem smaller than I remember with invisible lashes and eyebrows.

Ordinary. That's what she – that's what I – look like. Not ridiculous. Not ugly. Just very, very ordinary. Ordinary is okay. Maybe that's what I should aim at for a while, just accept my very ordinary exterior as a cunning disguise for my increasingly awesome interior.

All this time I was afraid of my own face, but I didn't need to be. I just needed time away from mirrors, phones and selfies for a while to realise that it wasn't a big deal. I feel very, very stupid but also relieved. I'm not going to waste time on worrying what I look like in the future. I look into the mirror and make a promise to her that she's okay and I really have learned to like her. Maybe I don't love her yet but I'm sure that that will come with time.

My phone is next to my bed. I've not had it for over a week. After the first day I didn't miss it. My fingers trace my pin code but I don't activate it. All kinds of feelings bubble around.

That's when I decide to do something very odd. I turn off my phone.

Afterwards, I feel something. It takes me a while to identify it. I feel peace. That's when it comes to me. I'm going to take a break, from the vlogging, from the make-up, from all the constant googling. I'm going phone and internet free. The queen of the selfie needs a break to work out her next step.

Phoebe checks on me, we order room service and then I feel myself falling asleep on my bed. I drift off into strange dreams of falling, flying, talking fish and boats that sail through the sky.

At some unearthly hour of the morning, my door rattles as someone on the other side knocks as if their life depended on it. Disorientated, I fall out of bed and on to the floor. Where the heck even am I? Where are the birds and the trees? Then, it all comes back to me. I'm in the hotel and I have no idea what is going to happen today. I've still not seen Harvey. Hope flares inside. Maybe that's him at the door.

As my hand grabs the latch, the thought flashes through my mind that I've not brushed my hair this morning. I hesitate for a second but then realise that Harvey has seen me au naturale for over a week now so what difference does it make?

I open the door.

'Tulip, darling. I came as soon as they called. They sent a car for me and we've driven through the night. But it's okay. Mummy's here.'

Since when did I call her Mummy? I check in the corridor to see if this is being filmed but I can't see anyone. Though I've learned the hard way that I can't always trust that. But as she pulls me into a huge hug, it feels brilliant. I love smelling her perfume. It's lovely being touched again. I've missed hugging Rowan and Willow. I'm not going to tell her, but I've even missed her.

After the hug, she waves at me to go back in the room where she lounges on the sofa, so I snuggle back into bed.

'It's so good to see you,' she says. 'they tell me that you had the most terrible ordeal yesterday. I only let you go on this programme after they promised that you would be safe. I'd never have agreed if I thought you were in danger.' She pauses for a moment. 'I'm going to take legal action about suing them for emotional distress though.'

'Mum, you're not serious.'

'I am perfectly serious. They put you in harm's way. They should pay for that. Sirius has set up so many interviews for you when you get out. We'll see how you get on, but if money gets tight then I'll have to think about it.'

I'm lost now. She's back to controlling things and I don't like it.

'Sirius?'

'Yes, Sirius, your agent.'

Nope, not any clearer.

'I have an agent now?'

Mum laughs. 'Oh, of course you do. Tulip, you have no idea what's been going on since they started broadcasting the first episode. Everyone's gone crazy for you. You are the sensation of the moment. Sirius says the first few days after you get out are vital for establishing your media presence. He's going to arrange everything, of course, he's such a sweetie.'

My mind swirls in confusion. 'I still have no idea what you are talking about. And if you're here, who's looking after the twins? You haven't…' She wouldn't, would she? But then you never know with Mum.

'Left them? Don't be silly. No, your father is looking after them.'

Now I'm really confused. I have an agent and my father is in the same country as me. This is going beyond weird.

'Is this a strange dream?' I ask her. 'Are you my real mother or am I just hallucinating?'

'I know it's been awful for you, but you were so right to go on this show. This is going to be the making of you. This is going to save us all from a life of destitution.'

I start to say that no I've loved it and that I want to go back but I still feel that I'm really missing something here. 'If Dad's back, then surely he's paid you the money he owed. Isn't that enough to pay the mortgage?'

She sighs deeply. 'I know that you love your father but we both know he's unreliable. No, he flew home on his last few pounds. I'm not quite sure of the story but he's broke. I won't let him live in the house but currently he's camping in the orchard while he works out what to do next.'

I stare at her in disbelief. But the plan – the whole point of doing the show – was to buy time for Dad to come to the rescue. Slumping into the pillows, I turn away from her. How can he have let me down like this?

Mum comes and sits next to me, patting me on the back. 'I know it's hard. I know that you were counting on him. That's why it's such good news about Sirius taking us on. He's going to take care of everything. Just do what he says, and we'll be laughing all the way to the bank.'

'Really?'

She strokes the side of my face softly. 'Really. People love you, Tulip. They're talking about you on every social media site.

You are a meme. You should see the gifs of your reactions. I don't know how you did it, but you have made yourself into the story of the moment. And then the accident last night. When the TV company released the news, my phone nearly exploded. Everyone wants to talk to you.'

I'm loved? I try to take in what she's telling me. I feel a warm feeling spreading inside but I don't feel that I can trust it yet.

'People really like me?' I ask tentatively.

'Yes, people love you.'

'Wow,' I say. 'Okay. Right, so tell me more about these interviews. And why do I have an agent with the most bizarre name? And what exactly do people love about me?'

Her phone goes. 'It's Sirius. He's downstairs. I'll just go and chat and then bring him up later. You catch up with everything. Your phone's there. Now it will be busy. You do have quite the schedule for the next few days. But, Tulip...' Mum looks straight at me. It's only then that I realise that she never normally does, or if she does, then it's only for a fleeting, grudging moment. 'Thank you.'

'What for?' Her intensity is freaking me out.

'For saving us.'

'Mum, all I did was...'

'No,' she puts up a finger to stop me talking. 'I must admit that I did have my reservations about this whole thing, but I should have trusted you. There's so much interest in you. You won't believe it. Sirius has interviews and endorsements lined up, companies are falling over themselves to get you on board.'

'Really?' This all seems a long way from our little camp.

'Really. And so, I think we can safely say that our financial future is safe for the time being. And for that, I am truly thankful.' As Mum hugs me again, I feel her shaking. This is for real then. I didn't think vulnerable would ever be a word I'd use to describe Raven. Ravens normally follow the dying and then eat out their eyes to help them on their way to death. But not this Raven. There's so much reassessing that needs to go on. Perhaps now is not the time to tell her that I'm taking a break from the whole vlogging thing. Then I realise something. 'Mum...'

But she's gone.

Huddled up in my dressing gown, I lounge on my bed. It's lying next to my bed, all fully charged and shiny. My phone. My treasure. My precious. My best friend. My life-line. My encyclopaedia. My life. I was so lost without it and then I didn't miss it. Now, I don't even know if I want to pick it up. Mum says I'm an internet sensation but what does that even mean?

They say curiosity killed the cat. When Pandora opened the forbidden box, she let all kinds of evil in the world. Why is it that when you're not supposed to do something, then all of a sudden you just have to do it. Just like Adam and Eve and the apple. Though if I was going to unleash evil on the world, I think it might take more than an apple to tempt me.

But still my hand creeps out to the phone. The old control freak bit of me has to see what is being said about me.

I turn in back on. It's aglow with notifications. I'm not sure how to feel about this. Once it was a sign that I'd uploaded a good video but now I'm not the one who has created them.

Apparently, #Tulip is a thing. Fingers shaking, I click on and start to scroll through.

Yes, people love me. Apparently, I'm hilarious. Yes, I'm a meme. But people are definitely laughing at me not with me.

There's me being thrown from a helicopter, screaming. There I am, thinking I'm about to be eaten by a shark. Of course, I'm hunting through the forest looking for a shiny object to see myself. And finally, who could forget the moment I nearly blinded myself by trying to apply ash to my waterline with a stick. I am very, very entertaining. I can see that. But that's it. There's nothing about me coping, contributing, leading. It's just ridiculous Tulip. Why am I even surprised? I knew the TV company wanted me to be a certain way and I still just went ahead and was my fully ridiculous self.

Which is fine. But that's not all that there is to me and I want to be other things too. Sure, there are other bits – bits where I'm useful. But those aren't the bits that people are sharing over and over again. The public seem to want the Tulip of the first day. I need to talk to Mum about this. I need to know what this Sirius is up to and I need to know exactly what kind of companies that they want me to promote. I think it's fair to say that I have a very, very bad feeling about this. This is not the person I am. This is not the person I wanted to be. My future full of possibility is disappearing out of view.

CHAPTER FORTY-THREE

Word: Concede (verb)

One furious conversation with Mum and Sirius later, I bang on Harvey's door, tears streaming down my face. Bad Ass Tulip has just had her ass whooped by Mum. And reality. Bad Ass Tulip has disappeared and will not be seen for a while.

Mum's words ring around my head. 'It's just a part, darling.' 'I know it's not you, but we need the money.' 'Don't be ridiculous, this will be the making of the family. You're making a fuss about nothing like always.' And the killer line that I had no answer to. 'If you don't do it, I can't pay the mortgage. Do you want to live on the streets?'

Harvey opens the door and reacts to my face. 'What happened?' He drags me in, pulling me into a hug as he does. I hide my face in his shoulder. I feel safe here, like I did up after surviving the Klettersteig. I don't want to let go.

'Hey,' he speaks with such tenderness that I feel my heart break a bit more. 'What's happened?'

'It's Mum,' I hiccup. 'She's signed my life away. She's got me doing all kinds of make-up and product endorsements.'

'And?'

I look at him in desperation. 'And I don't want to do them. It's all set up for today. I've got to do an interview. She's signed up with some agent and he's even written down the questions and what I'm supposed to say in response to them. There's a whole list of endorsements that I have to get into the interview.' I wave a tear-stained piece of paper at him. 'Look. He's making me sound so stupid.'

Harvey starts to read, his face twisting in disgust. 'This is his idea of you?'

'Apparently it's what people are going to expect from me after the footage that they've seen, that I'm a stupid, vain girl who can't go a day without make-up and thinks that there are great white sharks off the Scottish shoreline.'

'What are you going to do?' He pulls me down so that we're sitting on his bed.

'I don't know,' I say forlornly.

'I'm not having that. You always have a plan.'

My heart sinks. I don't want to hear this. I just want sympathy. 'I'm outplanned and outwitted. She's got me completely trapped this time. There's nothing I can do.'

Harvey starts to walk about the room in agitation. 'Come on, that's not Tulip talking. You always have an answer for everything.'

I shake my head, silently. My brain is an arid desert of nothing. He punches me lightly on the shoulder. 'Just give yourself some time.'

'I don't have any time, don't you see? It all starts tomorrow.'

'But just say no, that you don't want to do it.'

'No. I can't.' Irritation is beginning to build up now.

'I don't get why not.'

'Because of the money. This is going to pay off the mortgage and set us up for life. If I say no, there's no other option. Dad's run out of money and come home. If I don't agree, then apparently we're looking at being homeless.' Tears start welling up again.

'But that's your mum's job, not yours.'

'Try telling her that.' I sniffle.

'No, I think you should try telling her that. In fact, don't try, just do it.'

I'm getting cross now. 'Like you say no to your dad?'

'That's not fair.'

'No, life's not fair. But don't start making out that you're braver than me when we both know that you're not.'

'What's got into you? The Tulip I know can do this. She can make a stand and do what she thinks is right.'

'Look, you don't get it, do you? Has your family ever been poor? Have you any idea what it's like to be told that you and you alone are responsible for the family's income? Poor little rich boy, the worst thing that's ever happened to you is…'

He struggles to keep calm. 'I know this is hard…'

'You don't…'

'Tulip, just listen to me…'

I've had enough. 'I'm tired of listening. I'm tired of talking. I'm just tired.'

As I go, he grabs my arm. 'You don't have to do it. You're better than this. You can think of a way out of this.'

'You expect too much from me. Maybe I'm not the girl you thought I was.'

He starts to disagree, but I shake my head sadly. 'No. I'm

done. I'm beaten. I'll just have to do this for a while, no matter how much I hate it.'

'Don't put your life on hold. What about…'

'No.' I wave the paper at him in defeat. 'This is what I've got to do.'

'But…'

'No, that Tulip has to disappear for a while. Old Tulip is back.' I pin on my biggest, fakest, cheesiest smile.

'Tulip,' he says slowly, 'I think you're making a big mistake. Don't be that person. You're so much better than that.'

'Who are you to judge me? Who are you to make any comment on what I do?' I say, the old fury at him returning. 'It feels like we're right back to where we were. I'm looking out for my family. What's so terrible about that?'

'I know it's hard but…'

I put my hand up. 'Shush. No. You. Do. Not. I don't even know why I'm letting you talk to me like this. After all, we're just…'

'We're just what?'

I sigh. 'We're just friends, aren't we? That's what you said. But don't friends support each other?'

He shakes his head. 'I don't think I can support you when you're making such a mistake.'

'Really?' I can't believe he's letting me down. 'If you liked me, even a tiny bit, then you'd support me.'

'I can't let you…'

'Don't you get it? This is not up to you. This is my choice. And I need you to tell me that it's okay.'

'I just can't.' I've never seen him so sad.

'Then perhaps we're not friends anymore,' I say.

'Tulip…'

But I don't stop; I walk out and slam the door.

I look but he doesn't come after me.

CHAPTER FORTY-FOUR

Word: Interrogation (noun)

'Wow, your skin is amazing,' the make-up woman enthuses as she starts work on me. It's the next morning and she's got her work cut out because I've hardly slept. 'What do you use?'

'Just fresh air, Scottish water and plenty of attitude,' I say.

'Tulip!' Mum gives me a look from the chair next to me. 'Don't joke. You know that you only use Skybliss skin products, available exclusively online.'

'Mum. We're not on air,' I point out.

'I know but you might as well get used to it, so you don't slip up. It's important to get this right.' Mum waves a list of the products that apparently I use in front of me.

The make-up woman stares at us, sensing the tension. I smile sadly at her. 'My mistake. I bathe in unicorn tears and drape myself in star beams. That's what gives me my inner glow.'

'Okay,' she says, 'but you've still got quite big bags under your eyes. Couldn't sleep?'

'Something like that,' I mutter. We're in the conference room where I first met Hugh before we began filming, ten days ago. So much as happened. I thought so much had changed. But here I am, with make-up being plastered on my face, being bossed about by my mother. Absolutely nothing has changed at all. I slump further down in the chair.

'Close your eyes. Look up. Chin down.' I do as I'm told. 'So unicorn tears are good for the skin but don't help you sleep?'

'Not really,' I reply.

The make-up woman leans in over me. 'Well, you've been through a lot in the last week. I have to say me and my girls have been watching every show. They have just loved you.'

'Thanks.' I don't know what else to say.

'You're their favourite but they also really love that Harvey boy. It's probably because he looks so gorgeous.'

Everything churns inside as I re-live last night's conversation. His face as he tells me that I'm 'so much better than this'. How dare he judge me?

'He might look gorgeous, but he can be a complete arse at times.'

She leans back. 'Steady on. Keep your face calm or I'll have to start again.' I try to do what she says but it's hard.

'I mean, he can be so judgemental. He thinks he's so much better than me.'

'Yes, but I thought you two might have a bit of a spark.'

'No,' I shake my head. I've said it once and I'll say it again. 'He is the last boy in the world I would ever go for.'

'Okay,' she says, a slight smile on her lips. Then she looks up at something behind me. 'Okay,' she repeats but this time she's not smiling.

Ignoring the whole 'keep calm' instruction, I whip round. Harvey's standing right behind me. He heard everything.

I try to say something but he starts first. 'I just came to wish you good luck.'

Oh.

He goes. I try to follow him. 'Harvey!' He doesn't stop. Just like I didn't stop last night. Why can't we ever listen to each other?

'I didn't mean…' But there's no point. The door slams and he's gone.

'No spark at all?' She's teasing me but all I want to do is cry. How did everything get so complicated?

Mum fusses over me and makes sure I don't leave the chair. But it's all so wrong. I'm like a doll being dressed up when all I want to do is chase Harvey down and talk so that somehow this stupid mess might get put right. But no, my hair is brushed, squirted with product after product, and then scorched and curled into an image of perfection. But I'm not about perfect now. I want to be about natural products that don't leave a mark on the world, not these products that are probably burned into bunnies' eyes and tested on baby otters. There are a million and one feelings whirling about me and the one that I feel most intensely is this: this is not what I want.

But everyone is poking and prodding me. A mic is attached to me, the room is hot with camera lights with huge cables snaking over the floor. Here I am, getting ready for my time in front of the cameras again.

'Ready, Tulip?' the runner says and takes me to my seat.

My clothes feel stiff and scratchy. I know they are designer, and that I've never worn clothes as expensive at these. But I miss my faithful boots and cosy fleece. I catch a glimpse of myself in a mirror on the other side of the room.

I look good. But I'm not sure if I look like me. Even though my make-up is beautiful, I can't look at this Tulip and think, you know, she's okay, really.

I sigh. I get a tap on the shoulder. It's show time.

I sit down on the slippy leather sofa that's been chosen for the interview. On the other side of the room stand Mum and the bonkers Sirius, both smiling manically and supposedly encouraging me with lots of thumbs-ups.

There's no time to think this through. The lights blind me and make my skin hot. I put a hand up to my face to wipe a bead of sweat away but remember that with all this make-up on, I mustn't touch my face. Back to worrying about what I look like.

'Five. Four.' Then the runner goes to a silent countdown with her fingers, as she shows three, two and one with rapidly diminishing fingers.

I sit awkwardly, alone on my shiny sofa, smiling directly into a camera. I'll hear questions from the presenters of the biggest morning TV show in the country, all the way from London, in my earpiece, currently cunningly hidden behind my skilfully curled hair and the camera will beam my response around the country.

I feel like an idiot but the red light on the camera is on which means it's live, it's on and it's fixed on me.

My ear starts to tickle. 'This morning we're delighted to welcome the girl that everyone is talking about. The girl with the extraordinary name who has been entertaining us with her extraordinary behaviour. A huge hello to the young lady who is Tulip Summer Acorn Taylor. Tulip, welcome! I bet you were straight on your phone the moment you got back, weren't you?'

'Hi, something like that.' I say, not quite sure what to make of this introduction.

'So, you've been through quite an ordeal these last few days, worse than being separated from your phone. We're very glad you've made it.'

'Not being dead is a real bonus I find,' I say.

Gales of laughter burst out in my ear, the camera crew smile. Was it that funny? I thought I was stating the obvious. I just keep staring at the camera, I daren't look at Mum or Sirius to see their reaction.

'Indeed, you are right, Tulip. Now we'll get to the drama, in a few minutes, but I think it's safe to say that you didn't have the best of starts, now did you?'

'That is one way of putting it,' I agree.

'Let's just remind ourselves of some of Tulip's highlights.'

Do we have to? But on the monitor next to the camera, I see a tiny Tulip doing a number of very stupid things.

'So, what did you feel when you were first in camp? As many of our viewers know, you were, indeed you are, famous on the internet for your make-up tutorials. How did it feel to be without all your usual make-up? You're looking lovely today, if I may say so.'

I ignore the compliment. It's all a bit creepy. 'It was a bit overwhelming to be honest. But that's what the show is all about. For the first day, one thing after another went wrong but then after that I think I began to settle in a bit more.'

I feel that this is not what they want. They want funny. They want ridiculous. But I can't be that to order. I try to remember what I'm supposed to say from Sirius' script but my mind goes blank.

'But what about trying to use ash for eyeliner? That didn't exactly go well now, did it?'

Eyeliner. I'm supposed to sell a product here. I know that. What am I supposed to say?

'Yes. No. It went badly. Fortunately, now I'm out, I'm back to using my normal products. I find Jamais' Bold Black Ink eyeliner is perfect. It stays in place a lot longer than ash.'

More laughter. This is what they want. But this is not me. Worse, I know Jamais' products are over-priced rubbish. Ash would be a lot more natural and not tested on animals. I'm lying on national TV.

'Sure, sure, but don't mention any more brands, Tulip, we'll get in trouble with the powers that be.'

'Oh sorry, I'm just so excited to become a brand ambassador for a number of products. It's a dream come true for me.'

Oh please. Can the ground open up and swallow me? Can a huge wind come down and blow the hotel away? Please, someone save me from this embarrassment. Doing the Klettersteig wasn't as bad as this moment. Selling myself, selling my soul, live on TV.

'And did we detect a touch of romance? There were a few lovely moments between you and Harvey, weren't there?'

What do I say? More lies? The truth? But the truth is so personal. As far as I know, we might not even be friends now.

'We've become quite good friends.' That's a lie whichever way you look at it.

This is becoming the worst moment of my life by far. I'd rather stick an eyeliner in my eye and take my chances with a great white shark.

But no one can save me, I think.

Then I think, but there is someone. There is someone who can put a stop to this nonsense.

I know someone who's good in a crisis and can be Bad Ass when she wants to be.

Me.

Deep breath. This isn't rehearsed but I'm going for it.

'Actually, it's not a dream come true. It's a nightmare.'

A muffled 'what' comes from Mum's direction.

'What do you mean, Tulip?'

'Well, the thing is that I'm proud of all I've achieved with my channel and my vlogs, but I think it's time for a change. This show has given me a different way of looking at life, an opportunity to think. And yes, I was obsessed with my phone. But I didn't miss it after a while. I still don't.'

'Interesting. So, you didn't go straight back on your phone?'

'No. And I didn't look in a mirror straight away. And I didn't want to put make-up on today.'

Silence. 'So, the show really changed you then? Made you see things in a different way?'

'Yes, not that there's anything wrong with what I was like before. I'm sure I'll go back to that at some point. But after a week without all the things that I thought were essential, I realise that I'm happier without them all.'

'No make-up?'

'No.'

'No channel?'

'No.'

'No phone?'

'No.'

I think Mum is silently screaming. A door slams. Is that Sirius leaving the building?

'Are you absolutely sure that you're giving up your phone?'

If you're going to do something, do with in style. 'Excuse me a moment.' I walk to where I left my phone on a table to one side. Picking it up, I stand in front of the camera again. My fingers flicker over the keyboard.

'So, I'm deleting my channel. I'm deleting my favourite account. Now, my photo account. I'm basically deleting everything.'

'You're turning your back on social media completely?'

'For now. Not forever. Just until I sort out what I want to say.'

'But the phone's still in your hand,' the interviewer's voice in my ear says. 'I'm not sure that people will believe that you can really give that up?'

'I generally do what I say I'm going to do,' I say. 'I've learned that. And I think the people behind the show realised that they underestimated me. Here goes.'

I throw the phone to the floor. Mum outright yells, 'Tulip, no!'

I stamp on it. The glass cracks and the screen goes black.

'Tulip, what have you done?'

I smile. 'I'm not sure. But it felt good.'

I make myself look at Mum. Her face is in her hands, her shoulders moving up and down silently. I don't think she'll ever forgive me.

The voice in my ear keeps on shouting at me but I rip the earpiece out and walk off.

What have I done?

I do know one thing. For the first time since I left camp, I feel okay. For the first time, I feel like I've made the right choice. But how do I put things right with Mum and then ... is it even possible ... how do I put things right with Harvey?

CHAPTER FORTY-FIVE

Word: Lineage (noun)

The journey home is awkward to say the least. I want to call Kate and Anjali. But I don't have a phone. Not surprisingly, Mum won't lend me hers.

But coming home is a glorious thing. As the black car drives away for the last time, and Phoebe waves like a puppet that's drunk twenty caffeine drinks, I find myself standing on the doorstep. The door opens as I put my hand on the doorbell and I find myself falling into the hall only to be jumped on by Willow and Rowan. 'Tulip! I haven't been through all your make-up, I really haven't,' Rowan begins.

'He's a bit fat liar. He's been in your room every day.'

Rowan's lip begins to wobble. 'Well, unicorns don't even exist. So there!'

Willow punches him in the face. 'I am a unicorn and I exist and this is my horn to prove it.' With this, she flounces off. 'I love you, Tulip, but I don't want to share air with that poo-poo head.'

I turn on Rowan with a fierce stare. 'Have you really been at my make-up?'

He nods. I pull him close. 'You can have it.'

He stares at me with wide eyes. 'Go on. Before I change your mind. You can take anything you want.'

'Really? Truly? Anything?'

'Anything. Now scoot.' I may regret this later but right now it's worth it to see how he skips down the hall, singing, 'It's all mine. My precious. My darlings. It's all mine.' Yes, imagine a cute Gollum who's obsessed with contouring rather than a magical gold ring and you'll have something like it.

Willow calls, 'There's a message for you. Dad wrote it down on a Post-it before he went to play on his bongos.' Right. I'll check that out later.

Back in my room, I cuddle my teddies but they remain silent. Because they are teddies. If they started talking to me then that really would be time to worry. I grab for my non-existent phone again to call Anjali and Kate. Stupid me. Fortunately, they're a step ahead of me and it's not long before they call round, desperate for news. They pile on me, I hug them back. I have missed them so much. There might be tears but the best thing is we chat for hours.

'But I don't know what to do about Harvey,' I sigh.

'What do you mean?'

'Well, I don't know if he's seen the interview. He walked out. I'll ask him at school, I suppose.'

There's a pause.

Kate says, 'I'm not sure if it's true or not but there's a rumour that he's not coming back.'

'What do you mean?' I say, my heart dropping.

'That's what Tiffany says. Apparently, he messaged Lottie and said that he wasn't coming back.'

'But why?'

Anjali gives me a hug. 'This is going to hurt. Take a deep breath. Apparently he said he had nothing to come back for.'

Ouch. But I can hardly blame him. To be rejected once is hard. To be rejected twice? No one is going to risk a third.

We try to chat some more but it's clear I've nothing much to say.

Kate tries to fill the silence. 'It's fine, Tulip. You'll find a way to sort this out. You always do.'

But this time I have no bright ideas and, to be honest, I just don't want to think about it. So they wave their goodbyes while I try to process it all but Rowan cannons in, closely followed by Willow.

'He's stolen my unicorn.'

'She won't lend me her sparkly top.'

'It's not a sparkly top. It's my unicorn fur, decorated with unicorn tears, gathered at midnight.'

'They. Are. Sequins. Tell her they are sequins, Tulip.'

'Unicorn tear thief. Unicorn disbeliever.'

I put my hands over my ears. It's all too much. 'Enough already. Just get out, the pair of you.' I put the laptop down.

Two pairs of round eyes turn on me. Two mouths fall open into Os of horror. 'You have to sort this out, Tulip,' Willow whispers. 'Or what will we do?'

Rowan nods. 'We need you to make everything okay again. That's normally what you do. We've missed you. Mum is no good at sorting out problems 'cos she's always on her phone with a face that looks like this.' He purses his lips and contorts his face to make creases on his forehead.

I'd laugh but it really isn't funny. He's right. She does look like that. All the time. I thought I'd been clever to talk to Dad, but he's let me down.

'I'm not in the mood to sort things out, I'm afraid.'

Rowan plonks down next to me on one side and Willow wriggles up to me on the other. 'Are you sad, Tulip?'

Suddenly, I find huge tears running down my face. I can't even speak so now it's my time to nod.

Two pairs of arms grab round me and hug. 'Don't cry,' Willow whispers. 'It's not like you to cry.'

'I like crying though,' Rowan says. 'I always feel better when I cry. Or kicking a rugby ball very hard, that helps sometimes.'

'I like putting all my unicorn stuff out and stroking soft things. That helps me. Or coming to talk to you.' Willow's hugging me so hard that I can't breathe.

I find my voice, though it's a bit wobbly. 'You're both great but can you let go a bit? Otherwise, I won't be sad, I'll be dead.'

'But we need to hug you to stop you crying. That's what you do to us,' Rowan points out.

'Yes, but there's a balance between stopping crying because someone's being nice to you and stopping crying because you're dead.'

'Well, we don't want to kill you. I suppose we better let go,' Rowan sighs. 'Also, as you think that's for the best.'

'I really do,' I say, 'but look – no tears.' I use my newly released arms to wipe my face. 'Thank you. You've made me feel much better. Now, do you two think you can sort out this whole top mess between yourselves?'

'I suppose,' says Rowan, 'we could do what you normally do.'

'What do I normally do?'

'You find a – thingummy bob. What's it called?'

'It begins with s,' Willow adds.

'A solution?' I suggest.

His face breaks into a smile. 'That's the one. Maybe I could borrow another top from Willow that doesn't have a unicorn on.'

She looks sad. 'That's not going to work. Everything I have has a unicorn on.' She pulls down her leggings to show us her pants to make the point. I nod but begin to feel a bit more like myself.

'Don't you have something with a rainbow on? I'm sure you do.'

She thinks and then she explodes. 'I do. You can borrow my rainbow top. That's got rainbow dust on not unicorn tears.'

Of course. Problem solved.

Hand in hand, they race off to get themselves sorted.

I have another half laugh, half sob. I'd better not tell them yet about the environmental damage that sequins create. I would quite like to be small again and to get this worked up about sequins. It all seems much simpler than money and parents and thinking about what kind of person you want to be in real life and who you want to be online. That's why I miss waking up in the grey dawn and listening to the birds, watching out for the rabbits. There was nothing complicated going on there. No distractions. Me. And my thoughts.

But last time I was out there, in nature, I was with Harvey.

Only a few nights ago, we slept side by side under a huge sky. Now he's just gone, without saying anything to me. Does he know I turned my back on the deal? Why has he left school? I just want to see him and explain. Maybe I should start sleeping in the orchard to re-create the moment, just tie a hammock between two scraggly apple trees and spend the night there looking at the stars. It would be better than nothing.

The beginnings of an idea start to grow. I can't think about Harvey now. It's too much. But the whole family/money thing – surely that's not beyond me. What if… We could… Mum would be brilliant at… And then I wouldn't have to…

Solution. Ideas.

Yes, I'm good at those. In fact, I'm bloody brilliant.

I think I might have found a way for us to make a living that's doesn't involve twenty-four hour cameras.

Tulip Summer Acorn Taylor – you are a genius!

CHAPTER FORTY-SIX

Word: Posterity (noun)

Time to find Mum and launch my wonderful plan. I go out to where it's all going to happen. The orchard. Yes, our future plans all depend on this half an acre of scraggy ground and even scraggier trees. But then it's all about how you look at things and making the best of what you've got. Bit like planning a good makeover really, only on a much, much bigger scale.

Of course, Mum is in her pod.

'Mum, give me your phone.' Mum is clearly taken back by my unusually assertive tone and starts to babble.

'Mum, the phone.' I give her the look. It normally works on Rowan, Willow and Kate. Anjali is made of sterner stuff and I'm not sure that Mum will fall for it either, but she is strangely quiet.

'Phone.' I repeat with my hand out. 'And stop talking. I can only explain if you listen and you have to stop talking in order to listen.'

This is clearly very hard for her. It's like I'm asking her to hand over her soul. But slowly Mum's hand edges towards mine.

Then her phone rings and she snatches it back.

But I'm too quick for her and I grab it, cancel the call and then turn the phone off.

'What are you doing? That's an important business call. Turn it on. Give it back.'

I turn to the door and throw her phone into the thorniest, most overgrown patch of ground I can find. I have a new super power – killing phones! 'Now, no distractions. Can I have your full and undivided attention?'

Mum has lost the power of speech which is an unexpected benefit of the whole phone tossing stunt. Her mouth is flapping open and shut in a way that reminds me of the trout-tickling episode. Which makes me think of Harvey and that makes me sad. But I can't be distracted by such things.

'Right, Mum. I have deleted all my accounts. Every last post has gone. I've been in contact with the companies and asked them to wipe any references to me for ever. All the vlogs, all the posts, all the photos will go.'

Her eyes are flicking round my face, searching for any flicker of a smile to suggest that I might be joking. She's clearly disappointed. She's about to say something but then words fail her.

I sit down next to her. 'Mum, it's not okay for you to ask me to do this. I'm not the one who should be earning money.'

Her shoulders start to go, and she hides her face. My stomach flips. I hate doing this to her. I've made my mum cry. What kind of monster am I?

'But what are we doing to do? I don't expect you to answer. You're right. You're a child. You shouldn't have to think about all these things.' She blows her nose. 'You're telling me what I already know.'

I pull her to her feet. 'Let's go outside. I might have an idea.'

Well, I do have an idea. It depends if she likes it.

Mum follows me and I stand in a small clearing next to one of the trees, in full green-leaved glory. With the right filter on Instagram, I could make this place look amazing.

'Ta da,' I announce and spread my hands out as if to reveal the trees.

Mum stares at me as if I've said that I'm going to become an accountant. 'And what exactly am I looking at?'

'The orchard.'

'I know it's the orchard. I bought this house because of the orchard.'

'I know but you've never used it for anything.'

Mum kicks at a dandelion. 'I hope your new idea isn't collecting apples and making scrumpy because I can tell you now that there aren't enough apples to make more than a glass or two and we can't live off that.'

'Of course not.' I did think about it for about five seconds, but a few simple equations soon showed me that it wasn't economically viable.

'Well then? What's the big idea?'

'Okay, but you need to use your imagination. Imagine this place after a good spring/summer clean. We hang fairy lights in the trees. There's a fire pit where people can chill out and listen to cool music in the long summer nights, wrapped up in sustainably sourced blankets to ward against the cold of course. Among the trees are beautifully painted teepees and maybe even a yurt. How does that sound?'

'It sounds like heaven. It's like going back to my roots, where I met your dad. But I don't see where we make money from it.'

'It's all in the teepees and the yurt. Can you or can you not perform reiki?'

'I can.'

'Do you or do you not know several people who perform different kinds of services like holistic massage and herbal facials etc?'

'I do.'

I'm on a roll. 'So, what I'm suggesting is that you set up your own business where you can do the things you like doing – aura reading, chakra stones etc, and then you could rent out the other teepees to other people and you take a cut. We could make this into a little oasis of holistic calm where stressed-out people can come and relax and be at one with nature.'

She's looking around. I go in for the kill. 'Look, Mum, it's what we both want. No more advertising things that neither of us believe in. We will genuinely be making people's lives happier and more in touch with themselves.'

She's not looking happy. She hates it. It's a stupid idea. Why did I ever think that this would work? I turn away, so I don't see the disappointment spreading over her face.

Mum grabs my arm. 'But how could we set this up? We don't have the money.'

Time to play my final card.

'I've just had a very interesting message which I think will get us going.'

CHAPTER FORTY-SEVEN

Word: Jamboree (noun)

The orchard is on fire.

Well not literally but every branch, twig and leaf is lit up and the place is buzzing with people. It's safe to say that it's been transformed from a greyish green kind of place that was in need of a serious makeover into something kind of wonderful.

Where did we get the money from? The TV company sent me a very big fat payment to say sorry for nearly killing me and to stop me suing them for any more money. I could have put it towards university or could have put it towards a gap year. Or I could help get this family back on its feet. And that's what we've done. Together.

Though the yurt that Mum's bought to fill the main clearing is beigey on the outside, it's covered with ribbons and lines of flags that flutter in the wind, stretching to every tree around it. In front of it, the flames of the fire pit leap in the summer evening. Above the trees, the blue sky darkens to velvet and the first, early stars peep through.

Through the dusk you can see the bright tips of the four teepees that poke up into the sky, apparently scattered in a haphazard way throughout the orchard but actually carefully planned and placed because that's where 'the crystals have spoken'. Mum is currently, gin in hand, talking excitedly about how she's dowsed the course of an ancient stream and now we have our own well and I know that before she's had a few more sips she's going to be telling them about how we're on a leyline and that's why the energy is so particularly wonderful here. She thinks everyone's buzzing because of our direct connection to a prehistoric burial site at Arbour Low. I think the gin and the general atmosphere are more likely to be responsible than a heap of old stones fifteen miles away.

But when everyone around me is having a great time, who am I to be a party pooper? And what do I even know? I've been offline a few months now. The odd boy has hinted at liking me and suggested that we go out, but I don't take them up on it. It's not them. It's me. And it's not their fault that I seem stuck on the one boy who I've completely lost contact with and, let's face it, I've never quite worked out how he felt about me. It's all such a muddle. I want to move on, but I can't.

Kate and Anjali are dancing next to the fire pit. They are particularly excitable this evening and keep giggling behind their hands, like a pair of kids. I'm not quite sure what the reason for that is but I'll find out later. Rowan and Willow are chasing each other around the trees. Rowan is dressed in full princess regalia and Willow is part unicorn, part dragon and part mermaid. Which let's face it should be every small child's goal. In fact, it's still my goal.

I wander away from the light into the dusk.

It's a lovely scene. A party next to a fire pit. Sparks fly into the dark. People laugh, hug and dance.

We did this. Me and Mum together. I've done so much recently, taking full advantage of the summer holidays, and I do feel great about it all. Why does one little piece of a big, complicated jigsaw feel missing? There's one thing that I didn't manage to put right.

'Looks a bit like our nights in Scotland, doesn't it? Just missing the midges.'

Heart in mouth, I turn to see who's standing next to me.

Tall, hair which shines with gold even in the firelight. Eyes warm with laughter and a mouth curved in a smile.

Harvey.

For once I'm speechless.

'Stuck for words?' While I seem to be frozen like a penguin to an ice cap, Harvey seems quite at home here. A smile plays on his lips. It's almost like he's enjoying my confusion. As ever. I'm not even sure how I feel.

'Strangely,' I manage. 'I didn't see your name on the guest list.'

'There's a guest list?' he jokes. 'I thought every new age enthusiast in the area knew it was happening by a movement in their chakras.'

I could be offended. But then that's actually quite funny, but still how...

He pushes a flyer towards me.

'I assumed this was my invite. You did send this to the centre, didn't you?' I take it. It's certainly our flyer, printed on recycled paper and with our new logo for the retreat, made up of a tulip, a willow and rowan tree and – you guessed it – a raven. But what

I don't expect to see is a handwritten message in the corner. 'Be great to see you. Sorry for everything. Tulip x'

I didn't send it. I wish I had. Should I tell him? But I'm so happy he's here I don't want to spoil the moment. There's something dancing around in my peripheral vision. I turn to see Anjali and Kate, leaping up and down with excitement, giving me the thumbs up. So that's why they are so happy this evening. They must have sent the flyer to Harvey on my behalf. I love my friends!

With my attention back on Harvey, I realise that my face has moved. I think my mouth is doing something weird. It might be called a smile. I am sitting on a log in the dusk, smiling with Harvey.

'That is what you're up to these days. I had no idea. You've become a woman of mystery,' he says.

'What does that mean? I've not gone anywhere. I'm not the one who's left school without leaving anyone their phone number. Now that's anti-social.'

'But you've deleted every social media account you've ever had. I call that pretty anti-social.' He looks around at the party unfolding. 'I think you also called that social suicide.'

I know that in the pause that follows I'm supposed to say I'm wrong. I don't like saying I'm wrong. I've spent the last few months proving to the world that I'm right. And now I'm supposed to say... 'I may have to reconsider my position on that one.'

I get a quick glance and half a glorious smile for that. At least I think that's what happens because it's getting darker and darker. Near the fire pit, the drumming is getting faster and louder as people dance round the flames. Something odd is happening in me too, as if my heart is trying to keep up with the dancers and drummers. I try to keep my face calm because if I don't, I think it might split in half with happiness.

'It's quite an event. I wouldn't have missed it for the world.'

But now I need to know why he has actually come here. Does this mean what I hope it means? I turn to him. 'What are you doing here? Do you want your aura cleansed or an astral massage?'

'What even is an astral massage?'

'Okay, I made that one up but I'm sure we could see to it.' I slap him on the arm. 'But don't change the subject.'

'I like the sound of an astral massage. Does that mean you float away and then angels do the actual massaging because if so that would be a bestseller.'

I hit him harder. 'Shush. And answer my question.'

'How can I shush and answer your question?'

'Will you stop being annoying?'

'Shall I stop breathing then?'

'Meaning?'

'Since we've met, you've found me annoying. Which I probably am. But you have your moments too. Shall I stop talking and breathing and then you'll be happy?'

'I'm happy now.' I take his hand. All those times away when I wanted to do it, but I couldn't. It's hard, rough in places but lies softly in mine. No cameras. No worrying about getting things wrong. Just doing what feels right.

'Me too.'

We sit for a while and watch the lights flicker around us, alone, together, in the dark.

'Why didn't you come back to school?'

He squeezes my hand. 'I didn't think anyone wanted me there, remember?'

'There was a line of girls waiting for you. They all wanted you.'

'I know. But it wasn't any of them that I was interested in. There was one I liked but she said twice that she'd never have anything to do with me. Not once, but twice. Now I don't know much about girls, but I know enough to take what they say seriously.'

I rest my head on his shoulder to show him how I feel. For a while, we just sit there.

'I'm sorry, Tulip.'

I look up at him. 'What for?'

'For not supporting you. For trying to tell you what to do. I should have just let you make your own choices. I know it sounded like I was judging you, I just found it so hard to watch you do something I knew was making you so unhappy.'

After a while, I trust myself to speak. 'I think I might need to reconsider my position on a few things.'

'Such as?' His hand is still warm in mine.

'Do I have to say?'

'If you have something to say, then I'll listen.'

'Okay. I am willing to reconsider my position on you being an arse. I am also willing to reconsider my position on you being judgemental and thinking that you are better than me. I might even be sorry for the things I've said.'

'So if I was the last boy on earth…'

'You might be in with a chance.'

'But only then?'

I shift around. 'I might reconsider my position on that too.' He laughs, puts an arm round me. I can feel his lips on my hair.

'What's next for you now you're offline?' he says.

'Not sure yet. I'll make my mind up when I've decided what kind of person I want to be.'

'You know, I'm still working that out too, since all the male role models in my family are so rubbish. Though Dad seems to be trying to deal with Hector for a change.'

'He does like a challenge doesn't he, your dad. Well, we're bonded by both having strange families.' I feel our fingers weave together.

'And our sympathy for fish,' he adds.

'And our liking for sitting in the dark watching sparks fly and stars dance.'

'And the fact we like each other?'

'Do we?' I can barely ask the question.

'I think so.'

'I agree. Now, shush.' I face him and put my finger to his lips.

'As a very competent person once said, I'm not shushing. Don't tell me to shush. Why should I shush?' he teases, pushing my hand away.

'So I can do this.' Our eyes meet in the firelight.

As for the rest, well, that's private.

Acknowledgements

First and foremost, I have to thank my agent Anne Clark always having faith in my writing. Thank you to Penny Thomas and the team at Firefly for loving Tulip and giving her life. To Niki Pilkington – thank you for creating such a gorgeous image for my girl! – and also to Anne Glenn for the cover. A big shout-out to Megan Farr for all your support with the publicity.

Tulip Taylor would never have got to this stage with the support of a range of amazing people. I've been lucky enough to be a member of the north west group of SCBWI and I cannot say how grateful I am to have you all in my life. Being part of the 'Tween' group was a joy and an education – Cath Nichols, Susan Brownrigg, Lois Johnson, Jayne Fallows and Marion Brown – your early feedback and support with Tulip kept me going. Though the YA group didn't directly help with Tulip, your comments on an early synopsis of an ancient draft were all part of the very long journey from first concept to publication – thanks to Catherine Whitmore, Mel Green, Kim Hutson, Sui Annoukka and Helen Lapping. To Lucy Taylor, thank you for lending me your surname and forty years of book-based friendship. To Dave, thanks for the wine in times of need.

Finally, I would like to thank my daughters, Grace and Beth. It was you who educated me on the ways of make-up and vloggers and opened my eyes to how creative cosmetics can be. Without you, I would not now be in possession of quite such a range of high brand (and very expensive) make-up. Yes, I do notice when you take it. But without you, I would not have learned to love the beauty hall in Selfridges quite as much as I do. I'm sorry I often shout, 'Go away, I'm writing' or 'No, you can't borrow my laptop to do your homework', and that I steal the stories that you tell me. I hope you know that I love you very much.

About the Author

Anna Mainwaring read *The Lord of the Rings* when she was seven and hasn't stopped reading since. After studying English Literature she spent a brief time as a banker before realising this was a bad choice for someone who someone who can't even write down a phone number correctly, and became an English teacher. She lives in Cheshire, UK.